THE FEAST

Randy Lee
Eickhoff

A TOM DOHERTY ASSOCIATES BOOK
NEW YORK

THE FEAST

This book is printed on acid-free paper.

A Forge Book
Published by Tom Doherty Associates, LLC
175 Fifth Avenue
New York, NY 10010

www.tor.com

Forge® is a registered trademark of Tom Doherty Associates, LLC.

Designed by Lisa Pifher

Library of Congress Cataloging-in-Publication Data

Eickhoff, Randy Lee.
    The feast / Randy Lee Eickhoff.
        p.   cm.
    A retelling of: Fled Bricrend.
    "A Tom Doherty Associates book."
    ISBN 0-312-86647-X (hc)
    ISBN 0-312-87299-2 (pbk)
        1. Heroes—Ulster (Northern Ireland and Ireland)—Fiction.   2. Tales—Ulster
(Northern Ireland and Ireland)—Adaptations.   3. Cúchulain (Legendary character)—
Fiction.   4. Epic Literature, Irish—Adaptations.   I. Fled Bricrend.   II. Title.
PS3555.I23F4   1999
813'.54—dc21   98-44013
                                                                           CIP

First Hardcover Edition: March 1999
First Trade Paperback Edition: February 2001

Printed in the United States of America

0 9 8 7 6 5 4 3 2 1

Praise for Randy Lee Eickhoff's *The Feast*

"Historical storyteller Eickhoff turns out tight, compellingly grand novels....A fine retelling of an ancient Irish saga."
—*Kirkus Reviews*

"Eickhoff is a welcome addition to the ranks of modern Irish storytellers. His earthy, witty translations of these sagas are a joy to read and should appeal to fans of Irish culture as well as those who like a good adventure and/or tragedy. I hope we'll see more from Eickhoff soon!"
—*Rambles* magazine

"Continuing his expansive retelling of the ancient Irish epic...Eickhoff spotlights the swashbuckling and humorous tale of the feast of Fled Bricriu....Readers of mythology and lovers of the richness that is Irish literature will find this retelling accessible and most entertaining."
—*Library Journal*

Praise for Randy Lee Eickhoff's *The Raid*

"*The Raid* is one of the world's great adventure tales. Rollicking, bawdy, sometimes hilarious, ultimately both tragic and glorious, the tale is of epic proportions yet never loses the human dimension."
—Morgan Llywelyn, international bestselling author of *1916*

"A resounding read echoing through the ages."
—David Nevin, *New York Times* bestselling author of *Dream West* and *1812*

"A tremendous achievement. You don't have to be Irish to be entranced by Eickhoff's earthy yet magical rendering of one of the world's most ancient epics."
—Jeanne Williams, Spur Award–winning author of *Home Again*

"An amazing piece of work. This version has the marvelous ring of authenticity. This is what those wild pagans were really like, before the priests got to them."
—Thomas Fleming, author of *The Wages of Fame*

BOOKS BY RANDY LEE EICKHOFF

*The Fourth Horseman**
Bowie (with Leonard C. Lewis)*
A Hand to Execute
The Gombeen Man
*Fallon's Wake**

THE ULSTER CYCLE
*The Raid**
*The Feast**
*The Sorrows**

NONFICTION
Exiled

*denotes a Forge Book

for Al and Elise King

For one armed man cannot resist a multitude, nor one army conquer countless legions; but not all the armies of all the Empires on earth can crush the spirit of one true man. And that one man will prevail.

—Terence MacSwiney,
Principles of Freedom

We must touch his weaknesses with a delicate hand. There are some faults so nearly allied to excellence, that we can scarce weed out the fault without eradicating the virtue.

—Oliver Goldsmith,
The Good-Natured Man

Un sot savant est sot plus qu'un sot ignorant.

—Jean-Baptiste Molière,
Les femmes savantes

An Invitation to Bricriu's Feast
for Randy Lee Eickhoff

There will be
a grand feast tonight
and you are
cordially invited.
The whole green world
will be there. Please
be part of our
fabulous dinner.
Afterward you
can play
a little game
but first
you must know
the rules:
Search every corner
of your every room.
See that they are all
cleaned and dusted.
Bring everything that
you find. Everything
of worth and meaning.
Soon you will
find yourself
falling farther than
you have ever
fallen before.
You will not
be able to rise
even if you try.
But don't fight it.
Let yourself go.

It is too late now
to be uninvited.

Relax.
Take heart.
Be brave.
This is only a game
that only a loser
will win, only he
with nothing to lose.
That is why we
thought of you.
Only he
who humbly
gives away all
that he owns,
even his name,
even his soul,
even his hand—
some little head
will not go home
empty-handed.

—Micheál O'Ciardhi

INTRODUCTION

THE ULSTER CYCLE IS a large corpus of tales about the deeds of a legendary band of warriors led by Conchobor Mac Nessa who lived in the area now known as Ulster. They were originally called the *Ulaidh* but referred to themselves as the *Rudhraighe,* or "rightful owners," and from this, the name of Conchobor's house took its name: the *Craeb Ruad* of Emain Macha. The *Craeb Ruad* was only one of the three houses of Emain Macha, which included the Hostel of Kings at present-day Navan Fort, Co. Armagh, and *Craeb Derg*, where the skulls of enemies slain and other war trophies were stored. The exploits of these warriors, commonly called the Red Branch (*craeb*: branch; *ruad*: red), make up the corpus of the Ulster Cycle.

The central tale of the Cycle is *Táin Bó Cuailnge*, or "Cattle Raid of Cooley," of which a few recensions exist, the newest titled *The Raid* and translated by this author.[1] The earliest surviving recension dates from roughly the eleventh century, but it appears to be a conflation of two previous texts that have their origin in the ninth century, with clarifying material added by the newest author. As near as we can reckon, it appears that the basic material of this tale came from writings in the seventh century, although it seems to have had its genesis in the oral tradition, or bardic tradition, that dates back to the eighth century B.C.

The Ulster Cycle portrays a warrior-aristocracy that was organized along the lines of a heroic society and provides an excellent and authentic picture of the Iron Age Celtic culture.

Fled Bricrend, or "Bricriu's Feast," appears to be one of the oldest of the Ulster Cycle tales, dating back to the eighth century, and it survives today in several texts that have constantly been emended in order to explain some occurrences and parts of the tale that were common knowledge among the early Celts. Perhaps one of the more characteristic tales of the Ulster Cycle, *Fled Bricrend* is comprised of a mythic subtext, a heroic competition, and visits to and from the Otherworld that predate other stories in other cultures, suggesting that the Ulster Cycle may have been a major source of information for the compilers of such tales as *Sir Gawain and the Green Knight* and others.

Bricriu appears to be somewhat of an Irish Lóki, a mischief-maker, although he seldom perpetrates any pranks that cause severe damage or death. He is more humanistic than Lóki in that he appears to be misanthropic and does not seem to be capable of magic, although his threat to send the breasts of all women in Ireland banging together like empty bladders is taken most seriously by his peers. Unlike his Scandinavian counterpart, Bricriu cannot get out of difficulties through the use of wizardry or magic, but must depend upon his own wits. He suffers from bellyache, the gripe, and bitterness, all human conditions.

The central figure of the Ulster Cycle, however, even in *Fled Bricrend*, is not Bricriu, but Cúchulainn, the Boy-Warrior, who became such a strong metaphor for the people of Ireland that today a statue of the mythical youth can be seen in the Dublin post office as a symbol of those who were forced to stand alone while attempting to achieve Ireland's freedom from British rule. We cannot find any historical evidence that substantiates the existence of Cúchulainn, although his king, Conchobor, does appear in records as the ruler of ancient Ulster sometime around 30 B.C.

At the time, Ulster was a difficult land to travel in, what with dense fog and heavy undergrowth, almost surrounded by river and bog and mountains.

Although for the majority of Ireland in the seventh and eighth centuries, these stories were so familiar that simple reference to the main characters was enough to provide background for the listeners, this is not true today, for few people are aware of the "Ulster Curse" as it may be or what precipitated it, or of the birth of Cúchulainn, or of the general cultural background that gives meaning to the story. Consequently, I have been forced to intrude into the text in order to add a few points for clarification in the following story.

Those who would like to further their studies of the Ulster Cycle may wish to consult other translations of the tales such as Joseph Dunn's *The Ancient Irish Epic Tale Táin Bó Cúalnge,* London, 1914; Winifred Faraday's *The Cattle-Raid of Cualnge,* London, 1904; Cecile O'Rahilly's *Táin Bó Cúalnge from the Book of Leinster,* Dublin, 1967; Thomas Kinsella's *The Táin,* Oxford, 1969, and Lady Augusta Gregory's *Cúchulain of Muirthemne,* London, 1902.

Of course it is much better if the reader can read the original work, which shows ancient life in all its raw sensuality. But with the recent rapid decline in the Celtic language, this is almost an impossibility. Even in Ireland, where the Ulster Cycle is part of the national heritage and tradition, barely one-tenth of the people are capable of reading the original text.

Much of early Irish literature has been lost, for it did not exist in a written form but was handed down over the centuries through the oral tradition: from singer to singer, *seanchaí* to *seanchaí.* Certain sections of the central story were undoubtedly altered by the singers or storytellers of the various provinces, who focused upon what was important to their particular people or clans. These snippets underwent constant alteration until the central story all but disappeared. In certain cases, as we can tell from a careful study of the Ulster Cycle, some stories undoubtedly disappeared, for great gaps exist between some of the stories, gaps that logic tells us probably were once filled by stories or minor episodes that provided a transition from one tale to the next.

Eventually these stories were written down in the seventh century by medieval monks in illuminated manuscripts, on parchment in some cases, then later transcribed into more formal units. Basically, the ancient Irish stories can be subdivided into four groups: those pertaining to the *Tuatha Dé Danann*, the Ulster Cycle, the Fenian Cycle, and what we may call a post-Fenian Cycle.

The *Tuatha Dé Danann* refers to the various tribes that supposedly traced their lineage from the goddess Anu, or Danu, a Mother Goddess associated with fertility celebrations. According to legend, the Tuatha came from four cities in the northern islands of Greece—Failias, Goirias, Findias, and Muirias—bringing with them their knowledge of the Druidic arts (a possible reference to the Eleusinian Mysteries), and defeated the Fir Bolg for control of Ireland. They were discovered by the Fomorians ("sea-comers," or "those who live under the sea"), and the ensuing battle suggests a struggle between darkness (the Fomorians) and light (*Tuatha Dé Danann*), a common theme in stories from ancient cultures. The Tuatha are those who are commonly referred to as the gods of Ireland. According to legend, they came to Ireland from Greece, bringing with them the *Lia Fail*, a stone that utters a shriek at the inauguration of the rightful king; the invincible spear of Lugh; the deadly sword of Nuada; and the ever-plentiful cauldron of the Dagda, the "Good God," or "Father God," of Ireland. This story can be found in the account of the third invasion in *The Book of Invasions* (*Lebor Gabala*).

The Ulster Cycle concerns itself with the exploits of the Red Branch knights, led by their king, Conchobor. These stories are probably the best known, and they form a nucleus from which one could show a relationship with the *Mabinogion* (especially with five of the tales added by Lady Charlotte Guest from *The Red Book of Herest*). Most assuredly, we find similarities in heroic elements between the *Táin* and *Beowulf*, which could suggest a transient myth, but nothing more closely related than the beheading

game found in *Fled Bricrend* and "Sir Gawain and the Green
Knight." *Fled Bricrend* was composed, we believe, sometime
around the eighth century, while "Sir Gawain and the Green
Knight" appears to have been composed in the late fourteenth
century. In Sir Gawain, we find knightly attributes similar to those
in Cúchulainn, although Cúchulainn appears to be a much ruder
form of knightly warrior than Sir Gawain. This could suggest that
the cruder knightly elements in Cúchulainn were refined when
transferred to Gawain, when definitive chivalric rules, or rules of
etiquette, became more important to the people than the rules of
warriors.

Cúchulainn's personage apparently was developed from Lugh,
the Gaelic Sun God, the god of genius and light. Perhaps Cúchulainn's patronage is one of the reasons that his body is transformed
by the *riastradh,* a seizure ("warp-spasm"), that causes him to shake
uncontrollably from head to foot and revolve within his skin. His
features become blood-red, one eye growing almost cyclopean in
size while the other becomes tiny, his mouth stretching into a
grotesque form and issuing sparks, his heart booming in his chest
like a *bodhrán*, and a nimbus, or "warrior-light," rising from his
brow. It is this warrior-light that I have elected to translate as a
"hero-halo," which reminds one of the glorious light that emanates
from Lugh's own forehead. This emergence of light suggests an
attempt to bring light into the darkness of the ancient Celtic world,
but the usage of light in reference to Cúchulainn is also seen in
Gawain. Gawain's name is derived from the Welsh Sun God
Gwalchmei, and means "bright-haired." Consequently, we have
this common reference between Cúchulainn and Gawain in regard
to divinity, or to a mystical divinity, together with a divine light.
Both heroes become warriors of the light, or protectors of the light.
A remarkable similarity.

The Fenian Cycle refers to stories of Finn Mac Cumaill and
his son Oisín, along with other heroes of the *Fiana,* a group of
heroes *(laochs)* locked together by passing a series of tests that
formed them into a *curaid,* the "comitatus," if you like, of *Beowulf.*

The post-Fenian Cycle consists of a group of stories roughly from the third century B.C. until the eighth century A.D.

In ancient epics, certain warrior traits eventually fell out of practice, but because of Ireland's isolated location, those warrior traits may have continued for many ages, even up to the introduction of Christianity in the fifth century. I refer here to the practice of cattle-raiding, fighting from iron-wheeled chariots, and the cult of the severed head.

Although beheading one's enemies and retaining the heads either as trophies or for offering in shrines may seem barbarous by today's standards, one must always judge literature by the parameters of the time in which it first appeared rather than by imposing modern sensibilities upon the work. Literature, it must be remembered, is a window into the past. Consequently, one must look at the practice of beheading among the early Celts as a way of controlling the soul, or spirit, of the defeated warrior. The ancient Druids believed that the soul, or consciousness, was located in the mind, and thus the cult of head-hunting became a vital part of Celtic society, for by taking the head of the enemy, one captured his spirit and consciousness, keeping them from being used against oneself.

The Ulster Curse, or the "Pangs of Ulster," which made it necessary for Cúchulainn to defend Ulster's boundaries alone from the Connacht army, led by Maeve and Ailill, came about when Crunniuc Mac Agnomain, a rich landlord who lived with his sons in the mountains, found his bed suddenly visited by a beautiful woman who mysteriously appeared out of nowhere. She identified herself only as Macha.

One day Crunniuc went to a fair in Ulster with Macha, who acted as his wife, and after drinking more than he should, bragged that his wife was fleeter of foot than the king's horses. Although Macha warned him to cease his bragging, he continued with his boast until word reached the king.

The king demanded that the woman and her husband be brought before him. When they appeared, he told them that if the woman did not race his horses, Crunniuc would lose his head. Macha protested that she was heavy with child and her time was near, but the king was adamant: either she raced the horses or her husband died.

"I will race your horses," she said grimly, "but only evil will come out of this. My name and the name of my children will be given to this place. I am Macha, the daughter of Sinrith Mac Imbaith."

The race began, and as the woman and the king's chariot neared the finish line, she felt the first pangs of birth and screamed out that henceforth all who heard that scream, as well as their dependents, would suffer from the same pangs as she for five days and four nights during their times of crises, and that the place would never know peace. She gave birth to twins: a son and a daughter, and with her dying breath, cursed Ulster for nine generations. The place became known as "Emain Macha," the Twins of Macha. And from that moment on, those who had heard the scream suffered the same pangs in times of trial. Strangely enough, Ulster, to this day, has not seen peaceful times.

Macha is seen as one of the Mórrígna, along with Badb and Mórrígan, a sort of "triple goddess" of the battlefield. The three function as goddesses of war and symbols of promiscuity. The suggestion is that war and sex are interlocked, each an integral part of the other.

Badb (I have maintained the original spelling here to avoid possible confusion with Maeve) appears sometimes as an old hag or *caílleach* (a shape-changer from old hag to young woman) and at other times as a crow (the *Badb Catha*, or "battle raven"). She represents the destructive element of battle whose power is mainly psychological. When she appears on the battlefield, those whom she has chosen become confused and terrified. In the *Táin*, she wreaks havoc among the Connachtmen as a prophetess of doom.

Although she strongly resembles Badb, Mórrígan (the "She-Phantom") is a harbinger of death, but her prophecies are not always filled with doom as are Badb's. She is the most powerful sexual image among the three goddesses, as can be seen when she appears to Cúchulainn as a beautiful woman, fervently demanding his sexual attention. She is also considered a fertility goddess, for she is identified with Anu, "the Mother of the Irish gods." Once while washing herself standing with one foot on the south bank and the other on the north bank of the River Unius during the great pagan feast of Samhain (Halloween), she met Dagda (the "Father God" of the Gaelic pantheon of gods). Here, they mated over the water as part of an ancient fertility ritual. From their mating, this place has come to be known as the "Bed of the Couple" in County Sligo.

The translation in this book is taken primarily from the *Lebor na hUidre (Book of the Dun Cow)*, although others have been consulted as well. It is the *intent* of the early tale-tellers, with their vague references in epic similes, that one must remember while translating, for it is not only necessary to pay close attention to the literal *detail* of the original work, but to its connotations as well. When we consider the sexual imagery that is suggested by the appearances of the Mórríganí, and by Maeve herself, a type of euphemerized divinity whose promiscuity is legendary, we become aware of the complex sexual attitude the Celtic men had toward women. We can see this in *Fled Bricrend*, where Maeve greets the heros:

> Mná finna fornochta friú
> Great breasts bared and bouncing . . .

Other tales from the Ulster Cycle continue the action, and the reader is directed to them for further study. Chief among these are:

Cath Ruis na Ríg, or *The Battle of Ros na Ríg*, which is the story of Ulster's war for the raid after the Brown Bull. In this piece, Cúchulainn kills Coirpre, the king of Temair, in a classic battle;

Serglige ConCulainn ocus aenét Emireí, or *The Sickness of Cúchulainn and the One Jealousy of Emer*, explains the goddess Fann's love for the Warped One and how she lures him into the under-world;

Aided Con Roi, or *The Death of Cúroi*, shows the tragic flaw of Cúchulainn when he uses treachery to murder Cúroi after he shamed Cúchulainn in battle;

Brislech mór Maige Muirtheimne, or *The Great Slaughter on the Plain of Murtheimne*, explains how Ulster's united enemies join forces to defeat the Red Branch;

Aided ConCulainn, or *The Death of Cúchulainn*, explains how Cúchulainn is killed by the sons of Coirpre, Cúroi, and Calatín, and shows how even in death, Cúchulainn refuses to give total victory to his enemies;

Dergruather Chonaill Chernaigh, or *The Red Slaughter of Conall Cernach*, explains Conall's revenge for the death of Cúchulainn.

Two stories that are very interesting for study are sometimes grouped under the heading of "death tales," although they are not so much death tales as an attempt to explain the aftermath of Ulster. *Togail bruidne Da-Choca*, "The Destruction of Da-Choca's Inn," is concerned with the struggle by the warrior-heroes for the successor to Conchobor following his death, and *Siaburcharput ConCulainn*, or "The Dream Chariot of Cúchulainn," explains how the spirit of Cúchulainn is called up by St. Patrick to help convert Loegaire (aka Lóiguire), then High-King of Ireland, to Christianity. In the latter, we can see the merging of Christian elements into a pagan story in much the same manner that an ancient cleric inserted similar elements into *Beowulf*.

Fled Bricrend, however, is one of the most humorous tales in the Ulster Cycle and gives us a sense of the humor and wit of the ancient Celts. The story is a rollicking account of three men, each striving to be named Champion of Conchobor's realm and thus win the right to all the privileges accorded that status. Although some sensibilities may be offended by what follows in my recounting, one must remember that such times were not chivalrous (although a certain etiquette did, in fact, exist), nor had Christianity extended into the lands held by Celtic armies and warriors.

. . .

The question, of course, exists as to why an author should bother working in an almost dead language to reproduce something that on the surface appears to have little value today. The answer is that ancient literature provides us with a window into the past through which we can look and thereby ascertain the type of people who were the progenitors of today's society. We can see, through literature, how they lived, their beliefs, their lifestyles, their fears, their ambitions, their loves, their humor—everything that encompasses a culture that has had a profound influence upon our own.

We can see, for example, that the ancient Celtics generally built their houses inside a fort that was surrounded by earthen breastworks or wooden stockades, usually circular in design. The walls of the houses were of stone or wood, the roof supported on wooden poles and probably thatched with straw, reeds, or rushes. Unlike most ancient civilizations, the Celtics of this period were extremely particular about their appearance and washed and bathed frequently. Guests were provided with tubs and a fresh change of clothing by hosts. Soap was made by burning bracken and briars and made into cakes.

Knowledge of such practices is important when one considers what they suggest as far as a culture is concerned. We can see that the Celtics, for all their pagan beliefs, were an advanced form of civilization during a time when much of northern Europe was peopled by barbaric hordes whose belief in one bath per year was endemic. We can suggest, therefore, that the ancient Celts had already determined a link between personal hygiene and sickness, and had advanced to the realization that bathing was imperative to maintain a healthy body.

We can ascertain as well the role of women in a Celtic society. Women were not considered simple chattel slaves by the Celtics. Indeed, they played an active part in everyday affairs and often were consulted in regard to matters of state. They had legal rights, and rights to own and inherit property, whereas their counterparts in England and Europe were, for the most part, considered appreciably less important than the male.[2]

The woman often accompanied her husband into battle and in some cases, even joined the battle. Cúchulainn received a vital part of his training from two women: Skatha and Aife, who were so famed for their battle skills that kings would send their best warriors to them for training.[3]

The Celts had rather liberal views about marriage. Although most Celtic men had only one wife, provisions had been made in the Brehon Laws[4] for a man to have a chief wife and a second wife. Divorces were easy to obtain and by mutual consent. In some cases, couples could be married for one year only.[5]

Additionally, we can see that fosterage was an important aspect of the Irish life in that a man would often send his son or daughter away to be raised by a family that would undertake the responsibility of not only rearing the child, but of instructing the child in matters of social responsibility. The Brehon Laws even provided fees for this practice in accordance with an individual's societal standing.[6]

Guests were valued greatly among the ancient Celts, and strangers who might seek shelter at an individual's home were given food and drink before being asked their business. Anyone who refused a guest who requested shelter would be disgraced. Quite often a feast was held on the spur of the moment, and special animals were kept for impromptu occasions, as when honored guests unexpectedly appeared. The animal was carved in accordance with Brehon Law, and the portions handed out in accordance with an individual's rank, with the champion warrior being given the best portion of meat (the tenderloin), while particular joints of meat were reserved for other individuals.[7]

These banquets, or feasts, were accompanied by poetry and storytelling, which were important parts of Celtic life. A careful study of the large corpus of tales remaining from the various periods indicates the value the Celts placed upon such a practice. Those sections of a story that they considered to be purely background or informational were often given in a narrative prose fashion, didactic and terse in the manner of a modernist whose growing dissatisfaction with contemporary culture is shown in the language and the deliberate cultivation of the brutal and primitive. But the storyteller, the *seanchaí,* used poetry for those aspects that he thought to be important—love, descriptions of heroes and ladies, battles, laments—anything that represented an essential aspect of the society. The characters of the story, therefore, become symbols of historical significance.

The poetry, although of a simple form, reflects epic imagery, and although epideictic to a degree, it was instructional, and composed as commentary on the concerns of the audience.[8] The storyteller was ranked by the extent of his repertory, of which the highest class had committed to memory no less than three hundred fifty stories. The stories themselves were divided into numerous classes, or types: cattle-raids, wooings, adventures, voyages, visions, battles, elopements, feasts, exiles, destructions, and slaughters.

Consequently, the study of literature is necessary in that it gives the student and reader a sense of cultural identity, not only of ancient times, but of modern as well. If we look, for example, at *Loinges Mac n-Uislenn,*[9] we can understand the genesis of today's political picture in Ireland. So important was this story that it provided offshoots for other stories, including a play by William Butler Yeats, *Deirdre of the Sorrows.* Deirdre is so important to Irish culture (as is the story itself) that she became a symbol for Ireland during the country's struggle for independence. Deirdre is both an Irish Helen whose beauty disrupts a kingdom and an Irish Isolde who elopes with one of her king's warriors. This elopement shatters the peace and harmony of the kingdom and ultimately brings about a split in the political structure of the time when important heroes leave the Red Branch for exile with Maeve and Ailill in Connacht.

To understand the Ireland of today, it is necessary to look into its past, and to understand its past, it is necessary to look into its literature. For the modern political and cultural theorist, this provides a problem as that literature is found primarily in the Gaelic language. Despite the many years that early Irish literature has existed, relatively little of it has been satisfactorily translated into English. The reasons for this are many, certainly xenophobic in part, for the Irish rebellion in the early twentieth century brought about an almost fanatical rejection among the patriots of anything connected to the English, including the language. Understandable, as the English had, for hundreds of years, done their best to promote cultural genocide upon the Irish people by banning the teaching of the language in the schools, along with any study of Ireland's past.

Today, however, it has become necessary to look into Ireland's past in order to comprehend what has contributed to the present societal structure. To do that, it is necessary for the literature of the past to be translated not only in an exact manner that will adequately reflect the syntax of the times, but in connotation as well in order to *explain* the times. Although several purists insist that the emendation of a text is tantamount to creating sacrilege, one must remember that one does not have at one's fingertips those texts and commentaries necessary to comprehend the *why* of certain occurrences within story lines. Consequently, translations must be made today by specialists, technical writers who have had training not only in the language, but also in historical interpretation. Today's translator must not only work to give the words, but to explicate those words as well in order to provide as precise a picture of the past as possible for the present-day student.

---

1. Randy Lee Eickhoff, *The Raid: A Modern Translation of Ireland's National Epic.* New York: Tom Doherty Associates, 1997.

2. See Mary Wollstonecraft, *A Vindication of the Rights of Woman.* New York: W. W. Norton Co., Inc, 1975.

3. The Roman historian Ammianus Marcellinus writes: "Almost all the Gauls are of tall stature, fair and ruddy, terrible for the

fierceness of their eyes, fond of quarrelling, and of overbearing insolence. In fact, a whole band of foreigners will be unable to cope with one of them in a fight, if he calls in his wife, stronger than he by far and with flashing eyes; least of all when she swells her neck and gnashes her teeth, and poising her huge white arms, begins to rain blows mingled with kicks like shots discharged by the twisted cords of a catapult."

4. The old Irish laws. These were not established by a parliament or such, but rather were records of the old customs of the society and were orginally handed down in the bardic, or oral, tradition. They were finally written down sometime around the seventh century and were quite exact. Due compensation was awarded for any injury done and given on the basis of rank. A king, for example, had a higher honor or compensation price than a slave. Justice often could be obtained by an individual without having to go to court. For example, fasting was one way to obtain justice. If a man had a grievance in law against another, the man could sit outside the defendant's house and refuse meat and drink. If the defendant ignored him, he lost his honor and would be rejected by society. In a culture where society was needed for survival, this was tantamount to a death sentence.

5. Extract from Brehon Laws: "What are the marriageable ages? At the end of fourteen years for the daughter and at the end of seventeen years for the son."

6. The son of the lowest order of chief would require a fee of three cows, while a king's son would command a fee as high as thirty, depending upon the wealth and importance of his father. Higher fees were commanded for young girls. "How many kinds of fosterage are there? Two: fosterage for affection and fosterage for payment. The price of fosterage of the son of a chief is three sets; four sets is the price of fosterage of his daughter. [A set is half the value of a milk cow.] There are three periods at which fosterage ends: Death, Crime, and Marriage."—Brehon Law.

7. Posidonius (135 B.C.–51 B.C.) wrote, "The Celts sit on dried grass and have their meals served on wooden tables raised slightly above the earth. Their food consists of a small number of loaves of bread together with a large amount of meat, either boiled or roasted on charcoal or on spits. They partake of this in a cleanly but leonine fashion, raising up whole limbs in both hands and cutting off the meat, while any part which is hard to tear off they cut through with a small dagger which hangs attached to their sword sheath in its own scabbard. . . . When a large number dine together, they sit around in a circle with the most influential man in the centre. . . . Beside him sits the host and next on either side the others in order of distinction. . . . The drink of the wealthy classes is wine imported from Italy or from the territory of Marseilles. . . . The lower classes drink wheaten beer prepared with honey, but most people drink it plain. . . . They use a common cup, drinking a little at a time, not more than a mouthful, but they do it rather frequently."

8. Sometimes the poetry takes the form of a "paraphrase" that amplifies or clarifies a strange prose passage. Although the followers of New Criticism condemn what they call "the heresy of the *paraphrase*" by suggesting that the essential nature of a poem is incommunicable in terms other than its own, the paraphrase that exists in Irish literature is necessary as a "teaching tool," not only for the ancient listeners, but for today's audience as well.

9. *The Exile of the Sons of Uisliu*, from the ninth century, a part of the Ulster Cycle.

Chapter 1

THE HOUSE
OF BRICRIU

POISON-TONGUED BRICRIU LOOKED sourly around his spacious house, Dún Rubraige. Although he had built it in roughly the fashion of the Red Branch at Emain Macha—exceeding it in richness, however—he took little comfort from it. And now his stomach felt even more sour than usual, for the time had come for him to hold a feast for the king of the Red Branch, Conchobor Mac Nessa, and his knights to celebrate the finishing of his house.

Behind him, workmen stood respectfully, waiting as a wagon team hauled the last beam up the slope to the house to affix it within the mead-hall. Seven men stood by to receive the beam and raise it and anchor it firmly to the frame under the supervision of thirty artificers, who gnawed fingernails and worried hangnails, hoping that their plans would allow the beam to fit properly and not need wedges to snug it into place. Bricriu's tongue-lashings made the hardiest of them fearful, for they knew well his satirist's tongue could make them live forever in ignominy.

At last the team drew level with the door frame and the appointed seven grunted and strained, lifting the mammoth beam of oak from the wagon. Carefully, they rotated it so that the *Ogham* carvings faced the sun, then carefully seated it in the footings dug for it. Two stepped forward with hand rules and plumbs to check its trueness, then stepped back with satisfied nods as a workman carefully levered it firmly into place.

"Good!" exclaimed one artificer, then looked half-fearfully at his master to see if he shared his opinion. Bricriu stepped forward and eyed the beam critically, then slowly nodded in grudging consent.

"Yes, it appears to be settling satisfactorily. Yes," he said in a voice as thin as blood. The men winced from its nasal sharpness. "But we'll see. We'll see."

He stepped into the house, modeled on the plan of Tech Midchúarta, the mead-hall of Tara, and slowly walked through it, considering the columns and facades and carved decorations and pediments. Three fountains sparkled at one end, and great swathes of saffron and blue tumbled down from the high walls, billowing gently in the light breeze. A soft swath of emerald-green grass led down from the back of the hall to a garden with arrangements of flowers and bushes artfully planted to form a maze through which a man might chase a serving wench and bed her. Swans swam lazily at the pond in the center of the garden, along with several ducks.

No expense had been spared. The best marble and granite that quarries could provide had been purchased. Several hundred pilasters had been provided, each requiring a team of men to erect. The seven main oaken pillars and seven frontings glowed softly from hand-rubbings of oil, the carvings and lintel-work showing in deep bas-relief the tales of the Red Branch. Between the columns were long, shady colonnades. Each wall of the nine apartments had been covered with bronze thirty feet high and overlaid with gold and gold leaf.

He paused, looking sourly at where a royal couch had been erected especially for Conchobor, high above the whole house in the forepart. Around the couch, carbuncles and rubies and emeralds and carmelite and tiger's eyes had been cunningly set in white and red gold and silver so that they gleamed with the radiance of the day from either sun or fire, changing night to day at all times, unless a curtain of heavy brocade was drawn around them. Twelve couches, one for each of the twelve tribes of Ulster, had been carefully arranged so that Conchobor had only to turn his head to gaze at any.

Bricriu hawked and spat on the ground, reflecting on the cost of building a feasting-hall where he knew the Ulstermen would not allow him to sit for fear that his bitter tongue would incite them to fighting. And so it would, he reflected with satisfaction, for he had long been excluded from other feasts held by the knights of the Red Branch. This time, he thought with satisfaction, things would be different.

He turned and looked at a tower and balcony that had been erected on the same level as Conchobor's couch and was as high as those that would be occupied by valorous heroes. Its decorations were equally as magnificent as those of Conchobor's couch, but more important, windows, the first of glass in all of Ireland, had been placed around his couch so that he and his wife could watch the celebrations below them, the castle courtyard and Great Hall, without rising from their couch. He nodded in satisfaction. Yes, this would be most advantageous for him.

Reluctantly he left the hall and walked slowly to where the workmen and artificers waited. They watched as he paused in front of them, his mouth pursed tightly in distaste, his black eyes hard and suspicious above his nose, smashed and tilted to the side, a wart hanging from one nostril like a drop of snot. A purple boil dotted the middle of his forehead; it would grow to the size of a man's fist if he kept his thoughts to himself. His black hair, streaked with gray, hung in dank ringlets to the collar of his food-spotted tunic. His head stood on a scrawny neck, tendons like strings with a large Adam's apple bobbing between them. He glanced over at the washroom to the left of the hall, where seven oaken tubs had been erected for bathing (a chuckle escaped him as he thought of how the twelve heroes would argue to go first), then to the right, where a long, narrow stable stretched away from his tower like a middle finger extended from the palm. He nodded slowly.

"All right," he said. He motioned, and four slaves carried a cask of beer to his side. "You may drink in celebration of a job well done."

"Better to drink pig-piss," someone grumbled.

Bricriu's eyes flashed as he looked over them. "What's that? Who said that?"

The men remained silent, most looking away, pretending indifference. Bricriu's eyes crawled over them like slugs, but no one met his eyes. The Poison-Tongued One had well earned his reputation. Once he had composed a story about a man who was so bitter and vile that his name had passed with him into oblivion after he hanged himself from the rafters of his mead-hall. No one knew the man or remembered the slight he had given Bricriu, but they knew the story and that was enough.

"The wind," one said at last. "Must've been the wind. You left the doors open."

Bricriu sharpened his gaze at him. The man paled and looked away, walking to the cask of beer and fumbling for a cup. A slave pulled the plug and thin beer waggled out in a tiny stream, hissing as it hit the bottom of the cup.

"Yes," Bricriu said. "That was it." He turned and walked away stiffly, his head canted to one side as if listening to the secrets of the earth. The workmen watched his stiff gait until he disappeared around the corner, then they heaved a sigh of relief.

"You fool," one said, turning to a burly man with clay matting his beard. "You nearly brought him down on all of us. Keep a civil tongue behind your lip when he's around."

"He's right, though," said the one with the beer. He spat a mouthful of beer onto the ground and poured the rest after it. "As weak as a spider's crawl. Sour, too," he added as an afterthought. He glanced hopefully at the slave, who smiled and shook his head.

"None more," the slave said. "Master keeps the good stuff in the storeroom for himself. Never drinks it, though."

"What? Why keep it?"

The slave shrugged. "Same reason why he keeps concubines and cows. It's the owning that's important. Not the drinking."

"Unhuman, that's what it is," another muttered, shaking his head at the cups offered. "Pour it on the shit pile by the stable. It'll mix well there."

"Tell you what," the first muttered, pulling at his beard with gnarled fingers. "I'll be glad to get away from here, that's speaking the truth. Get down to Muirtheimhne on the plains. What about you?"

"I'm off to Laighin. Man down there wants four more out-buildings with souterains running to them. I figure the whole project will be good for the season. Be a welcome shift from here, I say," he said, glancing darkly around. He shivered and leaned closer to his friend. "Last night, I swore I heard a *banhsídhe* moan."

"No!"

"I did. I did," he said. "Nigh near made me piss my bed, it did."

"That does it!" a third man exclaimed. "I'm out of here." He bent and shouldered a hod and dumped it into a cart. "You can stay if you want, but when the *Sídhe* get to roaming around the place at night, the *bocánach*, the goblins of the air, will be flying soon after, and you can bet your pecker that the fairy folk have given their mark to the place. One need not have the *imbas forasnai* to know that." He shook his head. "Aye, I could tell that. And isn't it being that only crows we're seeing flying around here? None of the other birds come near the place." He picked up a clod and threw it at one resting on the peak of the roof. The crow called mockingly as it jumped up and settled back down. "You see that? They know. They know." He shook a dirty finger at them. "And if we hang around longer, then we'll be here for the old hags. Samhain's coming, and that's a time for a man to be at his own home or in a friendly house behind a stout *rath*. Better yet, a *cathair*."

"I'm with you," his friend said. They looked over at the man who was off to Laighin. "Would there be work for the two of us down there?"

"I've seen you bevel the joints and carve the doodles," he answered. "I'll speak for you."

"Right. And me mate?"

The man eyed the other critically. "Strong back and large hands. He'll do to dig the souterains. I'll speak for him, too."

Their eyes were drawn by a stream of slaves led by Bricriu's *ben urnadna,* his contract wife for the year, and dressed in stained and tattered clothing, emerging from one of the old buildings, their arms piled high with quilts and blankets, beds and pillows. Others carried roasts of pork and beef, ducks and chickens plucked and gutted, and ale in casks made of finer wood than the one standing in front of the workers.

"Yes," the man said who was afraid of the *banhsídhe,* "I reckon it's time for us to be off. Collect our wages, will you? We'll gather your tackle and put it in the cart with ours. The old horse ain't much, but she can pull a bit more."

The two left hurriedly for the common hut. The man watched them go, then sighed deeply and squared his shoulders, heading for Bricriu's house. His insides churned with fear.

Chapter 2

THE PLOT

SUNLIGHT SLANTED LATE UPON the ground in front of Conchobor's pavilion where he and his Red Branch knights took their ease in the heat of the afternoon, relaxing back against cushions with huge cups of ale in their meaty fists. Serving wenches bustled back and forth between the couches, keeping each mug filled with the frothy ale made from honey, occasionally shrieking with delight when one of the heroes pulled them down upon the couches for a quick caress.

Conchobor drank deeply from his cup and eyed his wife Mugain, whose body built strong lust in the most celibant of warriors. She felt his eyes upon her and glanced up, then lazily leaned forward, her large breasts rolling over the top of her gown, showing the deep valley between. Conchobor felt his *bod* swell. His mouth went dry as she rose, winked saucily at him, then walked slowly away, hips switching sensually with promise. He drained his cup and started to rise to follow.

"My king!"

He groaned and fell back against his couch as a messenger

rushed in. He glanced at the doorway leading into his private rooms, then frowned.

"Yes, yes. What is it?" he snapped.

The young lad blanched from Conchobor's waspish tone, swallowed, and said, "Bricriu Nrmthenga has arrived."

"Shit," Fergus Mac Róich mumbled from his seat to the right of Conchobor. "That Poison-Tongued One. I knew the day had gone too peacefully!"

Conchobor groaned inwardly and gestured irritably with his cup. A young wench hurried forward to fill it, her cone-shaped breasts pushing hard points against the front of her dress. Conchobor glanced at her, made a mental note, and gestured for her to stand beside his couch, then turned his attention back to the young boy standing in front of him.

"Well?" he demanded. "Has he come through the gate yet?"

"He begs admittance," the boy stammered.

"To spread more of his damn flibbertigibbet!" Fergus said in disgust. "Tell him to go away, Conchobor."

"You do it," Conchobor said.

"You're the king now," Fergus reminded him. He grinned, but his eyes were bright and accusing, reminding Conchobor of how his own mother, Ness, had tricked Fergus into giving up his throne for a year so Conchobor's children would have royalty after their name. Fergus had enjoyed that year, for Ness was wise in the ways of the bed and for once, Fergus, whose bed normally held seven women a night, each exhausted by morning, had found himself well-mated. But during that year, Conchobor gave the heads of the clans all that they could possibly want and when it became time for him to step down, the clan leaders supported him against Fergus, who had to be satisfied with the title of *seneschal* instead.

"You're the *seneschal*," Conchobor rebutted.

"That isn't the king," Fergus said stoutly.

"Would you have when you were king before me?" Conchobor asked, annoyed.

"Damn right, I would have," Fergus said. "And with my boot up his arse to hurry him along the way."

"Despite his tongue?" Conchobor said.

Fergus growled and raised his cup, draining it. A short, buxom woman upended a pitcher over the cup, refilling it. When Fergus slapped her backside, she giggled and moved away, big breasts bouncing bawdily.

"My lord?" the young lad asked timorously. "Bricriu?"

Conchobor sighed. His temples began to throb. He collapsed against the back of his couch, yanking hard on his earlocks.

"Show him in," he said. "Might as well beard him in my own den as let him geld me in his."

The young boy nodded and scurried away. Conchobor cast a longing look at the doorway through which Mugain had disappeared, felt a tugging on his *bod,* then drew a deep breath and held out his cup for the young girl to refill. Absently, he contemplated her young breasts and slim shanks, then turned his attention to the front as Bricriu strolled in, his small paunch, like a pig's bladder filled with air, artfully concealed beneath a four-threaded, saffron-colored cloak stitched at the hem with purple, a color reserved for royalty. Conchobor pretended not to notice.

"Welcome, Bricriu," he said graciously. He indicated a seat below the champion's place at his knee. "And what brings you to Emain Macha? I thought you were busy with your castle, at Dún Rudraige, isn't it?"

Bricriu smiled thinly. Everyone knew about the building of his castle. Some even called it "Bricriu's Folly." He bowed, though, keeping his thoughts to himself, feeling the purple boil on his forehead beginning to grow.

"Of course, my lord," he said smoothly. "But it is finished now, and I have come to invite you and your valiant warriors to its inaugural feast. Come and partake of a banquet never before served. Cooks have been preparing it for three weeks now. Twenty boars and twenty shoats have been slaughtered and roasted slowly with honey basting. Ten steers and fifteen deer turn on spits even as we talk. A hundred fish wrapped in seaweed bake in coals. I have purchased a whole ship's cargo of red wine from Iberia, and twenty tuns of honeyed beer and ale have been made ready. That," he said modestly, "is for the first day of feasting. I have other plans for the next four," he added.

"Ah," Conchobor said awkwardly. "I see. Well." He paused uncomfortably, then breathed deeply through his nose and hastily backed away as a fecal cloud floated silently up from Bricriu. He gestured around the room.

"Of course I will come," he said, blinking rapidly as his eyes watered. "That is, if that pleases the men of Ulster. What say you, Fergus?"

Fergus eyed Bricriu frostily, then shook his head. "You know my *geis*: if I am asked personally, I must go for I cannot refuse an ale-feast. But I have not been asked, *you* have, so I say no. If we go, our dead will outnumber the living. Then our enemies will be swift on our throats. You know we're having problems with our southern neighbors." Murmurs of agreement rose from the warriors on their couches in the shadows.

"We are?" Conchobor asked, then hastily amended: "Oh. Yes. Of course. I had forgotten." He grinned sheepishly at Bricriu. "Well. I guess you have your answer. State security and all that, you know. Must remain here. Yes. Must."

Bricriu compressed his lips into a thin line and stared first at Fergus, then at Conchobor. The purple boil on his forehead began to pulse. Slowly, he turned to face the other warriors, but none would meet his eye. He knew well the sobriquets given him in the dark by these warriors: "Poison-Tongued," "Fish-Eye," "Dog's Breath," "Pus-Face."

"I see," he said, turning back to Conchobor. "I don't suppose you'd be willing to change your mind?"

"Oh, I wish I could," Conchobor said expansively, relieved at the excuse Fergus had invented. "But, I must think first of my people."

"Ah. The people, is it?" Bricriu said. "Then let the people be wary. If you don't come, worse things will befall you than you can possibly imagine."

"Is that a threat?" Fergus asked narrowly, straightening his bulk on his couch. He reached down and scratched his genitals, five times the size of an ordinary man's, and his *bod*, the size of a man's two feet placed heel to toe. "Sounds like a threat to me."

"Of course it is," Bricriu snapped. He turned back to Conchobor, muttering, "Dolt. Well?"

Conchobor swallowed, and sipped from his cup. "And if the Ulstermen do not go? What then?"

"Oh, well. A few minor things," Bricriu answered. "I will cast the name of every man here into a satire that will stir brother against brother, neighbor against neighbor, kings against clans, valorous warriors, and peasants. I will bring down the wrath of all against all. I will—"

"That is about enough!" Conchobor said sharply. "This is not the way to earn our friendship."

"Well, then," Bricriu said, "I shall pit father against sons and bring about mutual slaughter across your lands. Waters will rise up and boil across the plains, leaving barren earth behind. Mothers will quarrel against daughters until all meals gel in sour fat in cauldrons. I will set women's breasts to banging together until they flap like empty bladders and become putrid and pus leaks from their nipples. I will—"

"Ah," Fergus growled. "You poets always speak in frigging metaphors. Give me the meat of it." He turned to Conchobor. "Why not kill him? He farts around telling his shit-ass stories and we grin and do whatever he wishes."

"May I remind you of the Rules of Hospitality?" Conchobor said quietly.

"Those rules go both ways," Fergus said.

"He has the satirist's tongue," Seancha, Conchobor's chief poet and son of Ailill, said mildly, reminding Fergus of Bricriu's reputation.

"Words," Fergus said in disgust, shaking his huge, shaggy head. "Always words. Then tear his tongue from his throat. Like to see him talk teats into flapping then."

"I will talk men's ballocks into air and all will walk around like eunuchs," Bricriu continued, ignoring Fergus.

"That's enough," Fergus said. "Sure, and isn't it better to come, then." He reached down covertly, feeling his balls like boulders reassuringly.

"I suggest that we counsel with the warriors of the Red Branch straightaway. This is going too far," Seancha whispered urgently to Conchobor.

"Hmm," Conchobor whispered back. "Perhaps this is something we should do. Otherwise, mischief may be the consequence. If not Bricriu, then surely someone like Fergus."

He turned to Bricriu. "I think it would be best if I talked with my warriors alone before I give you my answer. I see that you are dusty from your trip. Perhaps you would care for a bath and a change of clothes?" He gestured at the young girl beside him. "See to him." Her eyes flickered in terror to his. "No. Bad idea," he said, correcting himself. He gestured to Ness, sitting at the far side of the room. "Mother, would you be so kind as to take care of Bricriu?"

"Now wait a minute," Fergus began.

"Oh, do be quiet!" Ness said, coming forward. "I think you've said about enough for one afternoon." She paused beside the Poison-Tongued One. "Well, come on, then. Let's take care of you before dinner." She sniffed. "From the smell of things, I don't think you've had a wash in a week."

"Onions," Bricriu said apologetically. "My stomach can't take them anymore." He farted softly and all leaned hastily away from him.

"Then why eat them?" Ness said. "Whew! Smells like something crawled up your robe and died."

She led him firmly from the hall. Men reached hastily for their cups and drained them and clamored for more beer. Seancha shook his head and sat down at Conchobor's right hand.

"Well, this is a fine mess," he said.

"I still say rip his tongue out by the roots," Fergus growled. "I'd like to hear the words he says with his bare lips flapping like birds' wings, then. Maybe that boil will burst from his forehead and his brains will leak out onto the ground."

"It would make the ground barren, then," Seancha said.

"Then let's just kill him and be done with it," Fergus said.

"That wouldn't be moral," Conchobor said.

Seancha sniffed. "Morals are a tyranny against nature and reason. Know instead yourselves as part of the world. And know
what can happen if that balance is upset."

"Urk. Metaphysical speculation," Fergus complained. "The
next thing you know, you'll be speaking in mad, mock-elegant
dactyls. Give me another cup or two of this honey-beer and a good
sharp dagger, and I'll do the rest. Shit! I wish Cúchulainn was
here. He'd tear the ballocks off that ram and make him a wether.
Why, he'd—"

"Yes, yes. We all know what the Hound would do," Seancha
said. "You're becoming sententious. Let's get on with it." He
turned back to Conchobor. "Now, the way I see it, the best thing
to do is to go to the feast."

"Gods' balls," Fergus rumbled.

"But," Seancha continued, casting a withering look at Fergus,
"we can make conditions. Rules of Hospitality, remember? First,
we'll demand he give over hostages from his own family."

"Fat lot of good that'll do," Fergus said. "That worm-tongued
rat-fucker will set us all against each other with his honeyed
words. You watch and see. Watch and see."

"Not," Seancha said gently, "if he isn't at the feast."

"What's that? Oh, I like that," Fergus said, sitting up
straighter.

"But will he go for it?" Conchobor asked, worrying his lip
with a forefinger.

Seancha shrugged. "Of course. We'll simply set eight swordsmen on him to compel him to retire from the feast for the safety
of all. Rules—"

"—of Hospitality," Fergus finished. He clapped Seancha upon
the shoulder, staggering the slighter man. "Now, that is the way
to have a feast!" He smacked his lips, as if suddenly remembering
Bricriu's description of the feast preparation.

"Yes," Conchobor said doubtfully. "But it still seems a little . . ."

"Dubious?" suggested Seancha.

Conchobor nodded. "Yes. That's it. Dubious. I suppose, though, that it's the only way." Seancha nodded. Conchobor sighed, gnawed his lips for a moment, considering, then said, "Very well. We'll put it to him."

He looked around the room until he spied his son Furbaide Ferbenn sitting in a corner by himself, eyes hungrily watching the serving wenches bustling around the hall. He motioned to his son and Furbaide rose and sauntered up to his father.

"Yes?" he said, deliberately omitting the salutation. He resented his placement at the foot of the Red Branch while Cúchulainn occupied the Champion's Seat whenever he came to the Red Branch. Longer times passed between his visits lately, now that he had married and moved with his wife to the fortress of Dún Dealgan. Yet Conchobor kept the seat vacant beside him, steadfastly ignoring all hints by Furbaide that he be allowed to fill it.

"Yes?" Conchobor said, his eyebrows shooting upward. "That's all? Just 'yes?' " Syllables clicked like marbles in his throat.

Furbaide glanced at Seancha and Fergus, caught their reproving frowns and tossed his long, fine hair out of his eyes. "Yes, Father?"

"Father now," Conchobor said. "That's an improvement, wouldn't you say?" He glanced at Seancha, then back to his son. Tiny white lines of fury appeared on either side of his nose. His fingers drummed on the arm of his couch. Furbaide tried to meet his eyes, but couldn't. He shuffled his feet and dropped his gaze to his toes.

"Yes, my lord," Furbaide said sullenly.

"Better," Conchobor said. He leaned forward on his couch. "Honors will come to you *if* you are an honorable man. You cannot demand respect. You must earn it by giving it first. Do you understand?"

"I understand."

"I wish I could believe you," Conchobor said. He leaned back in his chair and took a deep drink from his cup, holding it out to the young girl to refill. "But I don't. Again," he said as Furbaide's head jerked back, "that is something you must earn. But never mind for now. Go to Bricriu, whom you will find in either the washhouse or the guest house, and tell him that I will be pleased to attend the feast to celebrate the building of his new house. I will be accompanied by Cúchulainn, Loegaire Búadach the Triumphant, son of Connad Mac Iliach, Conall Cernach the Victorious, Fergus, Seancha, and my usual *curaid*." His eyes flickered around the room. He began to chant:

"Celtchar Mac Uthechair,
Eogan Mac Durthacht,
Fiacha Fíachaig,
Fergna Mac Findchoíme,
Fergus Mac Leti,
Cúscraid Mend Macha Mac Conchobor,
Tri Mac Fiachach,
Rus Dáre Imchad,
Muinremur Mac Geirrgind,
Errge Echbél,
Amorgene Mac Ecit,
Mend Mac Salchadae,
Dubthach Dóel,
Feradach Find Fectnach,
Fedelmid Chilair Chétaig,
Furbaide Fer Bend,
Rochad Mac Fathemon,
Connad Mac Mornai,
Erc Mac Fedelmthe,
Illand Mac Fergusa,
Fintan Mac Neill,
Ceternd Mac Fintain,
Factna Mac Sencada,

Conla Sáeb,
Ailill Miltenga."

Conchobor paused and looked around. "All you will go. Our wives and their attendants will attend as well. Tell Bricriu that I hope the numbers will not inconvenience him."

"It shall be done. My lord," Furbaide said. He inclined his head and stepped back and away, seething as he left on his messenger's errand. "Damn and double blast," he mumbled as he stepped out into the glaring afternoon sun. "You could have sent one of the servants to do this. Not a knight of the Red Branch."

He found Bricriu lolling in a wooden tub in the washhouse. a clean tunic and robe laid out neatly for him. He glanced into the greasy gray water and shook his head.

"My father, Conchobor the King, has instructed me to inform you that he will be pleased to attend the feast in celebration of your new house and that he will be attended by Cúchulainn, Loegaire Búadach the Triumphant, son of Connad Mac Iliach, Conall Cernach the Victorious, Fergus, Seancha, and his usual *curaid*. The wives of the champions and their attendants will attend as well. He begs your pardon and hopes that the number will not be too great for you to host."

Bricriu grinned and made a wide, sweeping gesture with his hand. "It is happily arranged," he said. "Tell Conchobor that he may bring more if he wishes. It is all the same to me."

"There is one thing," Furbaide said, enjoying himself.

"What's that?" Bricriu's eyes narrowed suspiciously.

"Hostages from your own family must be given by you to insure your poison tongue does no harm to your guests."

"Done," Bricriu said, the smile disappearing from his face.

"*And* you will be escorted from the hall by eight swordsmen as soon as you have laid out the feast," Furbaide said.

Bricriu's face slipped into a mask of stone. Tiny muscles clenched and released at the corners of his jaws. His fingers turned white from his grip on the edge of the tub. Then he forced a laugh and shrugged. He farted, and gas bubbles appeared on the surface of the gray water and broke, releasing a foul stench. Fur-baide stepped back hastily, his nose burning.

"Tell Conchobor that such is my respect for him that I agree to all of his terms," he said.

Furbaide bowed his head and fled the washhouse, pausing outside to draw deep breaths.

Bricriu watched him go, then slid farther down into the water. "Well now, Conchobor," he said softly. "Let us see what mischief I can do with this insult."

He farted again.

Chapter 3

THE JOURNEY TO BRICRIU'S HOUSE

THE NEXT DAY, THE men from Ulster set out from Emain Macha with their host, Bricriu, a battalion of armed warriors, and company under Conchobor, king, chieftain, and leader of the Red Branch. They marched excellently and briskly to the huge house erected by Bricriu.

Bricriu still seethed at the conditions that Conchobor had laid down for his acceptance to the feast. Giving the hostages up didn't matter to him, however, as much as the insistence that he absent himself from his own feast.

"Practically unheard of in the civilized world," he grumbled to himself, and the purple boil on his forehead began to bulge with the purulence of his thoughts, making his head ache and his temples throb.

"Why," he continued, "this is such that my disgrace will be heard throughout all of Ireland. Time and space. Time and space. Banning me from my own feast! Thinking to rend me impotent, are they? Well, we'll just see. Clearer to me is a whisper than to anyone else a cry."

"Did you say something?" Conchobor asked, leaning over from his chariot.

"Me? No, no," Bricriu said hastily. "Just clearing my throat. Too much dust. Not enough rain, you see."

"Yes, it is the dry season," Conchobor said soothingly. He reached down between his feet and produced a wineskin. "Would you care for a drink?"

"No, no," Bricriu said, shaking his head. "We'll soon be there. Then we'll all have a cooling draught."

"And be damned if I'll sip from your leavings," he mumbled under his breath.

He glanced over at Conchobor to see if he had heard him, but his words had been lost in the rattle of the chariots and Conchobor had turned his shoulder and was looking off to his right, up a ridgeline to where eagles sat on a lightning-struck tree. Sunlight glinted off his golden hair and shone on his white robe with the wide purple band running through it. Around his neck he wore a gold *torc*, and gold circlets gleamed on his heavy forearms and wrists.

Bricriu sucked in on his lips, chewing on them furiously like a hungry bull its cud. "Ah, yes. Look away from me. Look. Back again to where your Hound rides patiently, waiting for you to unleash him and his terror. Do you fear the moment that the Hound might turn on you?"

He cackled with laughter, but quickly looked back himself in fear that Cúchulainn might have heard him. It wouldn't do for that one to take on a rip and a tear. No, no. He had seen what happened when the Hound was a boy and took weapons for the first time and slew the sons of Nechtan Scéne and decorated his chariot—Conchobor's chariot, that is—and returned, lost in his battle frenzy. Oh, yes. That terrible transformation, the *riastradh,* that transformed men's blood into ice, numbing them with its terror. So terrible that Conchobor had been forced to send the women of Emain Macha out naked to greet the young lad upon his return before the men could seize him and plunge him into three vats to cool the burning of his blood. Bricriu rubbed his belly where an old scar hung like a white leech, the mark of a stab wound that should have killed him but didn't, leaving him nearly useless as a warrior. No, don't want that. Oh, no.

His eyes wandered over to where Mugain rode, noting her heavy breasts, her high cheekbones, the curve of her hip. Wouldn't mind seeing that naked again, though. He started to laugh, but a cloud of dust rolled up from his chariot's wheels and made him sneeze. A horsefly flew up from the withers of the horse in front of him and landed on his forehead next to the boil and bit deeply. He slapped hard at the fly, nearly knocking himself out of the chariot so that his driver was forced to grab his arm and jerk him back in.

"Now, sir, hold on tight! Road's a little bumpy. Don't want to lose you, now do we?" the man said. He hawked and spat over the side into the dust of the road.

"Urk," Bricriu said, shaking his head. He blinked against the tears in his eyes and used the edge of his robe to dry them, thinking desperately of something to say, something nasty.

"Keep your eyes on the road and both hands on the reins. Watch out for those rocks and potholes, clod!" he snapped finally. "Small wonder a gentleman has a hard time standing in one of these infernal contraptions, with drivers like you about. Damned dangerous to others on the road, I say! Be the death of someone someday, I'm thinking!"

"As you wish," the driver said, shrugging.

He released Bricriu so suddenly that the Poison-Tongued One had to grip the side of the chariot to keep from tumbling over onto the sunbaked road. He glared at the driver, thought to say something, then thought better of it. Why waste his words on a dolt when he had other prey waiting for them?

He looked back over the party following behind them, his eyes lingering first on Loegaire, then on Conall. Typical Ulstermen, with a bitter streak running through them. A *bold,* bitter streak, he amended. Maybe something could be done with them? He racked his brain.

Seancha frowned as he stared ahead through the dust at Bricriu's back. Not for one moment did he trust him. Bricriu had given in far too quickly with the conditions that Conchobor had set him for attending the feast. A black spleen resided in Bricriu's belly and spread its putrilage throughout his body. Seancha thought about the stories Bricriu had written in the past and shuddered when he remembered the damage that the man had caused. Could he have set the women's breasts to banging against each other like clapping hands? It didn't matter. The *thought* that he could was all that mattered. That he could ruin reputations, Seancha had no doubt, for that he had seen. But what was he up to now?

Seancha thought hard, remembering the conditions Conchobor had made. If Bricriu wasn't at the feast, surely no harm could come to anyone! Yet, a nervous thought prickled at the edges of his mind like a nettle worrying itself into the skin of the foot. There had to be something. Something.

"There it is," his charioteer said as they came above the ridge leading down to Dún Rudraige. Conchobor's chariot had pulled off the road onto a grassy knoll along with Cúchulainn's famous *Carbad Seardha*, the scythed chariot, its armament now absent. The two stared down at Bricriu's work.

"Pull over beside them," Seancha ordered, and the charioteer leaned back against the wheel-rein, pulling the horses over next to Cúchulainn's Black of Saingliu and Gray of Macha. Seancha looked at the horses: they seemed not to even be breathing hard, and Seancha remembered how Cúchulainn had gained the two steeds when the Black of Saingliu came out of the black Lake of Saingliu to test Cúchulainn, only to be ridden by the hero all over the country in one day. Black had torn huge chunks of sod from the land as he twisted and turned, trying to throw the Boy-Warrior from his back, but failing. Then came the Gray of Macha, appearing just as magically out of the gray Lake of Slieve Fuad. Cúchulainn had slipped his hands around the neck of the horse and ridden it all over Erin, the mount digging lakes with its hooves, storming over the Bregia of Meath, across the seashore marsh of Muirthemne Macha, through Moy Maeve, Currech Cleitech Cerna, Lia of Linn Locharn, Fer Femen Fergna, Curros Domnand, Ros Roigne, and Eo, until at last, weary from its effort, it halted and allowed Cúchulainn to harness it beside Black. Only Cúchulainn and his charioteer, Laeg Ríangabra, could harness and rein the two horses.

"Seancha!" Conchobor said. "Come and look at this!"

Obediently, Seancha stepped stiffly from the chariot and walked over to stand beside Conchobor. He followed Conchobor's pointing finger, then looked again in disbelief.

The roof towered more than thirty feet above the rest of the buildings behind the *rath*. Bright saffron banners hung from the eaves. The length and breadth of the building seemed ten, no, *twenty* times the length of any other hall he had seen, with the possible exception of the *Craeb Ruad,* the Red Branch, or Maeve's Cruachain, the Place of Enchantment in Connacht. Behind the house stood a maze of wonder at the center of which lay a pond with water so blue it hurt the eyes to view it in the sun. Sunlight glinted from the fresh wood and marble, making the building shine as if plated with silver. Rainbows hung in the air from three fountains casting sparkling streams high into the air, while exotic birds and animals prowled the gardens.

"I think," Seancha said, "that Bricriu has ambition."

Conchobor looked at him. "Why do you say that?"

"What need does a man like Bricriu have for such finery?" Seancha answered. "There's much to think about a man who dresses a pig in fine robes."

"Well, gentlemen, what do you think?" Bricriu asked from behind them.

Conchobor turned, clapping his hands together. "Well. What can I say? Magnificent, Bricriu. Truly magnificent!"

Bricriu smiled thinly and looked at Cúchulainn. "And what does our fine Hound say about it?"

Cúchulainn shrugged, folding his arms across his brawny chest. He wore a simple gray tunic with a red-and-purple border, and a gold *torc,* smaller than Conchobor's but equally as magnificent, around his neck. His sword, the famous *Cruaidin Cailid-*

cheann, leaned against his thigh. Sunlight glinted from the three colors of his hair, refracting a halo. "I wonder about the necessity of it."

"The *necessity?*" Bricriu said. "There is no necessity. Cannot one simply make something of beauty and enjoy it without thinking about *necessity?*"

"You asked me; I told you," Cúchulainn said softly. "I do not see any added defenses to protect it, though. That is what I mean by necessity."

"Ah," Bricriu said. He smiled sourly. "But that is why we have you guarding the passes, is it not, Cúchulainn? The king's champion looking after the kingdom? What need do I have for defense if I have you for protection?"

"One man cannot be in two places at once," Seancha murmured. "And only a fool would think otherwise. Or a dolt."

"Why have we stopped?" a voice broke in from behind them. They turned to see Conall Cernach of the Victories trot up beside them, along with Loegaire Búadach the Triumphant.

"We have arrived," Cúchulainn said. He gestured with his chin toward the house.

"That's it, then?" Loegaire asked. He eyed it critically. "No defenses." He hawked and spat. "Like a mouse eating its tail, a house without defenses."

Bricriu's eyes narrowed, then a cold smile spread his lips. "Well. What do we stand here for in the noonday sun when tubs of cold water and beer and wine wait below?" He gestured back at the party that had halted when Conchobor's chariot had climbed the knoll and stopped. "And what about your lovely ladies? Surely you do not want their beauty marred by the sun? I have lotions waiting for them in their chambers."

"You are right. And most gracious for reminding me," Conchobor said. He stepped back into his chariot and nodded at his driver. "Let us go, Ibar."

Ibar nodded, glancing over meaningfully at Cúchulainn. He lifted the reins and slapped them down on the backs of Conchobor's matched blacks. The horses leaned into their harness and the chariot clattered down the road. Cúchulainn leaped effortlessly into his chariot. Laeg lifted the reins and clucked soothingly at Black and Gray and the two horses surged forward, catching up to Conchobor's chariot with ease.

"Wait for us!" Conall called and turned to race back to his chariot.

"Damn and rat-shit," Loegaire snarled. "First we stop, then we go. Then we stop. I tell you, Conall, it's glad I'll be when this folly's over." His voice faded as they drew near their chariots.

"Well, my friend, Seancha," Bricriu said, turning to him. "Should we go and see how one dresses a pig?"

He bowed and turned back to his chariot. Seancha flinched from Bricriu's words.

"He heard," he thought. "Now what mischief have I brought upon myself?"

He heaved a deep sigh and climbed stiffly back into his chariot and nodded. He clung tightly to the rim of the chariot as the charioteer unfurled his whip along the backs of the horses and they lurched forward into a gallop.

A strange foreboding gripped Seancha's heart as they drew nearer Bricriu's house.

Chapter 4

THE
CONSPIRACY

BRICRIU STEPPED FROM HIS chariot and glowered at the
servant hastening forward to take the bridle and lead the horses
away to be unyoked. He glanced up at the balcony where his wife
stood, mouth puckered as if eating ripe sloe berries. She was well
mated to him, with her own sharp tongue capable of shaving thin
slices from a person's pride. His mouth pulled down in a grimace
and her eyebrow raised in question. A gas bubble rose and burst
in his stomach and he belched and turned to welcome Conchobor
as his chariot rumbled into the fort, followed by the Black and
Gray of Cúchulainn.

"Welcome, my king!" he cried. "Welcome to Dún Rudraige
and my home!" He motioned irritably, and young, scantily dressed
wenches scurried from the porch to take Conchobor's cloak. A
couple tugged for a moment over Cúchulainn's cloak before he
shrugged it from his shoulders and handed it to a black-haired
girl with full breasts bubbling over her gray tunic cut low, and
high to expose her thighs. She giggled with pleasure and hurried
away as the other—a slim, golden-haired girl with cone-shaped
breasts poking pertly at her tunic—sulked for a moment, then

smiled as Cúchulainn nodded at her.

Music began in the courtyard as pipers tuned their instruments, one to the other, until twenty-four began sweet melodies in perfect harmony.

Bricriu caught the exchange between the serving girl and Cúchulainn and noticed as well how other serving girls hastened to the chariots of Loegaire and Conall as they entered behind Cúchulainn, and an idea began to prickle at the edges of his thought.

"You will want to refresh yourself, no doubt," he continued smoothly to Conchobor. He motioned to the washhouse off to the side of the stable. "Fresh, cool water has been readied for you to rinse the dust of the journey from you. New robes have been laid out for your use and your men's. Likewise, your wives shall be well-treated with perfumes and oils scented with damask roses and lavender. When you are ready, I shall bring you into the feasting-hall."

"We thank you, Bricriu," Conchobor said formally after carefully considering each of Bricriu's words. He glanced at Seancha, who gave a slight nod. "You have prepared well and your gracious greeting shows your worthiness."

Bricriu bowed as Conchobor followed the lead of the young women assigned to him. Seancha trailed closely behind him, while Cúchulainn took his sword from his chariot and told Laeg, his charioteer, to give a double measure of oats to both Black and Gray, then followed his king to the washhouse.

Conall grunted after hearing Bricriu's words and stepped from his chariot, tossing his robe to one of the young women. Then, ignoring Bricriu, he sauntered after Cúchulainn.

As Loegaire started past, Bricriu gave a tight smile and said, "Hail, Loegaire the Triumphant, son of Connad Mac Iliach, mighty mallet of Brega and hot hammer of Meath, whose ferocious blows like the red-hot thunderbolt have brought him many victories for Ulster! What has kept you from being named the champion of all?"

Loegaire paused and eyed him suspiciously. "We may have been boorish and churlish before accepting your invitation, Bricriu, but this is no way to greet me, by questioning my right to be named champion."

"Oh," Bricriu said hastily, raising his hands in protest at Loegaire's words. "Do not misunderstand me! I meant only that surely if anyone deserved the right to be named champion of all Ulster, it should be you. Who can raise claim to as many victories as you? Who has placed as many heads in the hall of the Red Branch as you?"

"No one," Loegaire said, relaxing against the honey-flow of Bricriu's words. "And, if I choose, that title would be mine."

"Well," Bricriu said confidentially, leaning closer to the brawny-chested warrior, "if that is your right, then the Champion's Portion of the feast should go to your place at the table and the championship of the Red Branch would be yours forever, for nowhere will a better Champion's Portion be prepared than the one I have prepared here."

Loegaire's eyes shone with greedy interest. "And what might that be?" he asked. "I have heard many claims made by many hosts for the Champion's Portion, but their words have been built on air. None has been worthy of claiming in the name of my deeds."

"Do you think I run a fool's house here?" Bricriu asked scornfully. He drew away from Loegaire, folding his robe over his right forearm in an oratory manner.

"I meant no offense," Loegaire said, suddenly reminded of Bricriu's poisoned tongue.

"And none has been taken," Bricriu said graciously. "But let me tell you of its preparation, then you can decide if it is worthy of claiming. And then you will know that by claiming it, you will be the champion among the warriors of the Red Branch forever. That is, if you follow my advice."

"I will," Loegaire said eagerly. "Speak on."

"First, I have had a cauldron—so big that it will easily hold any three of the Red Branch warriors—filled with undiluted wine. I have also ordered prepared a seven-year-old boar that since it was a piglet has been fed nothing but fresh milk and finely ground meal in springtime, curds and sweet milk in summer, shelled acorns and nuts and wheat in autumn, and beef and broth in winter. Along with that has been prepared a seven-year-old cow that since it was a calf has been fed nothing but heather gleaned from twigs, and fresh milk and herbs mashed with sweet meadow grass and oats and barley. One hundred wheat cakes made from twenty-five bushels—four cakes only from each bushel—have been baked in a honey-baste. That is truly a Champion's Portion!

"Now," he continued, seeing the greedy light glow brighter in Loegaire's eyes, "you have called yourself champion and so I give it to you. Simply have your charioteer claim it in your name and my servants will bring it to you."

"And many will die if it is not so," Loegaire said warningly.

Bricriu laughed. "As I said, this is not the house of a foolish man! Have I not said it would be so? The Champion's Portion will be brought to the true champion of the Red Branch!"

Satisfied, Loegaire smiled and turned away, making his way to the washhouse. Bricriu watched him go, the smile slowly fading from his lips as Loegaire drew nearer and nearer to the house.

"Idiot," he said under his breath as the warrior's broad back disappeared through the doorway. He glanced up at his wife. She looked down at him from her perch on the balcony and nodded in satisfaction, for she had heard the exchange between Loegaire and her husband.

"I take it, then, that you have had difficulty?" she purred softly.

Bricriu grimaced. "More than I thought. Nuts and onion stalks! These ill-mannered churls believe that I planned mischief when I invited them to the feast. At first they refused to come! Think of it! All that planning, all that food! We would have been eating this stuff until Beltaine. And you know my belly cannot tolerate sweetmeats anymore!"

"Unheard of, refusing you," his wife sniffed, tossing her black-and-gray curls back from her wide forehead. Her double chins wobbled indignantly. "City manners, I tell you! There's a sickness that breeds there you won't find here in the country," she said heatedly.

"Well, they've come," Bricriu said. "But only after refusing me a seat at my own feast!"

"What? What's this?" his wife shouted even more indignantly.

"Yes, yes," Bricriu said, breaking in on her tirade. He had heard these complaints before and they tired him just as much now as they did then. "You would think that they thought I would cause a disaster like an earthquake."

He threw his arms wide and declaimed,

> "Come, Dagda!
> Shatter the air!
> Make earth tremble!
> Shake Conchobor
> From his gilded chair!"

He paused, then flicked his wrist disdainfully. "See? Nothing! I'm impotent!"

"Hmm," his wife said crossly. "Of that, certainly. No Druid, you. But surely there is more you have planned for this insult?"

He placed a finger beside his nose and blinked wisely. "Ah. Now that is a different story. We shall see. We shall see."

The door opened behind him and Conall the Victorious came out, running thick fingers through his wet hair, smoothing it back. His tunic strained across his thick chest with the motion of his arms. His blue eyes swept over Bricriu, dismissing him as he walked toward the feasting-hall.

"Hail, Conall the Victorious! Hero of countless victories and battles! Winner of many hurling matches over the Red Branch warriors! Leader of the Ulster warriors in foreign lands by three days and three nights across so many fords that your comrades see you only after the battle is nearly won! When they return, who remains behind to protect their rear but the great Conall so that no surprise attack may be launched upon them!"

"Enough," Conall growled. "I've heard of your sly words, Bricriu. No serpents live in our land because your words have driven them from here in fear for their own skin."

"A bad metaphor, though useful," Bricriu said glibly. "But, tell me, Conall, what keeps the Champion's Portion from your table?"

"Nothing," Conall said. "Except none has been made that is equal to me."

"Ah, none until now, you mean. Surely you do not mean for my Champion's Portion to go to a lesser man." Bricriu's eyes widened in astonishment. "Why, that certainly would demean your stature among the Red Branch!"

Conall furrowed his thick brow, his eyes squinting against the pain of thought. He pawed his fingers through his beard, looking for meaning behind Bricriu's words. Finding none, he shrugged.

"All right. What makes your portion so different from the others that have been laid across skimpy tables?"

"First, I have had a cauldron—so big that it will easily hold any three of the Red Branch warriors—filled with undiluted wine. And a cask of beer, freshly brewed from honey-soaked barley," he added hastily, remembering that Conall was not given to sups of wine. "I have also ordered prepared a seven-year-old boar that since it was a piglet has been fed nothing but fresh milk and finely ground meal in springtime, curds and sweet milk in summer, shelled acorns and walnuts and hickory nuts and wheat in autumn, and beef and broth in winter. And if that is not enough for the great Conall, then I have had prepared a seven-year-old cow that since it was a calf has been fed nothing but heather gleaned from twigs, and fresh milk and herbs mashed with sweet meadow grass and oats and barley. One hundred wheat cakes made from twenty-five bushels—four cakes only from each bushel—have been baked in honey. That is truly a Champion's Portion!"

"As you say," Conall grunted. His belly rumbled with hunger. He nodded. "So, then as you say, the Champion's Portion will be mine."

"Then tell your charioteer, Id Ríangabra, to claim it on your behalf when the feast begins, and you will be forever exalted among the heroes of the Red Branch," Bricriu said.

Conall frowned. "You have something up your sleeve, Bricriu. I don't know what it is, but I warn you to avoid your trickery. Do not play nuts and sticks with me or I'll crush your head like a ripe melon!"

He turned to stump away, but Bricriu purred, "And the Champion's Portion?"

"Is mine, by right," Conall said. His eyes narrowed as he nearly caught a thought, but it danced away on fairies' wings in the bright sunlight. He mumbled insults beneath his breath against Bricriu's patronage as he walked past the Poison-Tongued One.

Bricriu watched his broad back disappear into the feasting hall, then looked up at his wife. Light flashed from her heavily jeweled fingers as she clapped her pudgy hands softly together in admiration.

"Ah! Now I understand, my husband. Brilliantly done! You play one off against the other. Very subtle! Very subtle!"

"It is nothing," he said modestly. "Everyone is only an actor in the play. It just takes a director to change their ways with a few hints. You only have to remember that we live by the myths we impose upon ourselves. Tap into that myth and you tap into the man. Simple."

His face clouded for a moment as he stared back at the wash-house. "Of course, one must be careful of playing too much the fool with that Seancha around. Seers and prophets are no men to jug with. The wrong word and they'll dry a man out into a husk and plant him in an arid ground. They're as crazy as loons until someone can harass them into sanity."

"Wisdom!" his wife cried with tiny squeals from the balcony.

"Hmm. Well, we hope so, don't we? Otherwise, it might be a dry feast."

The door opened again and Bricriu whirled and pretended to be walking to it. He stopped, feigning to be awestruck as Cúchulainn moved out, gliding quickly, smoothly, on the balls of his highly arched feet. Seven toes he had on each of his feet and seven fingers on each hand. Seven pupils looked from each eye and seven jewels sparkled from each pupil. Four dimples dented each cheek—blue, purple, green, and yellow—while fifty tresses of hair rolled neatly between his ears and three colors were they, black, white, and gold. His chin was hairless. A tunic of purple with a white-gold border hung over him to his knees, while a white-hooded cloak with a flashing red border was held around him by a brooch of red gold. He carried his sword, the *Cruaidin Cailidcheann,* carelessly over one shoulder.

Behind him, Bricriu heard his wife sigh in yearning and his stomach gripped him painfully. He forced a smile to his lips and greeted the Boy-Warrior respectfully.

"Hail, Cúchulainn! Mightiest of Emain Macha's warriors! Victor of Breg, the bright banner of the Liffey, and darling of Emain, secret sweetheart of wives and young girls! Your name is no nickname, that is certain, for they flock around you like bitches in heat!" Bricriu laughed. *Hyuck, hyuck, hyuck!* Then he hastily controlled himself as Cúchulainn frowned. "That is to say, you are truly the champion of the Red Branch! You control the feuds among them and protect them when they rashly—shall we say too rashly, hmm?—charge into battle! Justice is forever in your thoughts when you arbitrate between two men, and such is your decision that no one goes away dissatisfied. But braver still are your exploits! You succeed where others fail and all the men of the Red Branch acknowledge your bravery, your deeds! Why, who else but you could claim the Champion's Portion that I have prepared?"

"By my tribe's gods, no one!" exclaimed Cúchulainn. "Only he who would lose his head would dare to contest with me."

"And so it should be," purred Bricriu. "Only have your charioteer, Laeg Ríangabra, claim what I have prepared in your honor at the feast tonight. First, I have had a cauldron—so big that it will easily hold any three of the Red Branch warriors, except, of course, you and Fergus Mac Róich, understandably—filled with undiluted wine. I have also ordered prepared a seven-year-old boar that since it was a piglet has been fed nothing but fresh milk and finely ground meal in springtime, curds and sweet milk in summer, shelled acorns and nuts and wheat in autumn, and beef and broth in winter. Along with that has been prepared a seven-year-old cow that since it was a calf has been fed nothing but heather gleaned from twigs, and fresh milk and herbs mashed with sweet meadow grass and oats and barley. One hundred wheat cakes made from twenty-five bushels—four cakes only from each bushels—have been baked in a honey-baste. And, knowing your *geis,* that which has been forbidden you by the ancients, all hounds and dogs have been kept from herding the animals! That is truly a Champion's Portion!"

"It will do," Cúchulainn said. "But what is it you want, Bricriu?"

"I?" Bricriu's eyebrows shot upward in amazement, black smudges nearly disappearing into his hair. He forced his eyes wide. "What could I possibly want or get from honoring you?"

"Each dog has its day," Cúchulainn said. "The wiliest licks its master's hands until the master turns his back, then hamstrings him and goes for the throat."

"Ugh. Er. Hmm. I suppose it's a meaningful metaphor, but not appropriate at this time. I but seek to honor you, Great Cúchulainn."

"I wonder," Cúchulainn said. Tiny muscles quivered along his eyes and Bricriu felt his heart lurch and thud in his chest as for a moment, he thought Cúchulainn's *riastradh,* his "warp-spasm" that made him feared and invulnerable in battle, was about to set upon him, but the warrior lifted a corner of his cloak and wiped his eyes as a breeze kicked a dust devil between them. Bricriu sighed as he remembered the "warp-spasm," when each hair seemed to be a nail hammered into Cúchulainn's head and fire tipped each hair to form a halo over him, and one eye became a needle's eye while the other bulged from his cheek, and his great heart boomed in his chest like a giant's *bodhrán,* and he twisted in his skin as his mouth gaped wide until his liver flapped in his gullet.

"Very well," the warrior said. "I accept your Champion's Portion. But no knavery, Bricriu!" he added warningly. "That would not settle well with me!"

Bricriu shuddered as Cúchulainn passed him, entering the hall. He remembered well the day, for he had been wounded in the battle and had made it to the walls of the Red Branch and watched what had happened. The Red Branch had been beaten that day and Conchobor and his son Cúscraid Menn Macha, the Stammerer, had been left for dead by the warriors. It had been the keening of the women that had awakened the Boy-Warrior from his sleep so that he stretched and cracked the two blocks of stone that served him as a pillow and footrest. Cúchulainn had gone out, armed only with his hurling-stick, and brought back Conchobor, but while searching the battlefield below the ravens and crows whirling overhead, Cúchulainn had come upon a half-headed man carrying half a corpse upon his back.

—Help me, Cúchulainn, cried the man. Carry my brother for a while.

—No, Cúchulainn said. I cannot. I must find my king.

And the man threw his burden at Cúchulainn, but the young boy dodged and grappled with the man. Cúchulainn was thrown down and it was then that Bricriu had heard the Badb, the most terrible of the Mórrigna, the warrior goddesses, cry: "A poor warrior it is who lies at the feet of a ghost!"

And Cúchulainn had reached up, struck off the half-head with his hurling-stick and driven it before him, playing ball with it across the entire plain of battle until he found his king.

—Is this my king, Conchobor? the boy asked.

When Conchobor answered, Cúchulainn found him in the ditch, where earth had been piled up on either side to hide him.

—And what brings you to this craven field? Conchobor asked the boy. Do you wish to know terror that well?

But Cúchulainn did not answer and pulled his king from the ditch and lifted him to his back.

—I am famished, Conchobor said. Go to that house and light a fire. And when Cúchulainn had done this, Conchobor said: Now, if I had a cooked pig, I would return to life.

And Cúchulainn went out and found a man beside a cooking-pit, holding his weapons in one hand while he cooked a pig upon a spit with the other. The man attacked Cúchulainn, but the boy easily killed him and carried back his head as well as the pig to Conchobor, who swallowed the pig.

—Now, take me back to the Red Branch, where my wounds may be washed, Conchobor said.

On the way back, they found Cúscraid sorely wounded, but Cúchulainn easily lifted him to his other shoulder and carried both his king and the king's son into the Red Branch as one.

Bricriu shook himself from memory and took himself to the washhouse to cleanse himself, trying to forget what Cúchulainn had done when only seven. He did not want to bring that fury upon himself now that the boy had become a youth. No, this he did not want. He had to proceed carefully with the rest of his plan. Carefully, indeed.

Chapter 5

THE

ARGUMENT

When they entered the huge hall, all paused for a moment to stare openmouthed at the fine furnishings. Half of the hall was set aside for Conchobor and his *curaid*, while the other half had been made ready for the wives of the heroes and their attendants who waited upon Mugain, Conchobor's wife and daughter of Eochaid Fedlech.

Tiny lights danced from polished wood as three fires crackled and roared in the middle of the hall, casting light into the far corners. Apartments had been laid with plump cushions and discreetly shielded from others with fine curtains dyed in brilliant colors of yellow, purple, red, gold, green, and blue. Conchobor's apartment was raised above the others, and artfully placed so that the king had only to turn his head to see into any of the apartments.

From somewhere, a hidden *cruitire* began to play his harp in soft, dulcet tones, while fifty naked *cumals,* with fine, young breasts, waited to do their serving. Servants began bringing in thick platters laden with food.

"This is truly a fine place," Conchobor said to Bricriu.

"Yes," Bricriu said. "Isn't it? Will it please you to take your place so that the feasting might begin?"

"Of course," Conchobor said, and led the way to the men's half of the hall. He seated himself and motioned for his warriors to take their places. Cúchulainn seated himself at the foot of Conchobor's couch on a special place made for the king's champion. His cousin, Conall Cernach, and Loegaire took their places across the hall from him. Their charioteers seated themselves at the feet of their masters.

Fergus took his place to the king's left, as was his right as the former king. He sighed as he arranged his bulk on the pillows, reaching beneath his genitals to make himself comfortable. He scratched contentedly and cocked an eye at the seven heavy-breasted women who had been assigned to him. They giggled nervously and the boldest licked her lips in anticipation of the night to come, for all had been told of Fergus's need for seven women a night to satisfy his lust. It was a part of his *geis*, as was the curse to never refuse an ale-feast.

"Now," Seancha said, whispering in Conchobor's ear from his place to the king's right. "Remember your promise to the warriors: have Bricriu removed so that we may proceed in peace."

"Aye, remember that!" Fergus growled. "Get rid of that dog-licker—no offense, Cúchulainn, my foster-son—before he causes any trouble or ill feelings."

Conchobor looked apologetically at Bricriu. "You see how it is," he said. "A man reaps what he has sown, and so forth."

"I know, my lord," Bricriu said, bowing. "It is my ill fate to be cursed with a tongue that makes men nervous."

"Yes, yes," Conchobor said and quickly gestured toward Furbaide Ferbenn to bring the eight warriors who had been designated to escort Bricriu from the feast. They rose and quickly surrounded Bricriu and his wife, two on each side, their swords drawn and held ready.

Bricriu smiled thinly and turned, graciously taking his wife's arm to lead her from the feasting-hall. All watched nervously as the pair marched formally the length of the hall. At the threshold,

Bricriu paused, then called out guilelessly: "Now, don't forget the Champion's Portion, for it is not the portion of a fool's house. Be sure that you give it to the most valorous among you that all elect. Wine, beer, beef, and pork. All of the highest quality that a man might want."

He smiled brightly and stepped through the curtained door, letting the saffron folds fall behind him. For a moment, all was silent in the hall, then the servants began to serve the food. Sedlang Mac Ríangabra, Loegaire's charioteer, rose from his place and said: "Here now! Be certain that you bring the Champion's Portion over here to Loegaire the Triumphant, for only he is entitled to sup from that among the other would-be heroes of Emain Macha."

"Not so!" Id Mac Ríangabra said hotly, leaping to his feet. "All here know that Loegaire is still licking the milk from the paps of his nurse. He isn't worthy to carry the spear of Conall Cernach. Bring the Champion's Portion over here or be ridiculed by the poets for not knowing a champion from a spalpeen."

"Spalpeen, is it?" roared Loegaire. "Why, you shittrel, I'll leave your tongue wagging in your ear!"

"Stop it!" Laeg Ríangabra said, climbing to his feet. "You all are playing a fool's game. Why, everyone here knows that the only true champion is Cúchulainn! Who else can lay claim to his deeds?"

"You lie!" Sedlang shouted, shaking his fist from across the room.

"Lie, do I? Why, you pup from a bitch's litter, I'll ram those words back into your throat with me fist!" Laeg swore.

"Oh, you will, will you?" roared Id, advancing out onto the floor. "I'll carve your liver from your worthless hide if you both don't back off! Now, bring that feast over here!"

"Gods' balls," Fergus swore, wearily shaking his head. "He did it anyway."

Seancha groaned, squeezing his temples between his hands. "Argh. Bricriu doesn't even have to be here to cause strife. He planted the seeds with his poisoned tongue before he left and now we reap the bitter harvest!"

The charioteers leaped onto the floor, brandishing their short-swords. They hacked and hewed at each other until half the hall glowed with fire from the clash of their blades, sparks flying on the costly draperies, where they burned holes in the linen. The enamel of their shields glowed whitely and the heroes sat back on their couches, warily watching lest one of the warriors fall onto them.

"By the gods!" Loegaire yelled as his charioteer was beaten back by Laeg. He jumped from his couch, drawing his sword as he swung down on the hapless Laeg, driving him back furiously to give his charioteer a breather.

"Fair play!" Conall roared and lashed out at Loegaire. To-gether, the two of them attacked Laeg, and then Cúchulainn joined the fray, his mighty sword singing dangerously as the music of its blade danced the length of the other warriors' blades.

Conchobor and Fergus shouted angrily as Loegaire and Conall turned like terriers upon Cúchulainn, attacking him violently, forcing his blade to leap in a rainbow of colors.

"Separate them!" Seancha ordered, and Conchobor and Fer-gus rose from their couches, stepping between the combatants. Seeing their king and former king between them, the warriors immediately dropped their sword arms to their sides and stood glaring silently at each other.

"So, your foster-fathers step in for you," Loegaire sneered at Cúchulainn. Seancha saw the red slowly climb into the hero's face and quickly stepped in front of him.

"Obey me!" he snapped. He whirled to face Loegaire and Conall. "All of you! Now! Or you will not enjoy the songs I sing tonight." Immediately they fell silent, stepping back from each other. "That's better," he said. "Now, listen to my wishes. Conall?"

"Yes," he grumbled.

"Loegaire?"

"As you will," he said, looking away, his eyes flashing angry bits of fire.

"Cúchulainn?" He had to speak twice before the Hound of Ulster answered.

"For now," he said.

"Good," Seancha answered, relief shining from his face. He mopped his brow. "Then tonight we will divide the Champion's Portion among the entire host. After the feast, each of you will travel to Connacht to Cruachain and obey the will of Ailill Mac Matach for his decision on which of you will receive the Champion's Portion at a feast to be held in your honor twenty days hence." He glanced over at Conchobor. "We may well hold that feast here as well, my king, for it is Bricriu's tongue that has brought chaos to this peaceful gathering and it is just that he should pay for that with another feast."

"We shall see," Conchobor said, frowning. "I must say, though, that the less I have to do with this man Bricriu, the better I feel."

"We can decide that later," Seancha said. "But for now, you will go to Connacht for judgment."

"To Connacht?" Fergus said, wrinkling his heavy brow in disbelief. "They are the sworn enemies of Ulster. You would have them choose the champion? Sheer stupidity, you ask me."

"Nobody asked you," Seancha said coldly. "And mind your tongue. You do not have the skill of Bricriu to play his lackey. It is unlucky for us to choose the champion after this free-for-all, for whomever we choose will anger the other two and their friends. A house, not even the Red Branch, cannot stand alone if divided three ways, and our enemies will fall quickly upon us if this is not resolved, and resolved to the satisfaction of all."

"But, Ailill?" Conall shook his head. "I have killed too many Connachtmen to receive fair judgment from them."

"I, too," Loegaire said.

"No one has hung more Connacht heads in the hall than I," Cúchulainn said.

"Each of you has slain enough of the Connacht host to be their mortal enemy," Seancha said impatiently. "They have a bone to pick with each of you. Therefore, there will be no favorites among their judgment. I have spoken so and such is my will. This matter will be adjudged in Cruachain. Now, return to your places."

Reluctantly, the three and their charioteers parted and returned to their couches. The servants scurried around among the warriors, dividing the Champion's Portion equally under the sharp eye of Seancha. Tentatively, the wenches moved into each apartment, carrying unguents and perfumed oils and scented water in brass bowls for washing, while above them, Bricriu glanced with satisfaction at his wife from his apartment behind the glassed windows.

"You see, my pet, they do not need me to worry their egos. They manage quite well by themselves," Bricriu said.

"False modesty," sniffed his wife. "You have done an admirable job of sowing the seeds, but now it looks as if the harvest has been reaped and the fields left for gleaning. What do you propose next?"

"Shouldn't it be time for the women to join their men?" he asked, rising from his couch.

"Oh, yes," his wife answered. "I had quite forgotten them. Oh, yes indeed. It is most certainly time for them to make their appearance."

Together, they walked out onto the balcony and looked down at the women as they readied themselves for appearing among the men. Honeyed wine had been served them while they bathed languidly in the washhouse, and now they laughed and giggled among themselves, half drunk with giddy glee. Bricriu noticed Fedelm of the Fresh Heart, the wife of Loegaire, as she emerged with her fifty women in attendance.

"Greetings, wife of Loegaire the Triumphant! Fedelm of the Fresh Heart is no apt name for one as beautiful and exquisite of breast and form as you. Your wisdom and lineage are without parallel among the wives of the heroes here tonight. Conchobor, your father, has ensured your presence at the head of all women in Ulster and I would deem it but a small honor to have you take precedence among the Ulster women in the feast-hall! All other women should follow at your heels as you lead them to your rightful place and enjoy dominion over all the ladies in Ulster forever!"

Fedelm looked up blearily at the figures of Bricriu and his wife standing on the balcony above. She hiccuped and straightened her shoulders and smoothed the white *sida,* the sheer silk imported from sea-traders, over her heavy breasts. Her nipples pushed visibly against the cloth, her dark triangle a seductive shadow.

"Yes," she said, her words slurring. "You are correct in all of this. What a bright man you are, Bricriu! And I thought your words to be only poisoned pits to sink into one's gall. So it shall be! But first—" she stirred uneasily and looked over her shoulder "—first I must empty my bladder, for I have drunk enough wine to give change to the tide of Mannanán's sea!"

"Ditches have been dug for the women on the third ridge over," Bricriu said, pointing to the south wall of the *rath.*

"Most gracious," Fedelm slurred and led her attendants away as Lendabair, daughter of Eogan Mac Durthacht and wife of Conall, appeared. She staggered as she stepped over the threshold of the bathhouse and caught her toe on the baseboard. Bricriu's wife nudged him gently in the ribs with an elbow. He grinned evilly at her in the twilight.

"Well, Lendabair! And how do you fare this fine evening?"

"Swell," she said, burping. "And I thank you for the fine wine that you furnished us. The sun was most hot today while traveling and made us very thirsty." Her attendants twittered like birds amongst themselves.

"You are most welcome," Bricriu said suavely. "But why should I not give the best of my wine for fair Lendabair? You, the darling and pet of all Emain Macha, you whose luster shines like the sun and makes mere moons of other women! As your husband Conall exceeds all men with his feats in battle, so have you distinguished yourself among all women! Now that I think about it, you should be the foremost among all women in Ulster and all should trail your footsteps into the Great Hall for feasting!"

"Most discerning of you, Bricriu," Lendabair said, preening. She pulled the neckline of her green *sida* down, exposing the creamy hillocks of her breasts. Bricriu strained his eyes through the twilight to catch the ruby glint of her nipples. "And so they shall. But first, I must pee." She looked around in vague confusion.

"We have dug trenches for the women on the third ridge over by the south wall," Bricriu said.

"I thank you for your courtesy," Lendabair said. She motioned to her attendants. "Come! Let us water! I swear by Fand that I alone could fill a ditch."

They staggered away. Bricriu's wife grinned whitely in the growing darkness. "Oh, you are very good," she said. "As you have done with their husbands, you are doing with their wives."

"Ah, yes," Bricriu said. "But now comes the biggest challenge."

She glanced down as Emer, Cúchulainn's wife, emerged from the bathhouse with her fifty attendants.

"Greetings, Emer, daughter of Forgall Monach, wife of the best man in all of the land! Emer of the Fair Hair is not appropriate enough greeting for you, for your head seems as if of spun gold!"

"Enough of your flattery, Bricriu," Emer said shortly. "I have heard of how you turn people's heads with your doggerel. You won't do that to me or my women!"

"Of course not, and why would I want to?" he asked in an injured voice. "You do me a great disservice, Emer, for whom Erin's kings and princes contend in jealous rivalry! As the sun is brighter than the stars of the heavens, so do you outshine all the other women in our fair country. Yes, all of Ulster and Connacht and Leinster and Munster should bow before your dainty white feet and listen in awe to your words. Your beauty and shape and elegance are the envy of all!"

"Stuff and nonsense," Emer sniffed, but her chin rose proudly at Bricriu's words and he could see that he had struck at the core of her vanity. She smoothed her white *sida* down over her cone-shaped breasts, the nipples bursting upon the cloth like ripe grapes.

Bricriu shrugged. "Be that as it may, it is the truth, elegant Emer. And all women should honor you by following you and treading in honor where your foot falls."

"I need to relieve myself before I go into the hall," Emer said, looking around.

"The third ridge over," Bricriu said.

Emer waved her thanks and marched off, her attendants following like a gaggle of geese. Bricriu smiled and spread his hands, shrugging.

"So easily done," his wife said. "You would have thought they would have seen through your words."

"The grape," he said modestly. "Wine turns men into idiots and women into vain fools."

"Not *all* women," she sniffed.

"Oh, yes," he said. "A jug of wine is the spice of wit. Much better than the muddy ecstasies of beer. It makes all vows false, the meek insolent, mocks the valiant, spurns the affectionate, turns the shy seductive and the seductive into whores. And that is the truth of what lies in wine."

"All inclusive," she said, "women know their limits far more than men."

"Perhaps. But men get drunk to feel drunk. Women get drunk to feel equal. And that is woman's tragedy. Watch and see."

They turned their attention to the far wall where the women came together, lifting their *sidas* as they squatted spraddle-legged over the cut trench.

"Good evening, Fedelm. Lendabair!" Emer called out. "And a fine soft night, is it not?"

"It is," Fedelm answered. "And will you be soon going to the feasting?"

"Of course. And you, Lendabair?"

"I wouldn't miss it for a cask of Bricriu's fine wine," the wife of Conall said. She sighed as her urine hissed against the earth of the ditch like the persistent buzzing of flies. "Grapes to vinegar. I could tan a cowhide by myself."

"And I could cut a new stream," Fedelm sighed in relief.

"And I a moat," Emer finished. She stood carefully and picked her way clear of the ditch. She smoothed her hair back with a touch of her fingers and began a stately march toward the Great Hall.

Fedelm noticed her going and hurriedly finished, rising and quickening her step away from the trench. Lendabair suddenly found herself alone and rose, taking quick steps to bring herself up to the others.

They glanced over at each other as they raised each foot, slid it gracefully, stately, in front of the other. As they came down the second ridge, their steps quickened, became shorter and shorter, then suddenly Fedelm lifted her skirt to her hips and began to run toward the house. Not to be outdone, Lendabair followed suit, with Emer quickly folding her hem around her waist and sprinting after the other two.

Their attendants followed suit, and Bricriu cackled with glee as he watched one hundred fifty-three beards winking in the moonlight from between flashing white thighs. His eyes lingered for a moment on the heavy beard of Lendabair, but Emer's golden fleece quickly drew his gaze as it sparkled in the white light of the moon. She rapidly outdistanced all the others, sprinting with her attendants down the final ridge leading to the feasting-hall to be the first to enter and become the queen of the whole province.

Inside, Conchobor lifted himself up on one elbow, cocking his head in alarm. "Listen!" he shouted. "I hear the rumbling of fifty chariots approaching! It must be the Connacht host crossing the border!"

The men quickly rose and barred the door to the feasting-hall as the whole hall shook from the thundering feet of the women galloping toward it. The men sprang to their arms.

"Nonsense!" cried Seancha. "If the Connacht host had come across the border, all of us save one—" he nodded at Cúchulainn "—would be suffering the pangs!"

The men looked quickly at each other. Slowly they nodded, slyly pressing fingers against their bellies to assure themselves that they did not suffer the childbirth pangs cursed upon them by Macha after they had refused to intercede on her behalf when she, about to deliver twins, was commanded by Conchobor to run a race against his horses to save the head of her husband. She had won, but at what a cost, falling across the line well ahead of the famed blacks and giving birth, her birthing shrieks mounting to the sky.

"For ten generations upon generations, all Ulstermen will feel the pangs of birthing during Ulster's darkest hours, when threatened by its enemies for ten days upon days!" she had pronounced before her death.

And so it had happened to all save Cúchulainn, who was not Ulster-born.

But it did not happen now and the warriors looked expectantly at each other.

"Lay up your weapons," Seancha ordered. "No enemy comes to this fort. It is only Bricriu, who has set the women to quarreling against each other as he did to you. By the gods, though, unless the doors remain barred to them, they will raise the dead with their words and set each of us at the other's throat."

The doorkeepers hastily added additional bars of fresh yew wood that bent with the onslaught of the women, but did not break.

Emer, daughter of Forgall Monach, wife of Cúchulainn, the fleetest of them all, outran the others and slammed her back against the door, calling out for the door to be opened to her.

"By the goddess!" she cried. "Open this door that I might enter and claim my right!"

Cúchulainn rose to open the door, but the gatekeepers stood five deep in front of it, keeping him away.

Lendabair arrived next and stepped quickly around to the side of the house and pushed against that door, crying, "I command you! Open this door to me and my attendants now!"

Not to be outdone, Fedelm huffed and puffed her way to the other side and cried out, "Loegaire! Quickly! Make them open this door to us before the others gain my right upon entrance!"

"Bad. This is bad," Conchobor said, shaking his head. "A very bad night." He raised his silver wand and struck it against the bronze pillar of his couch. The sound rang like a bell through the

Great Hall, and all the men turned to his bidding.

"Sit down," he commanded. "All of you. This has gone on long enough. Are we to be undone by the bitter words of Bricriu? Where's your dignity? Be men!"

"Listen to your king!" Seancha ordered. "This is not a war of arms, but a war of words that will soon be coming out of the mouths of the wives of Loegaire, Conall, and Cúchulainn. Let them settle their own differences with words. Quiet!" he roared. Slowly the clamor died down outside as the women heard his urgings. Bricriu chuckled with glee and leaned over the railing of his balcony to listen as the women made their claims.

"I claim the right of first speech," Fedelm of the Fresh Heart said quickly.

> "The woman who gave birth to me,
> she who was noble and free
> and equal to my father in rank
> and race, mated with him to make
> the blood in me royal and ensure
> that I was reared in good behavior,
> in courage, and in manly ways that
> would bring grace upon whoever that
> was chosen to be my husband. Loegaire
> was chosen for that. Look at Loegaire's
> deeds and see the truth of my words,
> for I could not be the wife to a ward
> or man who could not do what his red hand
> has done for Ulster. By himself alone, he defends
> the boundaries of Ulster, keeping its enemies
> from its borders. The Red Branch enemies
> quail in fear at his approach, for his strength
> is equal to the entire Red Branch strength.
> He is a defense and stolid protector
> against the wounds of Ulster. Greater
> are his victories than all the other victories
> combined, and greater still are his stories.

Why should not I, Fedelm, the beautiful, joyful
and lovely, be the first of the three
into the hall? All women should follow me!"

"I smell Bricriu's hand in this," growled Fergus. "Rules of
Hospitality be damned! I'll cut him in twain with my sword, the
In Caladbolg, whose stroke is like the rainbow!"

"Be quiet, old fool!" Seancha snapped.

Fergus's head jerked indignantly. "Be careful, Seancha. Poet
or not, I'll not be trifled with!"

"Shut up," Conchobor said tonelessly. "Let us hear what the
others say.

And Lendabair spoke, saying:

"She who just spoke, that fat pig,
laeks all my beauty! Sticks and twigs!
I am more beautiful than she
and have more good sense than she
and a fine carriage. I should walk first
into the hall and let others thirst
after my free, even steps and give Ulster
women my bearing as a measure.
My husband Conall of the Great Shield,
he who is the Victorious, he who wields
the greatest sword, the proud one who leads
all the others and their spears to deeds,
and he who is so proud coming back
to my white arms, bearing on his back
the heads of his enemies, is more than
worthy of all of you for my hand.
He brings his hard sword into every battle
for me and Ulster, defending all our cattle
and every ford, or destroying the ford
to keep it from our enemies. My lord
is the one hero who will have a column stone
like a tower etched in *Ogham*

raised over him, telling of his deeds.
Who can speak against the valiant deeds
of the son of noble Amergin? Who can
challenge his deeds? Only Conall can
lead all the Red Branch heroes and only I
can lead all the wives. All eyes
look upon the glory of Conall and stare
upon the beauty of the fair Lendabair.
Tell me now why would I not be
the first and all others after me?"

"Indeed, she speaks the truth," Conall growled.

"And mine lies?" Loegaire said threateningly. "Are you calling my wife a liar?"

"Thems the ones who don't speak the truth," Conall said stoutly, glowering, his face dark like a furnace's roar.

"Enough," Conchobor said wearily. "I have had enough of these nuts and stones. I don't want to hear another word from either of you."

They sat glaring at each other, eyes red with blood, as Emer spoke from her door.

"No woman here is more beautiful than I
in shape or wisdom. Any who says so lies,
for no one can challenge me for goodness
of form or brightness of eye, or kindness."

Loegaire and Conall both snorted at this, drawing a narrow look from Cúchulainn.

"No one has as much joy of loving
or the strength of loving as have I.
How could they? For think now, why
should they who have not felt the arms
of a man like my Hound? All Ulster
desires me! I have seen it fester

in the eyes of the other two husbands,
feel their stares undress me, their wands
growing hard, their thoughts upon my thighs,
my breasts, my hips. Hear their sighs
of longing as I walk across the room.
I am a nut of the heart! Doom
would fall upon the Red Branch if I
were a Cypriote, for then women would sigh
without their husbands tomorrow,
and give out many cries of sorrow,
for not even Fergus, who easily sees
seven women a night, could stay one with me!
But my husband is Cúchulainn, the Hound,
and so powerful is his sword that sounds
of longing come from wives for his arms
to hold them within the night! Arms,
though, that clasp me make us mates,
for no woman but I could share his fate,
his bed for one hour, let alone a night.
No toothless hound there! Blood cakes
his spear, stains his sword. Black
is his white body with blood and
his soft skin scarred and
welted with many sword cuts.
His thighs alone have so many cuts
healed now, that no finger can be
placed between them. All can see
the flame of his eye turn to the west,
to our enemies who seek to best
and enslave Ulster and turn its pasture
into arid fields. He is the protector
of Ulster when the pangs come upon
all others. It is he who fights upon
the plains and over the ears of horses,
over the breath of men and their horses,
only he who can make a salmon-leap feat,

and who can do many strange feats
such as the deadly dart-feat,
the feat-of-nine, the blind-feat!
The backs of proud armies he breaks
in single combat and easily takes
terror from the hearts and minds
of the ignorant peasants he finds!
None of Ulster's heroes have the brass
equal to a single leaf of grass
compared to Cúchulainn. They groan
among themselves on his deeds and moan
from their beds, clutching their bellies
in agony, while he opens the bellies
of armies while defending the borders
of Ulster alone when its borders
are defiled by enemies who dare to
cross them. Among those who think to
be his equal, he is like clear, red
blood, while they are like the scum bred
on ponds and in horse droppings. And I
say that the fine women of Ulster that I
see have cow udders instead of fine breasts
like mine and are shaped like the rest
of the cows compared to Cúchulainn's wife,
who is far better than any other wife."

With that, Loegaire and Conall each made a rush at the door
behind which their wives stood. When the doorkeepers stood firm
against them, each turned and broke a stave from the wall and
used it like a club, trying to batter his way through the men to
unbar the doors.

Cúchulainn, however, stepped to the wall beside the door
guarded by the doormen and bent at the waist, gripping the base
timber with both hands and, straining, lifted the palace wall until
the light of the stars gleamed beneath its edge. Emer drew a deep
breath and stepped past the wall. Behind her crowded her fifty

attendants and the fifty attendants of both Fedelm and Lendabair.
Belatedly, Loegaire and Conall managed to drive the doorkeepers
from their posts and fling the doors wide. Their wives marched
in only to find Emer and one hundred fifty attendants waiting for
them.

Cúchulainn let the wall drop until seven feet of the wattle
went into the ground, shaking the whole house. Silence descended,
then timbers cracked and fell.

"Ahhh!" cried Bricriu as he and his wife plunged through the
railing, arms and legs pinwheeling helplessly, his wife's plump
thighs gleaming white.

"Ummph!" they grunted as they landed in the pit of soupy
night soil from the stables and night trenches, all fermenting
slowly for use in the fields.

"Ah, shit!" Bricriu cried needlessly. He floundered to the surface, a turd clinging to his matted hair. He stared at his wife; a
strand of undigested hay clung to her cheek.

"My husband!" she cried. "Help me!"

"Urk," Bricriu said, pulling himself from the pit. He reached
down and lifted his wife free. They stood for a moment, their wet
garments plastered by ordure to them, then his wife gave a great
cry and, bawling, ran for the bathhouse. Bricriu's stomach
cramped and he bent forward, spewing its contents into the pit.

"Gods' balls!" he swore, gasping. "Enemies have come into
my house!" He turned slowly around to view his house. It leaned
haphazardly to one side like a lop-eared feist dog. He swept his
hands down his sides, squeeging the soupy feces from his clothes,
then wrung his hands in despair and marched up to the door left
open when Fedelm fled inside.

The Ulstermen looked up in amazement as the bespattered
and befouled creature stumbled into the middle of the room.

"Good night! What is this?" Fergus exclaimed, wrinkling his
nose. A serving girl gagged and vomited into the basin of scented
water she held for a hero to dapple his fingers in and clean the
grease from them.

From the floor, Bricriu looked around in despair. He struck

his chest three times. "My fault! My fault! My fault! I thought to share my good fortune with you, my friends, and this is how I was treated? Betrayed! My fine house ruined! Well, let me tell you this: this house is the finest of all my possessions and I labored long upon its building. Therefore, no one will eat or drink or make merry, nor will you sleep or make love until it is set right as it was when you were welcomed into it! For shame! For shame! For shame!"

"You brought this upon yourself," Conchobor said. "Had you kept your words inside you until they welled and burst like pus from an uncleaned wound, you would not see your house in this manner."

"Yes, yes," Seancha said. "But the fact is that he has pronounced a *geis* and you all know what that means. Even if you wanted to, none of you will eat, drink, sleep, or make love without bringing disaster upon yourself until his bidding is done and the *geis* lifted."

"Ah, nuts!" Fergus mumbled and heaved himself from his couch. He settled his tunic over his broad shoulders and gestured at the rest of the men. "Let's do it, Ulstermen! The night doesn't grow any younger."

The rest of the Ulstermen followed him outside. They gathered timbers and made fulcrums out of boulders and tried to lift the house back into its original shape, but strain as they did until tendons and joints creaked like the timbers in their hands, the house did not raise so much as to allow the breath of wind to rush under it.

"All right, Seancha," Fergus panted, wiping a huge paw over his sweat-stained face. His eyes gleamed angrily in the moonlight. "What now?"

Seancha shrugged. "All I can suggest is that you beg the one who wrecked the house and left it lopsided to set it right again."

"Crab apples and thorns," Fergus mumbled. He looked over at Cúchulainn, who stood aside from the others, hip-shot, arms folded over his chest. "Why don't you help?"

Cúchulainn shrugged. "You asked for the Ulstermen. As you

all have suggested this night, I am not of Ulster."

"Damn your precious feelings!" Fergus said. "Come on, boy! You know the *geis* upon me. If I am to have my seven women, I must begin soon or the gods will damn me for certain! Give us a hand, lad!"

"Listen to me, Conchobor," Bricriu said. "And you men of the Red Branch. If you cannot set this upright, then no one in the world can. But my word stands along with the *geis* I pronounced upon you."

At that, the Ulstermen turned and looked silently at Cúchulainn. He stared back calmly, waiting.

"All right," Loegaire said. "I'm asking. Do it, Cúchulainn."

"Yes," Conall said. "So do I. Ask, that is."

"This has been thirsty work," another shouted from the crowd.

"Yes, thirsty!"

"And hungry, too," Fat-Neck said.

"You're always hungry," Seancha said.

"That's because there's more of me than any of you," Fat-Neck retorted.

"All right," Cúchulainn said. "Step back."

All bunched out of the way as the Hound stepped forward. He worked his fingers under the edge of the house, set himself and strained, but the house remained rooted in the dirt.

"I knew it," grumbled Durthacht. "His reputation is made of wind."

At that, Cúchulainn began to quiver. The others stepped well back and away from him, watching half fearfully as his *riastradh*, his "warp-spasm," claimed him. His hair stood straight out from his head, a drop of blood like a spot of flame appearing at the end of each hair, all merging into one color. Then he drew his hair inside his head so that the dark yellow tresses seemed shorn with scissors from above. The hero's halo rose above his head, shining like the sun, so that everyone there blinked and shaded his eyes with his hands. Cúchulainn's one eye bulged out, the other sank in, until it was the size of a needle's eye. His heart boomed in his chest like thunder and, rolling his shoulders like a millstone, he heaved until a warrior's foot could be placed between each rib.

Slowly, the house rose from the ground until, with a great sucking sound, it was freed from the earth.

"Come on, boys!" shouted Fergus.

And quickly they laid timbers beneath it so that when Cúchulainn slowly let it back down, the house righted itself and all appeared as it was before, except for the broken railing where Bricriu and his wife had broken through in their fall into the honey-pit.

"Very well," Bricriu said after eying the structure critically from all sides. "I lift the *geis*. You may return to your feast."

"At last," muttered Fat-Neck as he hurried inside.

Fergus paused to squeeze one of the serving wenches by the rump, then led the others into the feasting hall, while Bricriu plucked the last of ripe cabbage stalks from his hair and shoulders and took himself away to the washhouse.

The men of the Red Branch again settled themselves around Conchobor, while Fedelm of the Nine Shapes—nine shapes could she form, and each more beautiful than the last—and Findchoem, daughter of Cathbad the Druid, wife of Amergin of the Iron Jaw, and Devorgill, wife of Lugaid of the Red Stripes, besides Emer, and Fedelm of the Fresh Heart, and Lendabair also, took their rightful places in the hall among the other noblewomen.

"Did you see that?" whispered Durthacht to Celthair.

"Yes," the other nodded. "I saw something similar a few years ago. Near frightened the shit right out of me, it did!"

"I'll bet you mean that time when Ailill's men surprised him at the ford," said Furbaide. "I tell you, those Connachtmen saw him do that and the waters of the ford turned as brown as the shit that flowed from them like grease."

"I remember . . ."

Soon the hall buzzed with words like honey bees as men remembered times when Cúchulainn went through another "warp-spasm," while the women began praising their men as if to stir up another quarrel among them, until Seancha, son of Ailill, rose

and, shaking his hazel wand topped with a bell until all were
quiet, pronounced:

"There has been enough of this word-fighting.
Thanks to you women, men and their in-fighting
have made fools of themselves. It is the folly
of women that brings men to bruise their egos silly
by striking out at each other when they should be
embracing them as friends. Wives of the heroes, see
that you remember while I tell you to atone
and cease your nattering. Leave well enough alone."

But Emer answered him, saying:

"It is right for me to speak to you
on this, Seancha, since I am the wife who
is the wife of the most beautiful hero
here, who is beyond all others in wisdom. No
one can do his feats, the over-breath feat,
the apple-feat, the ghost-feat,
the screw feat, the cat-feat,
the red-whirling feat, the barbed-spear feat,
the quick stroke, the fire-of-the-mouth feat,
the hero's cry, the wheel feat, the sword-edge feat.
No one can do these, I tell you and I tell you truly.
No one is his equal in youth, form, brightness, truly
one of good birth, mind, voice, bravery, boldness.
No one has his fire, his skill, his hardiness.
No one is his equal in hunting, in strength,
in victories, in greatness. Along the breadth
of our land, there is no man here who can be
put beside Cúchulainn, my Hound, you see."

"Quite a mouthful of words, but they are all air," sneered
Conall. "If he is so great, let him rise and do all this to prove your
brag without the sleight-of-hand trickery he uses to amuse himself

and others. Let him fight someone in single combat. How about that, eh?"

Cúchulainn groaned. "Now look what you've done!" he said to Emer. "Why didn't you keep your mouth shut like you were told?"

"But—"

"No buts," he said firmly.

"Well?" Conall challenged.

"No," Cúchulainn said, yawning. He stretched until his bones cracked. "I am tired and will do no more of this nonsense until I have eaten and slept."

"Hah," snorted Loegaire.

"Enough," Conchobor said quietly. But the others heard the threat behind the word. "Let us eat and be merry. Tomorrow is another day for more foolishness, if that is what you want."

And so the heroes of the Red Branch stopped their quarreling and the women their bickering and all turned their minds to feasting and good times. But each knew that the matter was far from being settled as to who was the true hero of the Red Branch and deserving of the Champion's Portion.

Chapter 6

THE
CHALLENGES
BEGIN

FOR TWO DAYS AND nights, the feasting went well, but on the third day, the three champions took to quarreling once more about the Champion's Portion until Conchobor again struck the bronze pillar with his silver wand and rose from his couch.

"Enough! You are beginning to sound like fishwives, yammering and yelling your deeds at each other! We have heard your stories and, frankly, I am weary of hearing the same deeds told over and over with new embellishments. Earn yourselves new deeds! But as for now, I have changed my mind. I want you to stop this mewling and stop it now while I think what to do with you. I'm thinking about changing my mind about sending you to Connacht. Since," he added, glaring at Fergus, "there seems to be those who object to our using Ailill of Connacht as arbitrator."

"It is only right," Fergus said defensively. He took a quick swallow of beer to dampen the night's dryness from his tongue. "Why give our enemies a chance at discovering our strengths? You have seen what Bricriu can do with his tongue. Do you suppose that Ailill does not have a Bricriu at his house to do the same? Here, we can stop their bickering, but if they get to arguing thistles and nettles at Connacht, Ailill might let them fight until the matter is settled. Gods' brass balls! Wouldn't that be a sight? But it would weaken the Red Branch."

Seancha shook his head. "That may be what *you* would do if you were Ailill, Fergus, but Ailill knows better than to do such a matter. You forget—"

"Yes, yes, I know. The Rules of Hospitality. I still say it is a poor practice to put one's faith in words rather than a sword."

"Words will last longer than a sword," Seancha said sternly. "Once a sword weakens with age, it is useless. Words gain their strength with age. And more hear words than hear a sword's song."

Fergus grunted and turned his shoulder to the poet, showing that he had had enough of words for the time. He looked fondly at the seven women standing near him, hollow-eyed and worn from their night's exercise on Fergus's bed. One, a black-haired beauty, yawned and rubbed her eyes, saw Fergus staring at her and returned a tenuous smile. *Much better,* Fergus thought, *playing this game than playing with metaphors.* He arched an eyebrow and she brought him a bowl of grain and meat mixed in a mash, along with a fresh cup of beer.

"Yes," Seancha said, observing this. He cleared his throat and looked back to Loegaire, Conall, and Cúchulainn. "Well, we can give it a try, my lord. What do you have in mind to settle this hash?"

"Let them each find a new deed to do and we'll judge them on the basis of that," Conchobor said. He looked sternly at his three warriors. "Well?" he demanded. "Are you willing to do this?"

"I accept," Cúchulainn said carelessly. "It matters little to me, for the truth is known wherever we go or whatever we do."

"I agree," Loegaire answered.

"As do I," Conall said. He tweaked his nose between thumb and thick forefinger and blew vigorously onto the floor. He snuffled and hawked and spat. "Anything would be better than this poisoned place that has set friends to arguing."

"You don't have to argue," Seancha said softly. "All you have to do is agree on which is to receive the Champion's Portion."

"It's a matter of honor, you see," Loegaire asserted, shaking his head. He looked over at Cúchulainn. "I'd hate to mar your pretty face with my fist, so if you don't agree that I'm the one most deserving of the Champion's Portion, then we'd better go to this Cúroi."

"As you said," Cúchulainn answered, "it's a matter of honor. Stuff and nonsense!" he suddenly exploded. "Take the bloody portion if it means that much to you! All know that I am the better man anyway, so it matters little to me who eats and drinks Bricriu's swill."

For a brief moment, Loegaire was tempted to claim it, but then he saw how the others looked admiringly at Cúchulainn for his generosity and quickly changed his mind.

"No, you're right," he said. "Give it to Conall, if it means that much to him. I know I'm the better man. I don't need to show it by eating. My deeds stand by themselves on the walls of the Red Branch."

"What's this?" Conall said crossly. "You'd make me the dupe for all of this? Then Cúchulainn should take it, for he is the youngest of the three of us."

"Enough!" Conchobor cried again. "I can see where this is going, and I don't like it one twitch. The three of you will find a new deed to show your worthiness and then we will award the Champion's Portion appropriately! I have spoken!"

"Then let us go," Cúchulainn said.

"Yes, let's," Loegaire answered.

"Let us go, then," Conall said. "That is, if you two don't mind coming in last."

"Let the horses be brought and your chariot yoked, Conall," said Cúchulainn. "You may leave first."

"Why should I go first?" Conall asked suspiciously. "No, I don't think I'd like that."

A wide grin spread across Cúchulainn's face so that each of the four dimples in each cheek sparkled in the dim light of the hall. "I don't blame you," he said. "Everyone knows your clumsy-footed horses and wobbly chariot. Why, it is so heavy that each of the wheels plows up the sod on each side so deeply as it goes that for a full year the men of Ulster can know its track and your passage. Why, you should hire out to the farmers and plow their fields for them."

"Would you be listening to that, Loegaire?" Conall complained. "From a boy's lips, words of wisdom. Yes, the weakest chariot should go first. We'll let you get a head start, Loegaire!"

"Don't mock me," Loegaire said crossly. "I span all fords nimbly and am ready to face up to a breastwork of spears. I can easily outstrip the warriors of Ulster, so do not put upon me the pretense of kings and champions against single chariots in hard and narrow places. I can outrun all single chariots until even the champion of a single chariot will be afraid to pass me."

"Brave words," Conall sneered. "A challenge, then?" He glanced over at Cúchulainn, who shrugged and yawned his indifference.

"It makes no difference," he said carelessly. "I will still arrive first if I wish."

"Do not," Conchobor said, closing his eyes and gently rubbing his temples with the pads of his fingers, "turn this into a war. Loegaire, you go first. Conall, second. Cúchulainn, order your chariot to be yoked third and travel after the dust of Conall has settled."

So Loegaire ordered his chariot yoked, and Sedlang, his charioteer, brought it around. Loegaire leaped into it and ordered Sedlang to drive away from Dún Rudraige, over Magh da Gabal, the Plain of Two Forks,

> over Bernaid na Foraire, the Gap of the watch,
> over the Ford of Carpat Fergus,
> over the Ford of the Mórrigú,
> to Caerthund Cluana da Dam, the Rowan Meadow
> of the Two Oxen in the Fews of Fírbuide
> by the Meeting of the Four Ways past Dundalk,

across Mag Slicech, the Peeled Plain,
westward to the slopes of Breg.

A dim and dark mist, heavy and dank, overtook Loegaire
then, confusing the way. He ordered Sedlang to pull up while he
stood in the chariot, scratching his head in confusion, trying to
guess the road.

"Well," he said at last, "it's as good as the guess of a gilly-
watcher which way to take now. Best thing is to wait it out until
this infernal thing lifts."

"The horses could use a rest as well," Sedlang said, motioning
to where the pair stood, heads hanging, waiting for the charioteer's
whip.

"Might as well make camp here," Loegaire said. "At least until
the mist clears."

He stepped from the chariot, stretching and yawning. The
mist parted and through the streamers of wetness he saw a lush
green meadow. He pointed to it, saying, "Put the horses there
while we rest."

Sedlang scratched his head in wonder. "Now where did that
thing come from? I don't remember seeing it and I've driven this
road many times."

"Does it matter?" Loegaire said. "Gad, but I'm stiff with traveling. Just do it." He sighed and walked stiff-legged away, grim-
acing and stretching his back and legs.

Sedlang watched him, swearing softly under his breath. "Do
it, is it? Like I'm simply a walker-boy to be ordered and tossed
about at will?" He muttered as he unyoked the horses and led
them into the meadow, staking them out so they would not wan-
der very far.

"Hey, you! What do you think you're doing, picketing your
horses upon my grass?"

The voice startled Sedlang and he peered through the mist to
see a giant approaching him. *Ugly as sin!* Sedlang thought, looking
at the broad-shouldered creature with a fat mouth and thick lips
like the backs of slugs. His eyes hung lopsided in his face like

meal sacks, and tufts of black hair bristled like thorns from his chin. The flesh hung from his face, filled with warts and wrinkled like a whore's girdle, while bushy eyebrows stood straight up toward his forehead. He was hideous and horrible, stubborn and violent, arrogant and fat, and puffing with the efforts of his movement. Big sinews showed like cables from his strong forearms. His dun tunic was ripped, and black hairs peeked through like a briar patch. His tunic barely covered the ball of his rump, and on his feet he wore tattered and torn laced sandals. He carried a massive club over his shoulder like the wheel shaft of a mill.

"Well? Lose your tongue, gillie?" he asked, halting in front of Sedlang.

Sedlang reeled back from the reeking breath that rolled like a venomous cloud from the giant's mouth. "No, have you lost your manners? If you had any to begin with," he added.

"Strong words for a young whelp fresh off its mother's teat," the giant rumbled. He guffawed at his own joke. *Har-rumph, har-rumph, har-rumph!* Then he looked closely at the horses. "Rode a ways with those, I see. Whose are they?"

"The horses of Loegaire the Triumphant," Sedlang said. "And you would do better to mind your tongue around him."

"Mind my tongue? Oh, yes! I should mind my tongue! A fine fellow is this Loegaire!" And he raised the club off his shoulder and thumped Sedlang on top of the head with it. Then he dusted Sedlang's ribs and dropped the end of it on his toe.

"Ow!" Sedlang yelled. "Yowp! Dirty dealing! Help, Loegaire! I'm being attacked! Ow!"

Loegaire ran through the mist until he stumbled upon the pair, with Sedlang curled in a ball on the ground, one hand gently massaging his head while the other cradled his foot. Loegaire glanced at the giant standing calmly by, leaning on his club.

"And just what, dung-head," Loegaire said angrily, "do you think you are doing with my man?"

The giant laughed and shrugged. He lifted the club and twirled it between thick fingers. The shaft whistled like a dove's flight.

"It is a matter of teaching him manners," the giant said. "And giving him a penalty for damage to my meadow."

"He did this by my order," Loegaire said.

"Then you should bear part of the penalty," the giant said.

He raised his club to strike, but Loegaire, no shilly or weed, leaped upon him, grabbing the huge head in a headlock. Straining, he barely brought his arms together before the giant slipped easily out of the headlock and, grabbing Loegaire by the scruff of the neck as a bitch would a pup, threw him hard to the ground.

"Erk!" Loegaire squeaked as he struck hard. Only the soft meadow grass kept him from breaking bones.

The giant lifted a huge foot to stomp him, but Loegaire rolled quickly under the giant's foot and leaped upon the giant's back. He wrapped his arms around the giant's neck and seized the giant's ear between his teeth, biting hard.

"Yeow! No fair!" cried the giant, but Loegaire hung on grimly as the giant whirled and danced, and grabbed at Loegaire's hair with a huge paw. He plucked Loegaire from his back and threw him again to the ground, then leaped up in the air and landed hard on Loegaire's chest with the ball of his rump.

"Eek!" squeaked Loegaire as he slipped out along the wet grass. He clambored to his feet, saw the giant approaching, and turning, fled into the mist, running for his life, leaving his chariot, his horses, and most of all, Sedlang, behind. He ran until he arrived out of breath at Dún Rudraige and stumbled into the Red Branch hall, gasping out his story.

"Hah!" Conall laughed. "So, a wee giant made you tuck your tail between your legs and run, Loegaire! And you want the Champion's Portion for that?"

"I'd like to see you do better," Loegaire said, fingering the welts and scrapes and bruises left by the giant's grip.

"That I will," Conall said, and rising, he swaggered out, yelling for Id Mac Ríangabra to yoke his horses and bring his chariot around.

He climbed in and Id whipped the team away from Dún Rudraige, turning the leads so that the horses followed the same direction taken by Loegaire and his chariot. Soon they arrived at the plain, and a dark and dank Druidical mist overtook them, a hideous dark cloud smelling of old stable piles, moldering hay and manure, so thick that they could see neither the sky nor the earth.

"Unhitch the horses," Conall said. "I think this is where Loegaire found the giant."

The mist parted a bit and Id pointed to a meadow of lush green grass. "There, I think," he said. Conall looked and nodded.

"Picket the horses next to Loegaire's," he said, pointing to where the bays waited, patiently nibbling at the grass.

Id obediently took the horses over and drove a tent peg into the ground, tying their leads to it. When he straightened, he saw the giant coming toward him.

"Ah, another of the 'heroes' from the Red Branch," sneered the giant. "And what do you think you are doing?"

"What does it look like I'm doing?" countered Id.

"Tch-tch. Your tongue will trouble you, little man," the giant said. "Now again, whose horses are these?"

"Conall the Victorious, whom I serve," Id said proudly, then yelped as the giant casually dropped his club on top of his head.

"A good man, this Conall, but you need to keep a civil tongue in your head!" the giant admonished.

"What the . . . oh, shit!" Id exclaimed before the club bonked him on the head again and dusted his ribs. He yelled in pain. Conall heard his squeals and came running.

"What do you think you are doing?" he demanded of the giant.

"Drawing penance for what you have done to my meadow," the giant said, grinning. "And what's it to you, wee one?"

"Wee one, is it?" growled Conall, clenching his fist. "Mind your tongue or I'll rip it from your head!"

"Oh? Another challenge." The giant yawned and patted his foul mouth with his thick fingers.

Conall leaped at the giant, but caught the giant's fist on his chin and landed on his shoulders on the meadow. Dazed, he watched as the giant lumbered over and reached down to pluck

him up from the ground. He wrapped an arm around Conall and
squeezed. Conall gave a cry of pain and, bending his head, bit
hard on the giant's forearm. The giant howled and threw Conall
from him.

Conall landed hard, striking a heavy boulder. He rolled to his
feet and when he saw the giant bearing down upon him with a
face like a black cloud, his courage left him and, taking to his
heels, he dodged and darted his way through brambles, at last
making his way to Dún Rudraige, where he arrived torn and
bleeding, a huge bruise turning his face black and lumpy.

"I see," Conchobor said, grinning, "that you have met up with
the same fey fellow as Loegaire and fared as well."

"Stow it," Conall moaned, tenderly cradling his jaw in his
hands. "I think he broke my jaw."

"Let me see," Seancha said. He glanced critically at Conall's
jaw, then suddenly seized it and wrenched it to the left. A loud
pop! sounded and Conall howled.

"Oh, stop your whimpering," Seancha said. "It was only dis-
located. I've set it right."

"And for this," Conchobor said, "you want the Champion's
Portion?"

"He's a mighty man," Conall whined. "Mightier than any
here."

"Oh?" Cúchulainn rose from his couch, grinning. "We'll see.
Laeg! Ready my chariot!"

"You'll regret this," Conall said warningly as Cúchulainn
headed for the door. He raised his voice. "And watch his left. A
punch like an ox's kick, that one!"

Cúchulainn climbed into the chariot beside Laeg and the charioteer lifted the reins and let them fall on Black and Gray. The
two promptly raised hooves and galloped off, heading south toward Munster and the place where Conall and Loegaire had met
their match.

Soon they were climbing up into the mountains, then down
into a small valley, where a thick black mist, smelling like soiled
linen, crept over them. Slowly, Laeg drew rein.

"I think this is the place," Cúchulainn said. His white teeth spread in a pleased grin. "Take the horses over there and let them stand next to Loegaire's and Conall's horses."

"I wonder where he is," Laeg muttered, unyoking the horses.

"He'll show when he's ready," Cúchulainn said. He yawned and stretched out beside his chariot, resting his head on the tongue of the chariot. "Wake me when he comes."

"Wake you? Oh, yes," Laeg said. "I do the work and you get the rest. Fair enough. But who gets the blows?"

"Be civil to him and call me," Cúchulainn said sleepily. "Don't waggle your tongue at him like a proud puppy and you'll be all right. Proud words often bring about a shameful downfall."

Laeg mumbled incoherently and walked Black and Gray to the other horses. "There," he said. "Eat your fill. I expect we'll be here a while. Probably longer once he finds out that it's the Hound who's come to sink his teeth into his backside."

"And who might you be?"

Laeg leaped willy-nilly out of the way, twisting to look over his shoulder at the giant standing behind him. His nostrils twitched at the stench of the man. He shivered.

"I'm Laeg, charioteer to Cúchulainn, champion of champions, and you'd better mind your manners, you pecker-head, or he'll give you what-for," Laeg said, angry at having been frightened and forgetting Cúchulainn's warning.

"Oh? A tongue-twister, are you?" The giant reached out and walloped Laeg on the head with his club. "You'll keep a civil tongue in your head or speak from your ass!"

"Help! Cúchulainn! Hound! Tend to your driver!" Laeg yelped as the giant's club struck him in the stomach, doubling him over.

"Here, now," Cúchulainn said, coming up on the giant. "Is that any way to be friendly? Have you forgotten the Rules of Hospitality?"

"And have you forgotten that you are supposed to ask permission before taking advantage of the grass of my meadow?" asked the giant.

"Grass is grass and a little won't matter much here," Cúchulainn said. "What gives you the right to strike my man?"

"The same right that I take for striking you!" the giant said, swinging his club hard at Cúchulainn.

But the Hound dodged the blow and, dancing on the balls of his feet, delivered a blow from his fist that staggered the giant.

"Well done!" the giant cried, rubbing his jaw with his hand. He swung again with his club, swinging low to knock Cúchulainn's feet out from under him, but the Hound leaped up high in the air and landed lightly on the club's head. He danced for a quick second to gain his balance, then kicked the giant in the jaw with the horny sole of his foot. The giant fell backward, but quickly climbed to his feet.

"So," he said, tossing the club aside. He spat into the palm of each hand, folding his fingers to form huge fists. "It's fisticuffs you want, is it? A bit of dodging and darting?"

"Make it easy on yourself," Cúchulainn said. "I'm for you."

And the giant lunged, bouncing a huge fist off Cúchulainn's shoulder. The Hound delivered two more blows on the giant's chin, and then the rocky walls of the valley rang with the sounds of their combat as they fought back and forth over the meadow, first one driving the other back, then the other driving the first back. At last Cúchulainn saw his chance and, leaping high in the air, he delivered three kicks onto the giant's chin. The giant stood for a moment, wavering, then toppled over backward, lying cold upon the ground.

"Well done!" Laeg shouted. Cúchulainn grinned, his face bruised and puffy from his battle.

"Gather the horses and the chariots and we'll take them back to the Red Branch," he said through swollen lips.

"Watch out!" Laeg said warningly, and Cúchulainn whirled to find the giant sitting up. The giant hastily raised his hands, waving off his challenge.

"No more," he said. He touched the lumps on his homely face, wincing. "Sure, and if you're not the champion of the Red Branch."

"What's that?" Cúchulainn said. He advanced toward the giant, but a cold mist blew up suddenly between them and when it cleared, the giant had disappeared.

"Sure, and if it isn't wizardry at work," Laeg said, astonished. "Let us leave from this frightful place!"

"No fear," Cúchulainn said. He looked hard into the mist. "But I sure wish I knew who that fellow was."

When they arrived back at Dún Rudraige, Bricriu had entered, bringing another of the Champion's Portion with him. When he saw Cúchulainn drive through the gate with the others' horses and chariots and their charioteers, he waved his hand magnanimously.

"Surely this is the champion of champions!" he said to the heroes of the Red Branch. He glanced slyly at Conall and Loegaire, sitting forlorn upon their benches. "Well I know from your deed this day that you are in no way equal to Cúchulainn. His is the Champion's Portion."

"Now just one minute!" Loegaire said stiffly. "Luck doesn't make a champion, and that's all he's had. Blind luck."

"Or help from one of his fairy friends from the Otherworld," Conall said darkly. "We know your tricks, Cúchulainn! We haven't forgotten the stories of your birth!"

Cúchulainn flushed darkly, his face twitching in anger. He, too, had heard the stories about how his mother, Dechtine, Conchobor's sister, had been promised in marriage to Sualdam Mac Roig, when a man approached her on the rays of the sun as she sat dreaming by her window and bore her away. A year later, Conchobor and his men were sitting at a feast when a great flock of birds lit on the ground outside and began to eat up everything so that not a blade of grass was left. Conchobor rose and, accompanied by Fergus and Loegaire and Celthair, among others, with Bricriu bringing up the rear, chased the birds across Slieve Fuad, past Ath Lethan, by Ath Garach and Magh Grossa, between Fir Rois and Fir Ardae, never quite catching the birds, until at last, dark night came upon them.

—Find us a place to stay, Fergus, commanded Conchobor.

And Fergus went forward until he found a shack with a man and a woman in it.

—Bring your companions here, the man said. We haven't much, but you are welcome to it.

When Fergus took the biddings back to Conchobor, Bricriu said, Oh, stuff and nonsense! What is the use of going to a house like that where there're not enough bowls of soup for such as ourselves?

—Then you go and find us a different place, Conchobor said.

And Bricriu went forward, but when he came to the same house as Fergus had visited, he saw a grand, new, well-lit house with rich trappings. A young man wearing armor stood in front of it, handsome and shining, and said:

—Come into the house, Bricriu. Look about you and see that it is, indeed, worthy of you and your king.

When Bricriu entered, a young woman suddenly appeared beside him and welcomed him, and Bricriu recognized her as Dechtine, who gave him a purple cloak with gold fringes. When he brought the news back to Conchobor, they hurried forward and were made welcome in the house. The next morning when all awoke, they discovered Dechtine lying beside her brother Conchobor with a baby in her lap.

—Who is the father? Bricriu asked.

—Lugh, of the golden spear, the Sun God, Dechtine said.

And so they returned to Emain Macha and Dechtine married Sualdam, who claimed the son was his own. But there were some who believed that the boy—called at first Sétanta, then Cúchulainn after the boy slew the monstrous hound of Culann, the smith— was the son of Conchobor, a scandal violating the very basis of Brehon Law.

Cúchulainn looked levelly at Conall, the skin beginning to tighten over his face. "And what do you mean by those words, 'the story of my birth'?"

"Ah, none of that now," Conall said gruffly. "All I meant is that it was one of the spirit world you conned into pretending to be a giant. We battled with a spirit, a phantom made by the wee folk, not a flesh-and-blood man."

"I battled the same spirit," Cúchulainn said dangerously, pressing forward.

"All I'm saying is that you had help with one of your fairy friends who came out to play us mischief. I, for one, will not forgo my claim on the Champion's Portion until the challenge is made equal."

"Nor will I," Loegaire said stoutly, coming up to stand beside Conall.

"It seems to me," Bricriu said smugly, "that a champion of men should make his challenge among men, not in the fairy world."

"Oh, feathers and dirt-balls!" exclaimed Seancha. He glared over at Fergus. "This is your doing, you pigheaded dunce. All you think with is the goad between your legs and where you'll settle it next!"

"I resent that," Fergus said, shoving a squirming young girl with magnificent hips and breasts off his lap. She squealed indignantly, her bounteous breasts bouncing beautifully as she landed on her rump. He rose and started toward Seancha.

> "Here he comes, Fergus the Lout,
> ready to battle another bout,
> but with fists instead of words
> does this fat lord of lords
> expect to win. A dunce is he
> who battles best when a she
> sits on his lap or lies
> in his bed and gives sighs
> of gratitude for his goad.
> This is not a man, but a toad
> who pretends to be a man
> but lies about in his tan
> robes instead of riding to battle
> Ulster's enemies for their cattle.

What sort of man is Fergus the Red,
who does his best thinking in bed?"

Fergus drew up short at Seancha's quick words. A flush darkened his face as others laughed in derision at the picture the poet had painted.

"And that," Seancha said with satisfaction, "is what I have painted *extempore*. Think of what I can do if I put my mind to it!"

"Not a bad turn," Bricriu said musingly. "Have you given thought to giving it to a singer?"

"You do," Fergus said, whirling upon the Poison-Tongued One, "and I'll squeeze your scrawny neck until you cackle like a chicken."

He seized Bricriu by the throat and lifted him high. Bricriu's eyes bulged and his legs kicked weakly, one sandal flying off his bunioned foot to land in one of the clay water pots by the door.

"Put him down!" Conchobor ordered.

Grumbling, Fergus opened his hand and let Bricriu fall into a heap by his feet. He glared at Seancha, then returned to his bench and plopped down, sulking.

"Why, you . . ." croaked Bricriu. He swallowed painfully, but before he could get the words out, Conchobor ordered him to be quiet.

"Speak, Seancha," he said. "Tell us what must be done."

"You know what we must do," Seancha said. "Send the three to Ailill at Cruachain in Connacht for judgment, like I said first."

"Then that is what we will do," Conchobor said. "But the entire host will go this time. We'll have no more of these puts and pundits and false claimings of the spirit world shadowing a decision this time. We leave on the morrow."

And so the Red Branch dispersed as the warriors returned to their apartments in Bricriu's hall to make ready for the journey across Ulster to Cruachain, the Place of Enchantment, where Ailill and his wife, Maeve of the White Thighs, who needed thirty men a night to satisfy her lust, lived.

Chapter 7

THE PLACE OF ENCHANTMENT

THE NEXT DAY, THE heroes of the Red Branch readied themselves for the trip to Cruachain. Cúchulainn lounged in the shade of the mead-hall while he watched the bustling and hustling going on around him.

"Here now, little Hound," Loegaire said as he passed with his shield thrown over his shoulder and several javelins dangling loosely in his hands. "You'd better get ready. It's a goodly way to Ailill's house in Connacht."

"There's no hurry," Cúchulainn said, yawning and stretching.

"Hmpf," Loegaire snorted. "Well, it's all right for you to dawdle, I suppose. Especially since your horses will not be able to compete with mine on that long road. Or even with Conall's," he added as that hero clumped up.

"What's that?" Conall asked suspiciously. "Bandying my name about behind my back, eh, Loegaire?" He thrust a dirty forefinger into his nose, digging deeply.

Loegaire laughed. "Easy, big man! The little Hound thinks that there's no need to hurry to leave with the Red Branch. If he wants to come in third to you, then that's all right by me!"

"Second, you mean," growled Conall. "Those nags you stole from the knacker can't eat hay from the same bale as mine."

"Stuff and nonsense," Loegaire said, the red rising up his neck. His eyes glinted angrily at Conall. "My horses can run rings around yours between here and there."

"Pretty thing to say without risk," sneered Conall. "What do you think, Cúchulainn?"

"Oh, let Loegaire go first," Cúchulainn said carelessly. He picked up several clods of dirt and began juggling them, making one stand on top of the other in a children's game. "Everyone knows about your horses and rickety chariot. If you go first, you'll jam the fords when those wheels sink into the mud and sand."

Loegaire laughed. *Haw-uh! Haw-uh! Haw-uh!*

"Then we'll see who runs first through Cruachain's gates," he said. "Id," Conall bellowed. "Get your ass into the chariot! We leave! Now!"

He strode away. Loegaire grinned and flicked an arrogant forefinger toward Cúchulainn. "Better go, little Hound. If he gets to the Seven Hills first, it'll be a week before I'll be able to get around him on that twisting road. I'll give your regards to Maeve. She'll be glad that a man came first, anyway!" He walked away, while Cúchulainn stood up, brushed himself off, and sauntered over to where the women busily packed their men's kits.

"Oh, Cúchulainn!" one cried. "Do amuse us while we piddle around with this stuff!"

"Yes, do!" another cried. "Especially if you are not in any hurry."

He smiled and picked up a small sack of apples and, dumping them out, did nine feats with them while the women cooed in admiration over his dexterity. Then he did nine more feats with spears, and nine with knives without letting one touch the other. After he placed the knives neatly side by side in the earth, he took one hundred fifty needles from the women and threw them high into the air, one at a time, so that the point of each needle went into the eye of the one before it, until all were joined. Then he gave every woman back her own needle, smiling at Emer, who scowled at his familiarity with the other women.

Laeg, son of Ríangabra, watched this, his ire mounting as he looked over his shoulder at the host setting off for Cruachain. At last, he couldn't hold his bile any longer.

"You damn, pitiful squinter! You sorry simpleton! You've already lost your valor and bravery. The Champion's Portion is now long gone from your plate, make no bones about it. Why, the men of Ulster are halfway to Cruachain now, and you still play games of pins and needles with the women!"

Cúchulainn looked at him in amazement. "Why, do you really think so, Laeg? You know Black and Gray as well as I. Do you think that any horse in Ulster can beat them on that journey?"

"Not at an even start," Laeg said. He spat and watched his spittle ball in the dust. "But we ain't talking even start here. Loegaire and Conall will be whipping their horses into a frazzle to beat each other to Cruachain and you ain't even started out yet."

"Well," Cúchulainn said, rubbing his hairless chin thoughtfully, "if you feel that strongly about it, I guess you'd better yoke the chariot for me. Put Black and Gray in their harness while I gather my weapons."

"Now you're talking fine shakes!" Laeg said. He grinned and hurried off to gather Black and Gray from the stables and harness them to *Carbad Seardha.* Cúchulainn sauntered into the Great Hall, where he gathered his sword, the *Cruaidin Cailidcheann,* his shield, the *dubán,* crimson-red, with knobs and bands of silver that turned a terrifying black in battle, and his famous *gae bulga,* the ancient spear handed down from Ailill Érann that no one could escape once it was thrown at him.

He paused to give Emer a grin and a kiss. At first she tried to avoid his lips, but when his arms folded around her, she felt her heart melt and butterflies flit in her stomach, and she raised her lips to his. He kissed her and pulled back, swatting her on the rump and laughing when she squealed and jumped and struck him back on his chest with her fist. He winked at her and strolled out into the sunlight, where Laeg fiddled impatiently with the reins, their kit stowed by his feet in the chariot.

"Up, Black! Up, Gray!" he shouted when Cúchulainn's foot stomped lightly on the chariot floorboards. The young warrior had to grab fast for the chariot railing as the two horses, impatient to be off, leaned quickly into their harness and galloped through the gates of Dún Rudraige.

By the time Cúchulainn started off from Dún Rudraige, the Red Branch, led by Loegaire and Conall, who alternated taking the lead, had already reached Mag Breg. But the Gray of Macha and the Black of Saingliu raced so swiftly across the whole province of Conchobor, across Sliab Fuait and Mag Breg, that Cúchulainn soon caught up to the rear of the host.

"Take the cut across to Trego through the bog," Cúchulainn said casually. "We'll beat them there."

"What? You're crazy!" Laeg yelled. "No chariot can get through that bog!"

"Do it," Cúchulainn said merrily. "Black and Gray won't let us down."

With misgivings, Laeg pulled the lead reins, turning Black and Gray to the right. They caught a quick glimpse of the bog, then lowered their heads and began to dance their way so quickly along the water-covered trail that their hooves barely sullied the surface of the water. The chariot lurched and Cúchulainn's hair streamed out behind him as he stood calmly beside Laeg, whose eyes watered from the speed of the horses.

When Cúchulainn dropped down out of the mountains just in front of the host, Loegaire and Conall shouted angrily and whipped up their horses, urging them on toward shining Cruachain. Behind them thundered the host, horses straining against yokes as the Red Branch charged toward Cruachain's walls. So swift was their passing that the earth trembled violently in Cruachain, hurtling shields and swords and spears from the walls. The floor buckled and heaved, knocking stewards and slaves down, forcing the warriors to stumble and stagger along the great halls, weaving like rushes in high wind.

"Earthquake!" squealed one wench as she staggered forward, dumping a slop jar onto a warrior. He swore as his feet slipped out from under him and he landed on his shoulders as another wench stumbled over him, slipped, and fell with an *umph!* on top of him in a flash of naked white thighs. Another warrior lost his footing and trampled on the edge of the first wench's dress. She ran through the garment like a nymph racing through mist, her breasts bobbling, beard winking.

"Never have I heard such thunder!" exclaimed Maeve, pushing a guardsman away from her and wrapping her cloak around her naked body as she tried to stand from her couch. She glanced out the window. "But how could there be thunder without clouds?"

"Badb is angry!" one warrior yelled drunkenly.

"Oh, stuff it!" Maeve said crossly. "There's logic to this problem." She glanced over at Finnabair, daughter of Maeve and Ailill, beckoning to her.

"Come with me," she said as her daughter staggered up to her. The pair made their way to the balcony and looked out to the east.

"What do you see?" Maeve asked.

Finnabair shaded her eyes, looking into the distance. "I see a chariot, dear Mother," she answered.

"Well, describe it to me! Awk!" Maeve squawked, catching herself against the balcony wall to keep from being pitched over the side.

"Two fiery, dappled grays, well-matched with step and speed, draw it," Finnabair said. "Their ears are pricked and they hold their heads high proudly, wild, sinuous, narrow-nosed with flowing mane, tails curled. A bit thin-sided, but wide-chested. The chariot is made from finely laned spruce with wicker-wood highly polished and silver ornaments on the curved yoke. It has two black wheels, and yellow reins that loop softly along the backs of the grays. In the chariot I see a big, wide-chested man with red-yellow hair, dark brown at the base, and a long, forked beard that streams over both shoulders. He has a purple cloak striped with bright gold thread around him, and his bronze shield is gold-edged. He holds a five-pronged javelin in his red-flaming fist and wears a cover of strange bird-feathers over his head, encircled by three circlets."

Maeve shook her head, saying:

"A companion of kings, that bold
one! His victories are as old
as the hills! He pours a flame
of judgment upon all. But blame
no one for where his sword falls,
for he bears a long knife to cut all
who will oppose him here. He cuts through
men like a sharp knife slicing through
leeks. His sword stroke is the back
stroke of rushing waves. Loegaire Búadach
is his name and if he's angry, we will be
harvested like leeks and thrown to the sea!"

"Well, Mother, I don't know about that," Finnabair sniffed. "We have many fine warriors here at Cruachain."

"Oh, don't be foolish," Maeve snapped. "There are warriors and then there are warriors. Of the latter, we have none. For now," she added thoughtfully. "But . . . tell me, Finnabair. What else do you see?"

"I see a second chariot, as well-made as the first, coming over the plain toward us," Finnabair said waspishly.

"Well, describe it," Maeve demanded.

"A copper-colored horse with a white face, hardy, swift, fiery, is yoked to one side of the chariot. It takes long, strong, high strides over the fords and splashes heavily through the water and over banks and gaps and plains and hollows with the quickness of the birds that the sharp eye easily loses while trying to follow. On the other side of the chariot-spar is a bay horse of great strength that races at full speed across the plain, between stones, finding no hindrance in the land of oaks, trailing behind itself a chariot of fine spruce wood and wicker-work on two white-bronze wheels, its pole bright with silver, high-framed and creaking with a great, curving yoke, and fitted with looping yellow reins.

"In the chariot stands a fair man with wavy hair. His face is half white and half red, his vest clean and white, his cloak crimson and blue, his shield brown with yellow bosses and bronze-edged. He holds a shining silver-headed spear in one hand, and a cover of strange bird-feathers hangs over the wicker frame of his chariot."

And Maeve said:

> "Alas! I know that man, too!
> His cloak, crimson and blue,
> is the key! The growl of a lion
> is the last thing that dying
> men hear when his flame cuts heads
> from their shoulders. He heaps dead
> heads on each other. As we will
> cut a trout on red sandstone, so will
> Findchoem's son gut us if he's mad!
> Alas! This day has grown very sad!"

"Well, Mother, it doesn't look like it's getting any better. Another chariot pulls ahead of the first two," Finnabair said with relish as Maeve wrung her shapely hands beside her.

"What is it? What is it? Tell me!" ordered Maeve.

"Two horses of one size and beauty, fierce and filled with speed, ears pricked forward, nostrils spread wide, heads held high, spirited and powerful, wide foreheads, manes and tails curled, they leap with each other. One is a gray, handsome with broad thighs, eager, thundering hooves trampling the earth. As it goes, its fierce hooves throw sods of earth high like swift birds flying. A blast of hot breath bursts brightly from its curbed jaws as it gallops. The other, the dark one, small-headed, well-shaped, broad-hooved, thin-sided, with a lot of courage evident in its rippling muscles, takes long strides, leaping over streams, crossing the middle valley plains. They run easily together with fast, joyful steps, moving swiftly like mountain mist or the speed of a hill deer on level ground, rushing like a loud wind in winter!

"The chariot is of fine wood and wicker-work, with two iron wheels and a bright silver pole with bronze ornaments, high-framed, laden with iron, and a curved yoke laid with gold.

"In the chariot rides a sad, dark man, the comeliest of all men in Ireland." Her speech clicked for a second in her throat and she felt a weakness in her stomach and loins, her breast thrusting hard against her shift at the sight of the hero riding across the plain. "He wears a pleated crimson tunic fastened at the breast with a salmon-brooch of inlaid gold. A long-sleeved, white-hooded cloak of fine linen, embroidered in flame-red gold, streams in the wind behind him. His eyebrows are as black as a fire-spit. Seven lights shine from his eyes from red-dragon gemstones above his two cheeks, blue-white and blood-red, and seven colors flash from his head. Fire-sparks and burning breath come from his mouth, with love from his eyes! A shower of pearls gleams in his mouth. He holds a gold-hilted sword across his knees, and a blood-red spear stands ready to hand, a strange, sharp-tempered blade with a black shaft of wood. A crimson shield with a silver rim hangs over his shoulder, and upon the shield are beasts molded in gold. As they drive, he does the salmon leap into the air, and many other similar feats as well.

"Beside him in the chariot is a driver, very thin, tall and freck-led, with curly, bright-red hair held back from his face by a gold band. Patins of gold hold his hair on both sides. A short cloak folds over him, opening at the elbows. He holds a red-gold goad in one hand."

Maeve sighed heavily.

> "Ah, me! The other two are drops
> before the downpour. That one crops
> the heads of men with as much ease
> as you fall onto your pretty knees
> before handsome men! I know how he
> leaps like the sound of the angry sea,
> like the mounting of an angry wave.

With a wild whale's madness, he craves
his enemies' blood. They hear their death
in his war shout as he gathers a wealth
of heads and deeds. As in the mill
fresh malt is finely ground, so will
we be ground to dust by that man,
the Hound of Ulster, Cúchulainn!"

She sighed heavily, but Finnabair heard a familiar excitement
in the voice of Maeve of the Friendly Thighs too, and she smiled
to herself as she remembered her own lust.

"Well," Maeve said, "you might as well tell me. How are the
rest of the men who are coming?"

Finnabair drew a deep breath.

"Wrist to wrist, they ride!
Palm to palm, they ride!
Shoulder to shoulder, they ride!
And tunic to tunic, they ride!
They roll across the plain
like sea-tide, the same
way that the sea crushes
the sand, so they rush
forcefully across the land.
As their chargers speed and
chariots rumble, shaking earth,
so do the men shout, giving birth
to their valiant and noble names!
Ah, if only we could do the same!"

And Maeve drew herself upright, folding her red-and-green
cloak over her shoulders, baring her bold white breasts with hard
ruby tips, the trim tuck of her waist above her thick red-gold
beard, the white columns of her friendly thighs, and saying:

"Send women, all naked and flouncing,
great breasts bare and bouncing,

to greet them. Command baths drawn
of cold water and new curtains drawn
around the guest beds. Have the best
of our strong ale, with foamy crest,
well-malted, and sound made ready, too.
Let Cruachain's gates be opened, too.
With this army, we will well cope.
And then they won't kill us. I hope."

Finnabair left immediately to do her bidding as Maeve rushed
into her apartment and dressed herself in her most seductive gown,
the one that left the ruby tips of her breasts winking over the top.
She went out of the high door of the palace and into the cobbled
courtyard with one hundred naked maidens giggling in her train.
Three baths of cold water stood ready for the three heroes, now
nearing the gate in front of Cruachain and eager to ease the heat
of their journey.

"Greetings!" Maeve cried, carefully draping her robe around
her to show off her magnificent body. "Welcome to Cruachain,
the Place of Enchantment. We have made cooling baths ready for
you."

Loegaire tossed his weapons to the bottom of the chariot and
leaped down, stripping his clothes from his body as he walked
without words toward one of the baths, his goad swinging heavily
between his legs. Three naked women rushed to help him, carrying towels and robes.

"Looks all right to me," Conall muttered. He nodded at
Maeve, his eye raking boldly over her. "Well-meaning, aren't
you?"

"That we are," Maeve said archly. Her eye ran over his thick
chest and heavily muscled arms. Heat rose in her cheeks like lava
flow. She swallowed, adding huskily, "And all waiting for your
bidding."

"Uh-huh," he said. He slapped his hands across his tunic,
raising a heavy dust cloud. Quickly he stripped and stepped into
the bath. A young wench caught her breath at the sight of his

naked chest, his naked legs. He grinned and took the soap from her hands, lathering it across his hairy shoulders.

"I wonder," Maeve said as Cúchulainn came up to her, "if you would mind, that is, er, ahem . . ."

"Yes?" Cúchulainn asked politely as he pulled his tunic over his shoulders and stepped into the tub waiting for him. She caught her breath at the fine network of scars that laced across his shoulders and back, at his narrow waist and slim shanks, and last, at his manhood, heavy like a ship's beam, before it disappeared beneath the scented water.

"Well," Maeve said, her eyes roaming hungrily over his scarred body, eagerly devouring it. Her throat filled. A weakness came in her loins. "Would you three be wishing to share a house, or would you each prefer your own?" she finished huskily.

"A separate house," Cúchulainn said firmly. He glanced over to where Loegaire and Conall splashed in the water with the naked women. A weary grin touched his lips. "Yes, I think that will be much better," he said, nodding. "As for the rest of the host, well, a house for Conchobor and one for Fergus, for certain. The others can shift among themselves, I should think."

"So it shall be ordered," Maeve said, turning away. "When you have finished your baths, please follow the women to the houses I will have prepared for you."

"And *I* will lead you," Finnabair said to Cúchulainn, stepping in front of her mother. She wore a thin *sida*, so sheer that it appeared to have been woven from spider filaments.

"Well," Maeve said, biting her lips, trying to think of a way to supplant her daughter.

Finnabair pouted. "Oh, Mother. You know you have the rest of the host to take care of. And you heard that Fergus is coming. Is it true that he must have seven women a night or he goes sleepless?" she asked Cúchulainn.

He grinned and nodded. "Yes, that is true. And the seven women are truly worn when the sun rises."

"Oh, very well," Maeve said crossly, turning away. "I'll send food to your rooms."

"That would be good," Cúchulainn said politely, his eyes crinkling at the corners. Finnabair sighed.

When the Ulstermen arrived, both Ailill and Maeve met them with their whole household, promising them peace and bidding them welcome. Fresh water had been brought and more baths laid out for the men, with Ailill's own bath readied for Conchobor.

"We are pleased," Seancha said as Conchobor lowered himself into the water, sighing with relief. "We beg your pardon for not sending a messenger on ahead, but we hurried away from Ulster so rapidly that there was no time for the amenities to be properly observed."

"Oh?" Ailill said, his fine brow furrowing. "And what seemed to be the problem?"

"Well . . . oh, that is nice," Seancha said as a young woman helped him with his robe and tunic. He stepped into the water, sighing deeply. "Where was I? Oh, yes, nowhere. I had just started to answer when this delightfully young thing was so kind as to help me. You have been most kind, as I said, to prepare this welcome for us. I hope that someday we can return the favor if you should ever visit Emain Macha. That is, I hope that you will not look upon our sudden arrival as a breach of the Laws of Hospitality, for such was not our intent. No, no. I can assure you of that. Such was not our intent. No."

"You were saying?" Ailill said politely. A small pain began to throb behind his eyes.

"Was I? Oh, yes. Well, there is a problem, you see . . ."

And between his ramblings and side paths, Ailill and Maeve managed to piece together the story of Bricriu's feast and the plot he had carefully woven for the three champions. Ailill pulled at his lower lip with two slender fingers as he considered the story.

"Well, this is a pretty mess," he said. "I see that I have little choice, though."

"Oh, no," Seancha said. "Oh, I'm sorry. I see. I misunderstood. I thought you had already given thought to the problem. My fault. I was made so comfortable by, well, by this, this . . . no, my dear, not yet . . . *young* thing that I . . ."

"Quite all right, no offense taken," Ailill said. "Bathing strengthens a man's character. Leads him to new thoughts and all that."

"Quite so, quite so," Seancha panted. His eyes were very bright. "Well, shall we say . . . *shortly?*"

Ailill glanced over at Conchobor, who was grinning widely as three women vigorously toweled him dry. "Oh, yes. In a bit. Meanwhile, we'll ready dinner for you."

Seancha gurgled as he turned his attention to the soft ministrations of the young woman who had entered the bath with him, straddling him as she vigorously scrubbed his shoulders.

"That is a welcome relief," Maeve sighed as she and Ailill made their way into the house. "At first I thought they were coming for war. And with our armies scattered in the south collecting taxes. I hope," she said, glancing over her shoulder to be certain that no one was listening, "I hope that they do not discover how thin our ranks are at the moment."

"Don't worry about that," Ailill said. "I think you solved the problem well with your greeting. Quite thoughtful of you, my dear."

"Bah. It was nothing," Maeve said. She frowned thoughtfully. "Although I wonder about that Cúchulainn."

Ailill grinned. "It's lucky for you that you have married a husband who is never jealous," he said teasingly.

"That was the only reason that I would marry," Maeve said, dodging his groping hands. "Behave yourself. Until later, at least. You were the one man worthy of me who seemed to have no jealous bone whatsoever."

"Yes," Ailill said. "But be careful how far you push this. People change, you know. The gentlest dog sometimes snarls and barks at its master."

"Wisdom acts, stupidity labors to explain itself," Maeve said. "Now, what shall we do?"

"Do? Why, what we have been asked, I suppose. Seems the simplest thing to me. Truths move like trout, and like trout, they can dodge and dart here and there at whim."

"You mean," Maeve said acidly, "to play it by ear."

"Of course, my dear. Isn't that what I was just saying?" He took her by the arm and led her into their palace.

Hours later, the Ulstermen wandered into the stronghold. They paused, taking in Maeve's work in creating a Place of Enchantment out of Cruachain. Seven circles and seven compartments fronted each other from fire to partition. Each had been faced with bronze and carvings of red yew. Three bronze arches curved high overhead beneath the oak roof that had been carefully shingled with split pine. Twelve windows filled with glass—Bricriu looked enviously at this—stood on each side. Ailill and Maeve's couch stood in the center of the house on molded silver footings, and frontings with strips of bronze wrapped artfully around the posts.

Two statues of the *Síghle na gCíoch* stood at each end of the couch, while one hovered on a platform in back and above the middle of the couch, a sculpture of a naked woman, legs splayed, hands placed behind the thighs with her fingers delicately opening her vulva, proud breasts bared to the world, representatives of the *Mórrigna*—Badb, Macha, and Mórrigan, the triad of the war and fertility sorceresses. The likeness of Maeve could be seen in the high cheekbones, full breasts, and shapely thighs.

By the partition facing Ailill, there stood a silver wand that allowed him to check all the apartments and see that his guests were being well treated. Musicians played softly as the Red Branch heroes moved from door to door, considering the beauty of the palace.

Conchobor and Fergus Mac Róich had joined Ailill in his compartment, along with nine other Ulster heroes, as a great feast was laid out before them. For the required three days and three nights before business could be discussed—no king dare ignore the Laws of Hospitality as laid down by the Brehon—Ailill and Maeve entertained them at a feast that kept the ovens burning furiously every minute, every hour.

At last, Ailill decided that the time had come for him to formally inquire of Conchobor for the purpose of his visit. Seancha had related the matter briefly before, but now Conchobor dabbled his fingers in rose-scented water held for him by a plump, naked *cumal*, belched, and said, "We have come for your wisdom, Ailill. As a favor, if you will."

"Why don't you choose your own champion?" Ailill asked politely. "Your wisdom is certainly as great as mine."

"Ah, but that, you see, is why I have come to you," Conchobor said, grinning, lights shining from his greasy chin. "Only a foolish man creates a wind in his own house. Pardon." He farted gently and leaned back contentedly. "That is, only a foolish man picks one wife as more beautiful than another. You see—"

"Yes," Ailill said hastily. "I understand. If you pick one, the other two will be 'disgruntled?' "

"Madder than ten dogs after one bitch in heat," Conchobor said darkly. "I tell you, Ailill, it wouldn't take much for me to throw Bricriu to the wolves for all the trouble he's caused me."

"Why don't you?" Ailill asked curiously.

"Ah, well, he's a satirist. A poet, you know," Conchobor said softly, tapping one side of his nose with a forefinger. "Doesn't do to make a poet mad."

"Dead poets speak only dead words," Ailill said.

"Hmm. Yes. I'll have to think on that one. But what about it? Favor for favor?"

"What favor will you give me?" Ailill asked.

"It's just a saying," Conchobor admonished irritably. "The proprieties, you know. You'll understand after you've been a king as long as I. Come now, man! Will you do it?"

Ailill looked unhappy. He scratched his hair, working his fingers deep into his long, black tresses. "I don't like this, Conchobor. I mean, I shouldn't have to give this decision. Bones and crackling! You think you would have trouble if you chose one over the other, what about me? They owe me no allegiance. Nothing! What's to keep them from burning Cruachain and killing everyone if I make two unhappy? No, I shouldn't do it unless it's done out of hatred."

"Hatred?" Conchobor said darkly, furrowing his brow.

"I mean, only an enemy should be asked to do something like

this. And I," he said hastily, "do not wish to be an enemy of the mighty Red Branch. Indeed," he continued, frowning and spreading his hands in a supplicating manner, "what have I done that you should place this burden upon me and my people? Have we raided your borders recently? Do we not turn the correct side of our chariot to your people to avoid giving offense whenever we chance to meet upon the road? Why don't you give the choice to someone else? How about Da Derga of the Lagin? He's always ready to shoo-in his opinion on anything. Bit of a bragger perhaps, but by pussy willows! I think that he'd do it!" He added to himself. *And hanged if we all wouldn't be better if the other two burnt his hostel to the ground, for all of that!*

"No," Seancha said. "You are the one. Come on! Be a man! That's what kings are supposed to do! Make difficult choices and live with them. Think of it as an exercise in logic, in aesthetics. Remember the old conundrum: even pigs have to make aesthetic choices. We'd do the same for you, wouldn't we, Conchobor?"

"You would," Conchobor corrected, looking at his advisor's washed-out eyes and hair the color of milkweed pod.

"Uh-huh," Ailill said. "Well, of course. What are kings for?"

"That's the spirit!" Conchobor said, grinning. He reached over and punched Ailill on the shoulder, rocking him. "Now, how long will you need?"

"Yes, how long?" Seancha asked. "Do not make too long a delay. After all, we cannot spare our heroes long from us. Never know what might be brewing in the south and all that, you know."

"Oh, three days and three nights should do it, I would think," Ailill said, rubbing his bruised shoulder. *Asshole!*

"That would certainly be friendly," Seancha said eagerly. "Oh, yes, most friendly indeed! Shouldn't stretch our friendship at all. Shall we drink on it?"

"Oh, yes. Drink," Ailill said. He motioned to the serving wenches to refill the goblets. *Well,* he thought, *things could have been worse. Now all I have to do is figure out a way of making each one of them happy. Ugh. I must have done something to make the gods angry. Very angry.*

Chapter 8

THE CAVE AND
THE CATS

AILILL WATCHED SOURLY FROM the balcony of his bedroom as Conchobor and his Red Branch turned their chariots in the cobbled courtyard and thundered away, leaving Loegaire, Conall, and Cúchulainn behind. He raised his hand, smiling as Conchobor thrust his thick forearm into the air in salute, and said softly between set teeth to Maeve, standing beside him, "I'd like to stuff his chariot up his arse for this one."

"Oh, be quiet," Maeve said. Her eyes were puffy from the night she'd spent with Conchobor and his men. She smiled as a lusty warrior paused to wink up at her before his charioteer turned the horses toward the gate. Her thighs ached from the long night, but the hours had been worth every minute. She yawned and ran her fingers through her long, red-gold mane, remembering fondly how it had been wrapped around the throat of the young warrior, holding him close to her.

"Oh, yes, that's easy for you to say," Ailill sniffed. He looked down at her through half-closed eyes. "All you did was bed half his company."

"No," Maeve said wistfully. "Not half." Then she bristled as she caught the inference. "And just where do you stand, my darling, casting the witch's wand at me when your own hazel branch was waving delectably above that heavy-breasted wench sent to us from Munster?"

"She has been promised in marriage," Ailill said loftily. "You know the Brehon Law as well as I. The king has certain, er, responsibilities, and one of them is to see to the first night of the wedding. Ah, me!" He shook his head wearily. "It seems more and more weddings are being held in the fall than ever before. I swear that it'll make a eunuch out of me yet!"

"It's not like a cedar post, darling," Maeve said acidly. "Rubbing it won't wear it down to a peg. What's good for the gander's good for the goose."

"That," Ailill said crankily, "is not the point. The point is that you were . . . oh, forget it! Pussy willows and poppincocks! We have enough problems without these three popinjays poking their prickly prods in our best puddies. Why, that Conall nearly ruined three of our wenches by himself! And Loegaire two, and Cúchulainn, well, did you see how haggard our daughter looked this morning? Rode hard and put up wet, if I don't miss my guess. A fine thing to be teaching her!"

"Old enough," Maeve countered crossly. "And the Brehon, as you are so fond of quoting, is quite clear on that. Remember our bargain, Ailill. No jealousy! You know the *geis* placed upon me! Knew about it when I married you. Do you want me to bring the wrath down upon us now by denying it?"

"Handy excuse, that one, for diddling damn near every night like a mare in rut," he grumbled to himself.

"What's that?" she asked suspiciously, leaning toward him.

"Nothing, nothing," he said. "Piss and vinegar! You have a tongue like an adder this early in the morning. Go back to bed while I try to figure out what to do with this obligation."

"Well," Maeve said, mollified. She leaned close to him and hunched her shoulders so the neckline of her gown fell to the tips of her breasts. "We *can* wait for night, if you wish. There's enough around here to keep them occupied until then."

A strange clicking sounded in her throat. Ailill glanced down and swallowed heavily. "Ah, Maeve, you have the morals of a penurious strumpet!"

"Hmm," she said. A smoky fog slipped over her eyes. She grinned and arched her back, buddies threatening to burst from her bodice. "That is, if you haven't been worn out by your kingly duties?"

He gurgled and curled his arm around her. "There's much more to kingly duties, my dear, then predicated poking."

"Yes, yes," she answered breathlessly. "But why do men always insist upon talking it to death before producing?"

He growled and swept her up into his arms and, turning, hurried back into their sleeping rooms, tumbling her gracelessly upon the rumpled bed.

And where do you think our host has gone?" Conall asked grumpily, staring up at the empty balcony above them.

Loegaire shrugged. "If he's smart, he's giving that doxy a romp or two, he is." He sighed, glancing over at the women clustered together in a corner of the courtyard, watching the dust of the Red Branch settle over the plain. "Leaving the pickings to us, I guess."

"Pretty ripe pickings," Conall said. He winked, adding coarsely, "I swear, a few of them were ripe cherries ready for the pie last night."

"You wouldn't know nuts from cherries," Loegaire said. "Did you hear the tongue-lashing he gave that prick, Bricriu? Near peeled the hide right off him."

"Had it coming," Conall said. "Make him a gelding, what we should do. It'd calm him down if someone'd whack his clackers off." He scissored two thick fingers in the air. "Snip, snip. All it would take. That'd cut the poison from his tongue all right."

"No," Loegaire sighed. "Just make him meaner, I'm after thinking. Be always remembering what he'd lost, he would. Not that he's had that much. Man spends as much time thinking about mischief wouldn't have the time for poony-thinking."

"What wench would warm to those cockles?" Conall de-manded. "Bile from his mouth would blister her lips. Don't know why that hairy-legged wench he married takes to him so."

"Pair of a kind," Loegaire grunted. "So, what do we do now?" He looked at Cúchulainn.

"I think I'll take a walk around," the young warrior answered. He squinted up at the golden sun shining brightly overhead. " 'Tis a fine day for it. We might learn a thing or two if we keep our eyes open."

"No poony for you?" Conall said wistfully. He sighed. "Just as well, I suppose. Wear a man down, they will. Wouldn't do for that to happen, now would it? What with the challenge and all waiting to be settled. What d'yuh suppose it'll be?"

Cúchulainn shrugged indifferently. "Who knows? Does it matter? But I'd be careful. I suspect that Ailill might use this as a way of getting rid of one or all three of us."

"What? What's that you're saying?" Loegaire demanded, frowning.

Cúchulainn spread his hands. "Remember where you are. That's all I'm saying. Connacht has always been the enemy of Ulster. Little grows here but stumps and rocks. They'd like noth-ing better than to get the fine pastures of Ulster."

"Hmm. You might have something there," Loegaire said thoughtfully.

"What? What does he have?" Conall asked, his heavy brow furrowing. He stuck a thick forefinger in an ear, digging deeply.

"Yes, dig that cheese from your brain," Loegaire said. "Wouldn't it be just like Ailill to take advantage of our situation and use it to get rid of some, or even all, of us through challenges? Make things a bit simpler for him if we weren't there the next time he and that bitch of his raid our borders with their army. Speaking of which—" he added, looking around, speculating "—I wonder where they are. All I see here are the young boys who still think with their pods instead of their brains. Where are the warriors? A place the size of Cruachain should have at least a hundred or two more behind its walls, wouldn't you think?"

"I would," Cúchulainn said. "That's why I say we'd better be careful now. Remember that a challenge is a challenge, but there's more between apples and oranges than nuts and sticks."

"Ah!" Conall said loudly, slapping a huge hand across Loegaire's back. "Not enough warriors around to shovel shit. I get it. We need to watch our step, my friends!"

Loegaire closed his eyes painfully for a second, then looked at Cúchulainn, spreading his arms in pathetic appeal. "See what I mean?" he whined.

Cúchulainn laughed and walked away, turning his steps toward the stables to check on Black and Gray. After a moment's hesitation, Loegaire and Conall fell in beside him, arguing between themselves, but there was no heat to their words, only insults such as fighting men give each other.

That night, Ailill ordered three bullocks slaughtered, one in honor for each of the warriors so that none could argue over the Champion's Portion. Fifty women waited on each, bringing platters of meat from the spits as each devoured his portion. Others held damp cloths so the heroes could wipe their greasy fingers and lips, and still others, buddies bouncing, brought beer from a large puncheon for them to quench their thirst.

Ailill relaxed against the cushions of his couch next to Maeve, who was dressed becomingly in a red gown slit and laced wide to the arm on one side, soft and creamy skin showing between the diamonds of the lacings. Bright jewels bedecked her hair, and a heavy, golden *torc* encircled her neck, the weighty knobs at each end resting at the head of the deep valley of her breasts.

"You know, my dear," he murmured, "I think I've figured a way out of this mess, thanks to you."

"Thanks to me?" Maeve asked, her eyes clicking between each of the warriors, weighing, calculating.

"Oh, yes. It came to me while we were resting between battles." He looked over at the table where Crom Deroil, Maeve's

Druid, frowned over a *buanbach* board with his apprentice, his gnarled fingers combing slowly through his thick white beard. As they watched, his hand dropped from his chin and crept slowly across the board. His fingers opened like a crab's pincers, picked up a piece and dropped it upon a square. Then he leaned back and nodded with satisfaction at the apprentice, who shook his head wonderingly as he considered his move.

"Let's let Crom Deroil use a bit of his magic, his *draíocht an ealaín dubh,* if you will, to set the challenge."

"Black magic?" Maeve frowned. "You know what Druids think about that. A foul abomination. I don't know. I would hate to hurt him by asking him to do such a thing—although I know he'd do it for me. He's been with me a long time, and been kind to me since before my blood began to flow."

"Well," Ailill said, vexed by her answer, "we'll just ask him to set the challenge, and he can use whatever magic he wants. After all, it is the difficulty of the challenge that is important, not the challenge itself."

Besides, he added to himself, *if something goes wrong, Conchobor can't blame us for the old fart's mistake. We get the best of the two worlds. Our obligation is set and if we're lucky, we reap the harvest when one of them falls. And it's time the old fool earns his keep, sitting there in stony superiority, talking about omens and all that nonsense while he plays games with the next generation.*

Maeve nibbled thoughtfully at her full lower lip. "And if something goes wrong?"

Minx! Ailill thought. *Read my mind, will you?* "What can Conchobor do to a Druid?" he asked smoothly. He grinned. "It's perfectly safe, my darling. Trust me."

"Trust you? Trust a peacock's preening," Maeve scoffed. She raised an eyebrow and shook her head. "Ask him. Won't hurt to do that, I suppose. All he can say is 'no.' "

"To his king? I don't think so," Ailill said, rapping a heavy ring on the massive oak arm of his couch. "Who disobeys his king brings down wrath upon his own head. Brehon Law."

"From which," Maeve said, reminding, "all Druids are exempt

save for treason and rape, but no woman would refuse a Druid, for any child born from such a mating would produce a demigod. Of sorts," she amended. "Remember the story of Conchobor?"

"Don't remind me," Ailill said crossly, crooking his finger. "I'm trying to have a good time."

Crom Deroil rose obediently at Ailill's summons and, using his staff, moved stiffly across the feasting-hall. He paused, staring at Ailill with rheumy eyes.

"Yes?" he asked softly. "What is it you wish?"

"Well," Ailill said, shifting his weight on the couch, "we have a bit of a problem here that we hope you will be able to help us with."

Crom Deroil nodded. "Yes, I wondered how long it would be before you asked me."

Caught unaware, Ailill frowned. "What? Asked you what?"

"To devise a challenge for our three guests," Crom Deroil said calmly. He looked contemptuously at Ailill. "As good a way as any, I suppose, to avoid your obligations. And, you cannot be blamed if anything goes wrong. A mere mischance. Fate. Meanwhile, you can sit and moan about overcooked cabbage and leeks."

"I don't like cabbage," Ailill muttered absently.

"A metaphor, nothing more," Crom Deroil said. "You'll simply blame any mistake upon the doddering old fool. Never mind," he said, waving his hand tiredly as Ailill opened his mouth to object. "Truth is truth, and your prevarications cannot change hemp mats into silk. Cattails into oats. A cow to a sheep. Where was I?" He frowned. "Ah, yes. The challenge. What is it precisely you want done? And don't bandy words around trying to make a nail into a horseshoe." He shook his head, thinking to himself. *A pain, always looking for correct analogies to explain things to kings. A weakening of the blood, it is. That's it, a weakening of the blood. Zounds and bodkins! Inferior breeding brings the brain down to the prick.*

"All right," Ailill said, clearing his throat with a quick glance at Maeve. Her face seemed carved in stone as she stared back at him. He could read his plan in her eyes. "What we want is a workable challenge to separate the men from the boys..."

"Chaff from the wheat. Colts from the stallions. Use something original, if you can, besides dead metaphors," Crom Deroil muttered.

Ailill swallowed the anger creeping up into his throat. *Someday,* he thought, then quickly dismissed the thought on bat's wings before the old Druid slipped it from his mind and twisted it to use on him. "Look, let's be practical about the whole thing."

"Yes, let's," Crom Deroil said.

"I could send them somewhere, oh, I don't know...bring pearls back from the deep...kill a dragon, a troll...clean the stables like that Greek fellow. You know, something difficult, but would that be a challenge appropriate to warrant giving the Champion's Portion? No, no, we must have something much more difficult. Something to bring out the mettle in the man."

"Send them south," Crom Deroil said. "There's always a challenge down there. Award it to the one who brings back the most heads."

"Er...yes, we could do that," Ailill said. "But what would that prove? That one was lucky enough to find the most heads to cut, nothing more. Blind luck, not bold deeds. That's what we need. You see?"

Crom Deroil bowed his head, his eyes becoming as dark as the night before a storm as he turned his thoughts inward, considering. Ailill watched, half fearful that lightning might crackle forth from one of his gnarled fingers and crisp him like overdone meat, even though Druids seldom used such wizardly tricks, preferring more subtle methods, such as rhyme and reason. Playing with the Otherworld always taxed the strength and spirit of a man, aging him long before his time, although, Ailill remembered, there are those who say a Druid's time comes only when he is so tired he wants to go back into the trees from whence he came. For a moment, envy crept over him at the thought of immortality and all the wenches waiting yet to be borne for his loins, but then he clamped down memory when he saw the Druid's eyes flicker darkly at him.

"Don't interfere," Crom Deroil said acidly, "or I'll change you into a truffle and let a hog root you out."

"I don't think I would like that." Ailill swallowed hard against a suddenly dry throat. "Have you come up with anything yet?"

The Druid heaved a sigh that seemed to come from the callused soles of his feet. He stared down at the thick, yellowed nails on his foot.

"Yes, I think I can do something that will serve your purpose."

"Hard, but relatively safe?"

"Oh, yes. Very hard. And *if* they are champions, then it should be safe," the Druid answered.

"Uh, I don't mean to press, but how long will this take to set up? There is a time limit. That is, I said it should only take three days or so before we send them on their way back to Ulster. Wouldn't do to make a liar out of me, now would it?" He laughed—*heh, heh, heh*—then covered his nervousness by lifting his wine goblet and drinking thirstily.

"Tonight suit you?" Crom Deroil asked crossly. "Oh, do not act so surprised! A minor thing, really. Now, if you asked for something *really* difficult, such as turning lead into gold or a rose into a daisy—although why anyone would want a foolish parlor trick like that is anybody's guess—then I might have to think a bit more. But a simple challenge, why, that's nothing! A bit of imagination is all. Create a worthy opponent with the proper skills and attributes in a proper setting and you've got a proper challenge. Child's play!"

He turned and stumped back to the *buanbach* board. He stared down thoughtfully for a moment, then moved a piece and cackled gleefully as his apprentice's face fell in disappointment. "Think, boy!" he crowed. "Don't hope for miracles. You have to create them yourself!"

"Uh." Ailill rapped the arm of his couch again with his ring. "Where do I send them?" Crom Deroil glared at him. "The champions?" Ailill asked again nervously.

Crom Deroil sighed. He closed his eyes, wincing painfully. He pinched the bridge of his nose. "Now where do you suppose you'd

be sending three champions for a bit of a do against the magic?
To the room that joins the Hill of the Sídhe, of course."

Ailill's face flamed and he leaned back on his couch, noncha-
lantly lifting his goblet, pretending to sip. *Damn fool! He'd better
be as good as he says, or . . .*

—*Or what?*

Ailill's face whitened as the thought crashed in upon his, filled
with malice, threatening. He forced his anger down, feeling it
bubble in his stomach.

—*Or what?*

The thought returned, forceful, demanding, and Ailill drained
his goblet, trying to befuddle the thought with drink.

—*Fool! Think you to be a shaper? One like me? One who knows
the beginning, the present, the end? Everything? Faugh! You see only
the past and a bit of the present when you rest your cock, but you
have no higher faculties than memory and perception! If you could
only see once the passionate and the passive, the vision of the huge
blowout awaiting you, your bowels would turn to dust! You cannot
cause things to happen any more than you can cause the sun to stand
still!* A dry chuckle snapped like dead branches in his mind. *Nyeh!
Heh! Heh! Scared enough to pee in your tunic!* He winced.

—*But . . .*

—*Silence! Or I'll let loose the forked lightning you fear and fry
your balls!*

—*Sorry.*

—*That's better. Now, for your information, of course, it doesn't
have to be the Hill of the Sídhe, but why should I drain my life-force
by going into the Otherworld from here and bringing them with me?
Hmmm? Fundamentals, fool! The mouth of the cave will suffice!*

—*All right,* he whimpered, pressing the pads of his fingers
against his temples and rubbing hard to release the pain of
thought. *All right! I'm sorry! Enough!*

—*It's damned hard confining myself to thoughts that a creature
like you can understand. Talking in jargon, inventing worthless metaphors. Life, blockhead, can be found in the frustrations of natural order,
if you can push your way along the path from the deadening influence*

of your social comformity. See that jug of wine at your elbow?

Ailill opened his eyes, staring at the jug of fired clay resting by his right elbow. Automatically he nodded.

—*If you were to break that jug . . .*

Ailill's hand closed around the neck of the jug and dashed it to the floor. It shattered, sending a pool of red wine spreading like blood across the slate. Rubies glinted from the spare drops flung out from the pool.

—*Fool! That was to be a metaphor!*

He winced again, aware that the talk had died and eyes stared at him. But he was unable to give voice to his action for other words filled his mind, crowding out his thoughts.

—*An angry man does not shake his fist at the universe! Senseless gesture, that! As meaningless as boils and pimples! Now, you must pretend that you've had a vision and that the three champions must go to the mound of the Sídhe and there await what may occur.*

"I apologize," Ailill said swiftly before the thoughts could again converge within his mind. "A sudden spasm, a pain. You know." The others looked sympathetically at him. "But I tell you—Loegaire, Conall, Cúchulainn—that you will go to the room that adjoins the Hill of the Sídhe outside Cruachain and there wait for your challenge from whence judgment will be made."

—*Not bad. Better than I hoped. You have the makings of a good actor. Not much different than a king, you know. Just a ripple on the lake of Time. Nothing more.* A deep sigh soughed through Ailill's mind like a chill wind. He shivered. *Ah! What pathetic nonsense this is, man's cunning. As predictable as a baby's belch. As useless as a fart in the wind. Think of trees, my friend!* The image of a rowan grew in his mind, leafing out, spreading branches over the fertile earth. Black dirt. *Ah, there you have it! The letter "L." All knowledge begins with the alphabet. Now, repeat after me: Birch, rowan, alder . . .*

"Birch, rowan, alder . . ." Sweat streamed down his face as Ailill opened his mouth, obediently parroting.

— *. . . willow, ash, hawthorn, oak . . .*

"Willow, ash, hawthorn, oak . . ."

— *. . . holly, hazel, apple, vine, ivy, broom, blackthorn, elder, fir,* *gorse, heather, aspen, yew, spindle, honeysuckle, gooseberry, and beech.*

"I . . ."

—Say it!

"Hollyhazelapplevineivybroomblackthornelderfir . . ." He paused, mouth gulping like a fish out of water.

—Gorse, heather, aspen, yew, spindle, honeysuckle, gooseberry, and beech.

"Gorseheatheraspenyewspindlehoneysucklegooseberrybeech!" he gasped, finishing.

—Terrible, terrible. Tch-tch. At least try to remember the chieftain trees: oak, hazel, holly, apple, ash, yew, and fir.

"I will!"

"You will what?" Maeve said. She placed her cool fingers on his forehead, jerking them back as if she had touched hot iron. "You're burning up!"

—Yes, that is thought! And if I continue, you will fry as certainly as if a dragon's breath had encindered you! Bones to dust! Ashes to ashes! A black hole into eternity and all that nonsense!

"I'm sorry."

"For what?" Maeve said, wrinkling her brow. She grabbed him by the shoulders, shaking him. "Ailill! Stop it! You're making a fool of yourself!"

"I don't want to be a shaper," he whined.

"A what?" Maeve said loudly.

—Pathetic.

And the thoughts disappeared with the blink of an eye. He closed his eyes and dug his knuckles into them. Then he opened them and stared across at the Druid, standing placidly beside the *buanbach* board, his hands folded inside the large sleeves of his robe like a nightmare flower. He smiled benignly across at Ailill.

"I think," Ailill croaked, "that I shall retire. No, stay where you are. Enjoy yourselves. Just a touch of nausea. A bit of under-cooked pork, perhaps. A blot of mustard. Erk." He belched and farted. Maeve winced and hastily rose, backing away from the couch.

"Try some wine," Crom Deroil suggested. "Perhaps that will help."

"No, I think . . . water," Ailill said, tugging furiously at the collar of his tunic. "By Dagda's balls! I feel on fire."

He rose and staggered to the wide clay pots standing beside the door. He plunged his head into the cold water, feeling the last burning thoughts slip away through the rush of cool water. He ventured a cautious thought: *Of course, water stops all things!* Then he hastily banished the thought as he came up gasping and sputtering for air.

"I think," Maeve said slowly from beside him, "that you have dropped your senses." She stared into his eyes, as lonely as empty graves. She shuddered delicately, her breasts bobbling nicely.

"Come on, then," she said softly. "Let's take you to bed."

She took his arm to lead him from the hall. Obediently he followed, then stiffened and turned back to the hall.

"I do beg your pardon," he said. His stomach rumbled again. He belched softly into his fist. "Bad meat. Has to be. But you all enjoy yourselves." He looked at the three heroes, watching him. *Eyes like wolves,* he thought, and shuddered. "Your job is to wait at the mouth of the cave that is part of the Hill of the Sídhe. There, you will find your challenge."

He nodded, glanced over at the merry eyes of Crom Deroil, then hurried from the hall, his arm draped over Maeve's shoulders, hand cupping her breast, automatically registering the rise of her nipple against his palm.

Well!" Conall said loudly, looking from Loegaire to Cúchulainn. "What was that all about?"

Loegaire shrugged and looked at Cúchulainn.

"I think," the Hound answered, "that Ailill had a visitation."

"Visitation?" Conall's brows drew together, waggling like mating beetles. "What do you mean, 'visitation'?"

"From the Otherworld," Cúchulainn said.

"Gods' balls!" Loegaire swore. "Are you going to start again about this mystical crap of yours? The Otherworld?"

"We don't need any of that barmy talk," Conall said. He closed his huge fist and shook it at the smaller man. "Keep a current tongue in your head or I'll knock such thoughts out of it!"

"No you won't," Cúchulainn said softly. The seven pupils in his eyes began to glow like the sun viewed through jewels. "And mind your manners. You asked me; I didn't volunteer."

"That's right, that's right," Loegaire said hurriedly. Conall started to rise, but Loegaire grabbed his arm, pulling the huge warrior back onto his cushion. He leaned closer, whispering urgently into Conall's ear. "Now behave! We don't need to be fighting amongst ourselves. Plenty of that around here, if you want bloodletting!"

"All right, all *right!*" Conall said, snapping his arm away from Loegaire's grasp. "We'll save this until later. But, wee one," he said to Cúchulainn, "I won't forget this! We'll settle up later."

"As you wish," Cúchulainn said. "If you want a thumping that badly, I'll be happy to oblige you, I will."

Conall flushed darkly and started to rise, only to be pulled back again by Loegaire. Cúchulainn ignored him and glanced across at Crom Deroil. Their eyes locked, and a look of surprise flickered quickly across the Druid's face like a fairy's dance. His lips twitched. He picked up his staff, nodded at his apprentice to follow him, then slowly made his way across to the three champions.

"Well met, Cúchulainn," he said.

"*Samildánach*, Master of All Arts," the young warrior said respectfully. He made a curious gesture with his fingers and the Druid's smile broadened.

"I have heard stories about you, of your birth . . ."

"Here we go again," Loegaire muttered, rolling his eyes at Conall.

". . . and of Lugh, the Sun God," the Druid finished. His eyes looked reprovingly at Loegaire. The grizzled warrior fidgeted nervously under the Druid's gaze.

"So some claim," Cúchulainn said. He nodded at the apprentice beside the Druid. "I see you are preparing your replacement."

"Yes," the Druid said. He raised a gnarled hand and affectionately rumpled the youth's hair. "But he has a long way to go. I fear I have quite a few years left before I can retire into the trees." His eyes stared at Cúchulainn, dimming faintly as he looked past the present and into the future. "But you . . . I do not see at the end of this life."

Cúchulainn shook his head. "So it has been prophesied. A short life for honor and immortality." He shrugged. "A fair trade. The choice was mine."

"Ah," Crom Deroil said. "You may regret that at the end."

"Perhaps," Cúchulainn said. "But do any of us know what exists after our choices? Man can see only so far."

"True," the Druid said. "Such wisdom. You would have made an excellent Druid."

"Thank you," Cúchulainn said.

"Of course," Crom Deroil added, "it is too late now. The stones of the future have been set in place and now you can only walk upon their path."

"And where will this path lead?" Cúchulainn asked.

"Do you truly wish to know?"

"Not the end. But if your life eclipses mine, surely you can see what lies after mine," Cúchulainn said.

The Druid's eyes clouded, then cleared. He smiled gently. "What you wished for," he said. He motioned to his apprentice and turned toward the door. He glanced back at Cúchulainn. "*If you hold fast to your honor.*" He looked at the others. "My apprentice will return to lead you to the room beside the Hill of the Sídhe at the appropriate hour. If I were you, I would not drink any more wine or beer," he added acidly. "A clear head may be needed."

He nodded and turned to walk painfully on his swollen bunions from the hall. Loegaire and Conall exchanged glances, then laughed nervously.

"Prophecies!" Conall growled, snatching a foaming jug of beer from a passing serving wench. He raised it, swallowing noisily, draining it. He tossed it back to the wide-eyed girl, belching loudly. "I have had a bellyful of prophecies!"

"I'll drink to that," Loegaire said, seizing his mug from his table and putting action to his words.

Cúchulainn shrugged and asked the young girl to bring him a jug of water. He smiled at the other two. "Sometimes it is better to give heed to the blowing of the wind like the rushes do than to resist it like the oak," he said.

"Huh?" Conall looked bewildered.

"Another prophecy," Loegaire sighed.

"No, an adage," Cúchulainn corrected.

"Whatever," Loegaire grunted.

The Druid's apprentice returned for them near midnight and motioned silently for them to follow him from the hall. The three warriors rose, gathered their weapons and departed with a lone warrior's call of "good luck!" ringing in their ears.

"Ulstermen," one of the warriors spat as Conall's back disappeared through the doorway. "Wishing them good luck is like pissing in your father's beer! What'd you want to do that for?"

"Have you ever been on the Hill of the Sídhe at midnight?" demanded the other. "If you have, then you'll know why I wished them good fortune. A *banhsídhe*'s cry will freeze your blood, and that's nothing to what they'll see there when the witching hour is upon us." He shook his head. "And sure I am that you haven't been there or you wouldn't deprive anyone of luck, even if you were to fight him on the morrow."

The first warrior shuddered and lifted his mug, draining it, pretending that he hadn't heard.

The three warriors followed the apprentice through the halls of Cruachain. After a brief attempt at speech by Loegaire, they all fell silent as the apprentice silently pointed ahead of them, refusing words.

Cold air blew upon them with a hint of frost in its breath as

they stepped from the warmth of the hall. Stars twinkled overhead, winking coldly in the foreboding blackness above them. The
moon glowed blood-red, a harvest moon or a blood moon, they
couldn't tell. They hurried behind the apprentice, drawing closer
to each other for comfort as he led them through the woods. Stark,
black branches rubbed gnarly knobs against each other in the
wind, and dead leaves crackled beneath their feet.

At last they emerged from the woods and found themselves
facing a large building that came off from the main palace of
Cruachain and butted up against a large hill mounded softly like
a woman's breast. The apprentice walked to a door barred from
the outside at the end of the hall. He took down the bar and
opened it. At once a foul odor breathed upon them, like rotting
flesh. Torches had been set in sconces along the wall. They looked
into the cold room that butted up against the side of the hill. A
table laden with food stood in the middle of the hall. Three chairs
had been placed around the table, facing the base of the hill, where
a gaping cave opened its dark mouth, rocks studded around it like
rotting teeth in the mouth of a *caílleach*.

"Here?" Loegaire asked the apprentice, who nodded and
pointed to the three chairs at the table in front of the cave.

"You're sure?" Conall said.

Again, the youth nodded.

"Thank you," Cúchulainn said. "Will you wait with us?"

Wary movement flickered in the youth's eyes, and he shook
his head. He turned and jogged out of the room. They started as
the door boomed shut and the bar dropped down with an ominous
thud!

"Well, if that won't ruffle a billy goat's ruff," Loegaire said,
attempting a laugh. The sound echoed hollowly in the hall. *Har-
uh! Har-uh! Har-uh!* He stopped immediately. "What do we do
now?" he asked in a hushed voice.

"Sit and wait," Cúchulainn said.

"Oh, yes, I forgot. You have the *imbas forasnaí*, the future
sight. Tell us, will the *bocánachs*, come for us, or are we to see the
Donn?" Loegaire asked sarcastically.

"Don't be an *amadán*," Cúchulainn said. "Common logic tells me this. Why else would there be three chairs?"

"Don't—" Loegaire began, but Conall stiffened, raising his hand.

"Quiet! Listen! Do you hear that?" he asked.

The three fell silent, straining to hear behind the night sounds echoing softly in the hall.

"I don't hear anything," Loegaire said.

"Must've been the wind," Conall said at last. He looked at the table set with three places. He shrugged. "Well, might as well eat." He sat down and pulled a huge haunch of roasted beef to him and began slicing chunks from it with his knife.

"Oh, yes," Loegaire said. "Just like you to think of your belly at a time like this. What do you think, Cúchulainn?"

The Hound shrugged and sat beside Conall. "What else is there to do? Sit and stew in our own juices the rest of the night?"

"How do you know that meat isn't poisoned?" Loegaire demanded. "It would be just like Ailill to do that. Wipe all three of us out at once, he would."

"And how would he explain our death to Conchobor?" Cúchulainn asked. "If we die in battle, that's one thing. But poisoned?"

"*Ath ah gooth anther,*" Conall said, his words muffled by a mouthful of beef.

"Ahh," Loegaire said in disgust. He pulled out a chair and sat reaching for a platter. "Might as well die with a full belly if that's what's in store for us."

A faint scratching came to their ears.

"Shh," Conall said.

The three listened hard to the silence of the room.

"I think it's coming from the cave," Conall whispered.

"Where else would it be coming from?" Loegaire asked. "Damned fool!"

"Shh," Cúchulainn said. His eyes began to glow. He cut a piece of meat and put it in his mouth, chewing slowly.

"I don't like this," Loegaire complained softly. "I'll gladly face a hundred men, each armed with the *del chliss*, but these things that go bump in the night, well, you can keep them for stories while we're lying around the fire in the field, thank you very much."

"What is it?" Conall whispered as the scratchings grew louder. A stench began rolling like poisonous fog from the mouth of the cave.

"Phaugh!" Loegaire gagged and spat a piece of meat from his mouth. "Stinks like Bricriu's breath. What is it?"

Growls rumbled from the cave on the heels of his words, and suddenly three huge cats leaped effortlessly from the cave. Slobber dripped from their long yellow fangs, and their claws, as sharp as a barber's razor, clicked against the stone of the floor, leaving deep, sharp scratches in its surface. They crouched and began to creep toward the table and the food.

"Yowp!" shouted Loegaire. "Cats! Shit! Look at the size of those beasties!"

"Gods' balls!" swore Conall, dropping the haunch he was holding. It clattered on the plate, and one of the cats swung its massive head, its yellow eyes fixed upon him. "Enough of this crap!" he said, and dropped his weapons. He leaped upon the table and jumped high, grabbing one of the rafters and pulling himself up into a cross-brace.

Within seconds, Loegaire followed him, stepping on Conall's hand as he clambered up and over the bulky man. His foot came down upon Conall's head as the wiry warrior shinnied up a rafter-spar to the peak of the roof, where he wrapped himself around the beam and stared down with loathing at the animals.

"Ow!" Conall yelled. "Damn you, Loegaire! Find your own roost!"

"First come, first rights, I say," Loegaire said. He shivered, refusing to move. "I hate cats! Especially the size of them. Cúchulainn! Grab a beam. Quick now! That one's got his eyes on you!"

Cúchulainn swallowed, wiped his fingers upon his tunic and reached for a mug filled with beer, watching the cat, the biggest of the three, in front of him, while the other two cats crept warily over to the platters abandoned by Loegaire and Conall and began to bolt their food. The big cat crept closer, then suddenly stretched out a paw to seize the food on Cúchulainn's plate. At once, Cúchulainn's sword flashed brightly in his hand and he leaped to his feet, slashing at the cat's head. Loegaire and Conall drew quick breaths, expecting the cat's head to roll from its shoulders, for well they knew the power behind Cúchulainn's right arm. But the sword skidded off the cat's neck and struck the stone floor, ringing a high, clear note like a golden bell.

The cat shook its head and growled. Cúchulainn struck again and again, the sword glancing off the cat's neck each time. The other two cats growled and stopped eating. They began to circle Cúchulainn, but the Hound slipped his shield over his arm and placed his back into a corner of the room, facing the three cats. They paused, crouching, tails switching angrily, but Cúchulainn faced them calmly, waiting.

"Now you've done it!" Loegaire called from the ceiling. "You've gone and made them angry!"

Cúchulainn ignored him, his eyes glowing brightly as he stared into first one cat's eyes, then another's. One made a slight move, and instantly Cúchulainn's sword struck it hard, driving it back.

For the rest of the long night, Conall and Loegaire clung to their perch high over the floor of the hall while Cúchulainn faced the cats, driving them back whenever one made a move at him. At last they heard a cock crow faintly in the distance, and the cats moved slowly, reluctantly, back into the cave and disappeared.

"I think you can come down now," Cúchulainn said softly. He slid his sword into its scabbard and went back to the table, where he picked up a mug and drank thirstily.

"I'm not coming down until I see that door opened," Loegaire said.

"Me neither," Conall added. "Them cats weren't natural cats, they weren't. Sure and if they weren't from the Otherworld. I suppose they were friends of yours," he added angrily to Cúchulainn. "Otherwise, why wouldn't they have et you, and you only one against three?"

"Yes," Loegaire said quickly. "If you think this earns you the Champion's Portion, you're crazy."

The door creaked open and bright sunlight flashed into the room, dispelling the gloom. Loegaire and Conall dropped hastily from their perch and grabbed their weapons, scurrying for the door. Cúchulainn sauntered over and said a pleasant "Good morning" to the young apprentice silently holding the door open.

They returned to the hall where Ailill waited, white-faced but recovered from the night before. Maeve sat silently beside him. Crom Deroil leaned on his staff at the foot of the couch. His eyes smiled as the three heroes stumbled bleary-eyed from lack of sleep into the hall.

"What—" Loegaire began angrily, but the Druid raised a hand, stopping him.

"Did you face your challenge? Or did you flee from it?" asked the Druid.

"That wasn't a challenge," Conall said hotly.

"No," Loegaire said. "Magic and bedknobs maybe! But it wasn't fair!"

"Not fair," echoed Conall.

"We fight against men, not magic. That's for a Druid's art, and Druid's we ain't. Aren't," Loegaire corrected.

"A man fights with men," Conall insisted. "Not against nightmares."

The Druid smiled at Cúchulainn. "And you? What do you have to say?"

The Hound shrugged. "They were only cats. A bit strange, I admit, but still, only cats."

"Stuff and nonsense!" Loegaire said angrily. "Only cats, my aching arse! They was sent by your magic!" He pointed a trembling forefinger at Crom Deroil accusingly. "Admit it!"

The Druid turned calmly to Ailill and Maeve. "I think your answer has been given," he said. He dropped a hand lightly upon Cúchulainn's shoulder. "This man is he to whom the Champion's

Portion should be given."

"No!" Conall shouted.

"Absolutely not!" Loegaire agreed.

"I have spoken," Crom Deroil said. He spread his hands, shrugging. "It is, of course, up to you. As . . . king," he said. He smiled and left, shuffling with his apprentice from the chamber.

"That man gives me the creeps," muttered Loegaire. He pushed his shoulders back, easing a crick from his back. "Now you listen to me—if those cats would've been human, then I wouldn't argue and I'd say let Cúchulainn have the Champion's Portion and may it stick in his craw!"

"In his craw," echoed Conall.

"But they weren't human, and that's all there is to that. We demand to be judged on our own feats and not on a magician's whim. Besides, I'd say that you had a hand in this, with your Otherworld connections," he said to Cúchulainn.

"Don't speak foolishness," Cúchulainn said. He yawned. "The fact is, I stayed, you two left. Plain and simple. The Champion's Portion should be mine." He looked up at Ailill. "Well?" he demanded.

"Well?" echoed Loegaire.

"Yeah. Well?" growled Conall.

Ailill made a face as his stomach suddenly burned. He belched and gently rubbed his stomach. He scratched his head, then sighed, saying, "I'll have to think on this, I will. Go and rest. It's been a busy night for you. I'll give my decision later." A bubble burst from his stomach. "Argh!" he said, pressing his fingers gently to his belly. "Go, and I'll give my decision later. Rest for now."

Cúchulainn smiled and shook his head. "No, give your decision now."

"I can't," groaned Ailill, sinking his head into his hands. "I need to think! Enough!" he shouted as Loegaire opened his mouth to speak. He rose from his couch, his hand pressing against his stomach. He farted and sighed. "Later. I have spoken."

He walked resolutely from the hall.

"Oh, bother!" Maeve exclaimed. She stood abruptly, her white thighs flashing beneath her saffron gown. Her breasts bobbled indignantly. "Let me see to this! Meanwhile, the three of you go and bathe and rest. I'll . . . *we'll* send for you as soon as we reach a decision!"

She strode regally from the hall. They watched her leave, round buttocks twitching like a dog and a cat in a sack.

"Well," Loegaire said, licking his lips.

"Yes, well," Conall said. He sighed. "We might as well get cleaned up." He yawned. "I don't know about you two, but I could rest."

"Looks like we'll have to," Cúchulainn said. He shrugged his shoulders. Together, they left the hall, returning to the houses allotted to them, where cool baths awaited along with the white arms of the women assigned to them by Maeve. But in Cúchulainn's room, Finnabair waited anxiously, until the door closed behind Cúchulainn and a wide smile creased his face. She crossed gladly to him, her cloak falling to the floor beside her shapely white feet.

Chapter 9

MAEVE'S
DECISION

THE DOOR BANGED LOUDLY against the wall as Maeve flung it open and stormed into Ailill's room. He winced but did not rise from where he sat squatted on his heels, back against the wall, cradling his head in his hands.

"What," she said furiously, "do you mean by not awarding the Champion's Portion and being done with this mess? Send them back home and let's get on with our lives. Shocks and bolts! What has gotten into you, coward? If you do not decide, I will!"

He wearily lifted his head and looked at her. "And just what do you think the other two will do if I name the champion?" he demanded sulkily. "You heard them! Neither of them is willing to give in to the other. If I name Cúchulainn the champion—and rightly so, if I'm any judge. Cats, indeed!—then Loegaire and Conall will fill our Great Hall with the blood of our warriors, the majority of whom, if you *will* recall, are out on our southern borders dealing with that little difficulty that arose with Munster, remember, hmm? We have a handful who might, *might,* I add, have a chance with one, *one* of those Red Branch devils, but not with two or all three, for if the two began fighting, then by virtue of their oath, the other would support them. Other than that, we have a few would-be warriors, a dozen or two who want to be, and old farts in their dotage whose memories grow longer as their days grow shorter. We would, my dear, turn the Place of Enchantment into a charnel house if I named the champion."

"Hmm," Maeve said. She began walking back and forth, her gown swirling at each turn, white thighs winking momentarily through the slit up the side. She rubbed her neck, lifting the heavy, red-gold waves of her hair, exposing the column of her neck. But Ailill had dropped his head back into his hands, staring hard at the slate covering the floor, his brow furrowed in thought.

"The only thing I can see to do is to name another challenge," he said at last. "But there's nothing to say that we won't have a repeat of this again. Whoever wins will be denounced by the other two. Oh, my! I can see this going on through the entire year, challenge after challenge."

She paused in front of him, legs spread wide under the front of her dress. Sunlight streaming through the window behind Ailill struck her red-gold beard, sending bright glints into the dark corners of the room. A heady hint of rose-oil wafted gently to him.

"And what," she purred, "do men want most?"

"Ah, now that," he said, shaking his head. "True, a woman's soft breasts and white thighs have resolved many an argument, but a man's honor, well now, that cannot be trifled with. A momentary respite, my dear. That's all that can be earned from the bed."

"But," Maeve said triumphantly, "what if that was not all?"

Ailill frowned. His hands began to move automatically up her legs. Her breath caught in her throat. "What do you mean?"

"I mean there really is no difficulty in—hmm, *stop* that! No, don't stop! Hmm—between Loegaire and Conall Cernach, for they are as different as—*gasp*—bronze and silver, while Conall and Cúchulainn are as different as silver and red gold."

"You could be right," Ailill said, standing, his hands sliding beneath her gown to stroke her back. She arched her shoulders against the pressure of his hands.

"All we have to do is put them at ease," she said, drawing slow, deep breaths. "And then give them a trifle, a trophy representative of their worth. Of course we'll ... let me finish, where was I ... oh, yes ... we'll ask each of them to pretend to go through another challenge for the sake of maintaining peace among the others, claiming each of them has already been chosen."

"What good will that do?" Ailill asked, his hands suddenly still. He frowned. "They will know who won."

"Oh, we'll invent a few challenges that each will easily accomplish. Then we'll send them on their way home, telling them to stop and spend the night with Ercol, my foster-father, and his wife Garmna, while we send word on to the Red Branch about who will ... is ... the real champion. Of course we won't send any messenger, but they won't know that and each will have the trophy we have given him and will claim the Champion's Portion because of that."

"But won't they realize that we've played a trick on them when the messenger doesn't arrive?"

"It's a *long* way to Ulster, and longer to Emain Macha," she answered. "Anything could have happened to a simple messenger between here and there. Of course there is the possibility that what my foster-father arranges will resolve the whole matter, but that's only wine in the sauce. We will have the three of them out of Cruachain, with nobody the wiser that the champion hasn't been chosen."

"I don't know," Ailill said doubtfully.

"Leave it to me," Maeve said firmly, tugging him to the bed. They tumbled onto the rumbled bedclothes, all thoughts of the three heroes momentarily forgotten in the anxiousness of the moment.

Maeve sat in her tub of scented rosewater, racking her brain for an answer to the conundrum she had given Ailill. She had to be careful in her manipulations of the three Red Branch warriors; men like those were highly volatile, ready to explode at any insult, real or imaginary. Absently, she reached over for a glass of wine, sipping. She frowned and studied the wineglass, then a smile broke over her face, carving deep dimples into her cheeks. She stood up, water streaming from her naked body, and called for a towel.

Loegaire walked warily into Maeve's private chambers, glancing quickly at the rich tapestries and hangings, the carved chair of yew wood with its curved back standing on a dais, the huge bed capable of sleeping five persons at a time—and often had—tables covered with vases and various flowers and grasses, the two large, red-haired dogs whose coats matched the red hair of their mistress, waiting in the chair.

"You wished to see me?" Loegaire asked.

"Yes," Maeve answered. She made an impatient gesture with her hand, and her attendants slipped discreetly out, closing the door softly behind them.

"Welcome, Loegaire the Triumphant! I have long waited for this moment!"

"You have?" Loegaire asked suspiciously. He looked around him again, carefully noting the folds of the curtains and draperies to see if they hid waiting assassins.

"Oh, yes," Maeve continued. "And it is to you that we wish to give the Champion's Portion."

His head jerked around, his black eyes focusing fully on Maeve. "Now, what's this? What about the challenge? You know about that, don't you?"

"Stuff and poppycock," Maeve said, lifting her shapely lip in scorn. "The game of a foolish man. Only an intelligent man knows enough to wisely depart from mystical maneuverings of magicians! There is no sense in fighting wizardry—unless, of course, you are a wizard. You aren't a wizard, are you, Loegaire?"

"No, ma'am," Loegaire said firmly. "Me feet are firmly on the ground. I drink when I'm thirsty, eat when I'm hungry, fight when I'm mad, and fuck—beg pardon, ma'am—when I'm— again, beg pardon—horny. No shaman tricks about me. Plain and simple, I am. Nothing more, nothing less. Of course," he added modestly, "that is, if it's simple warrior stuff you are looking for."

"Oh, quite," Maeve said, trying to keep her smile from breaking out into guffaws at his pompous posing and preening. "Why, men are meant to fight men, not monsters and demons, the brash posings of a magician's nightmare. A champion is to be a champion among men, not among the Otherworld."

"Precisely," Loegaire said. "If I might add, ma'am, you are most observing. Most observing. You see right into the souls of men."

"I've had a lot of practice," Maeve said. Then she frowned. "Of course, we have a little problem with awarding you the Champion's Portion."

"Why's that?" Loegaire asked, his eyes narrowing into tiny slits as he stared at her.

"Well," she purred, holding up a well-manicured hand, "you see, if we make this award officially—you know, with pipes and harps and big feasting and all that rot that *ordinary* men like to stroke their spirits with—then we shall anger your two, er, comrades. You understand?"

"I think so," Loegaire said. "In other words, you want to make this a *private* presentation."

"Exactly!" she cried, clapping her hands. "Oh, how wise you are to think of this."

"Think of what?" Loegaire asked stupidly.

"A private presentation! Why, that's just the answer!" She rose and came to the foot of the dais, leaning forward conspiratorially. Her gown gaped, and Loegaire swallowed heavily as he looked down the deep valley between her heavy breasts, noting the shallow indentation of her belly.

"I shall give you a cup of polished bronze with an eagle in chased silver at the bottom. I will give this only to you, and this you may use to claim the Champion's Portion when you arrive back in Emain Macha. *But* you must promise not to show it or to tell *anyone* about our conversation. On the day that you show this cup to the other knights of Conchobor's Red Branch, they will know that you have been chosen from among the others to be the one true champion, for I will secretly send a messenger to Conchobor. That way, no one will be able to dispute your claim to the Champion's Portion! The cup will be a signal to everyone of our, *my,* token of the real champion among all of Ulster."

Somewhere in Loegaire's mind, tiny warning bells tried to alert him to beware her words, but the delicious view of her creamy breasts, the heady scent of her perfumed oils and unguents, the mesmerizing depths of her emerald-green eyes—as deep as the grassy, low-bottom fields along Shannon's valleys—washed over him, muffling the bells with the heat that rose from his loins, up through his stomach. He swallowed heavily as saliva gushed into his mouth.

"That, that would be . . . nice," he finished lamely.

Maeve took the bronze cup from a small table next to her chair and filled it with honey-wine, aged ten years in an oak cask that had been carefully charred with burning faggots of apple wood. She took a sip from it, then handed it to Loegaire, breathing deeply.

"To seal our agreement," she said softly.

He quickly gulped the wine, his eyes bugging out of his head at her beauty.

"Now, may you enjoy the feast of the Champion's Portion for a hundred years at the head of all of Ulster," she said, smiling with delight. She kissed him on the brow, and he felt his throat tighten with emotion. His brow felt on fire, as if a hundred needles had been pricking gently at it.

"Thank you, Loegaire, for understanding our difficulty and for helping me find a way out of this . . . mess," she said. She returned to her chair and sat, artfully arranging the folds of her gown around her legs.

"I . . ." Loegaire began.

"Was there something else?"

"Yes. Er . . . I mean, no. I mean . . . thank you, ma'am," he blurted.

"Please do me one more favor," she purred.

"Anything," he croaked.

She smiled. "Leave all fires out and your room in pitch-darkness tonight so none may see when I come to you."

"Yes, yes! Of course!" he cried, and blushing, he made an awkward bow and hurried from the room.

Maeve grinned to herself as the door closed with a large bump behind him. "Dolt," she said softly. "Now, for the next one."

She sent an attendant for Conall Cernach. The burly warrior came to Maeve's room, the door darkening with his bulk as he entered. She sat dressed in a light green *sida* that allowed the soft sheen of her body to glow through its diaphanous folds.

"You wanted to see me?" Conall asked bluntly without greeting upon entering.

"Why, yes," Maeve said, instantly softening her voice, recognizing that Conall would have to be handled differently from Loegaire.

"Well?" Conall's eyes raked over her, stripping her clothes away. His brow was heavy, a bony ridge extending over the hollows of his eyes like the jut of a cliff. His heavy cheekbones rose like angle irons, while his nose, broken so many times that it looked like a squashed slug, lay misshapenen to the side. His chin was solid, a massive boulder. She looked down at his thick thighs, muscles hanging like hawsers from them, at the cables of his arms, at his chest, his biceps so huge that she wondered how his arms could lift themselves.

"Well?" he asked again. "You didn't ask me here to play parlor games. What do you want?"

"A blunt man," she said admiringly, and in truth, she did admire Conall much in the same way primitive woman admired primitive man. "I like that. No wasted words there! Quick and clear to the point. Much to be admired over the posturing of would-be heroes."

"Hmm," Conall said. He twisted his head. The bones of his neck cracked like snow-weighted limbs in winter. "There's them that says I'm too plainspoken. But the truth of the matter is that

I have little patience with the modest airs of court and circumstances."

"Yes, yes. I can see that. Oh, yes I can," Maeve said. "And because you are just such a man, why I—that is, Ailill and me, you understand?—have decided to award you the Champion's Portion."

"About time," he grunted. "Wasted enough time on this bullpuckery."

"Um. Yes, of course. You are right. Well, we had to be clever, you understand, and I apologize for that, but we had no desire to make enemies of the other two. We want to remain at peace with Ulster, you understand, and we were afraid that *if* we gave you our blessing as the champion, why, then the other two would take out their vengeance upon us with their swords. As you can see—" she gestured around the room "—we are not warriors here. No indeed. Not warriors."

"Nothing to fear while I'm here," Conall growled. He flexed his arms, the muscles leaping into round mountains.

"Yes," Maeve continued. She rose and came down, bending from the waist as she had with Loegaire. She felt his eyes rake beneath her gown and caught her breath at the heat that began to rise in her throat.

"You see," she said softly, "we have to be very quiet about all of this. Our little secret, you understand? Now, I will give you a cup of silver with an eagle in the bottom chased in gold as proof of my choice of you as the champion. *But* you are not to show this to anyone until you return to Ulster. I will send a messenger on ahead of you to take word of our selection of you as the one worthy of the Champion's Portion to Conchobor, who will prepare an appropriate feast there among your friends for the naming. What do you think?"

"A bunch of nonsense," he said. He licked his thick lips and raised a heavy paw to touch her white shoulder. Her gown nearly split in two from his touch. She drew back from him, laughing.

"Now, is it the cup you want, or me?" she asked, teasing.

"Truth be told, I care little for fopperies," he said. He placed a huge foot on the edge of her dais. "Leave that for the cony-catchers and nances."

"Yes. That is the mark of a real champion, one who is so . . . so . . . earthy," she finished, quickly pouring a jot of the honey-wine into the cup she had designated for him and eagerly handing it to him. "Now, will you drink to our agreement?"

Conall took the cup and drained it. He started to reach for her again but she shook a finger admonishingly in front of him. "Now, now, now! You must be a good boy!" She lowered her voice at the sparks of fire that leaped into flame in his eyes. *"But,* tonight leave the fires out in your room and I shall come to you in the darkness."

"A lot of malarkey, you ask me," Conall growled. "Fucking's fucking and ain't nothing wrong with doing it dark or light if the mood's full upon you."

"But, you must remember my position here. I have certain, uh, responsibilities to uphold. Image, you know, to a king and his wife is everything. What would people think if someone were to catch us making love right under my husband's nose when the sun is at its zenith?"

Conall scratched his head, pondering. "Seems to me I remember hearing about other times and you."

"Stories," she sniffed. She tried to force a tear, but none would come from the merriment building up inside her at the role she was playing. "You know how people talk about such things. I'll bet they say the same things about Mugain, Conchobor's wife. And yours?"

A dark flush suffused his face. "They do, and I bury them," he said grimly.

"But you will leave your fires out and the room in pitch-dark for me tonight, won't you?" she breathed.

"That's the way you want it, that's the way you get it. All walnuts and acorns to me."

He turned on his heel and stalked from the room, the silver cup nearly hidden in his meaty paw. She sighed heavily and went to a sideboard, puddling her fingers in a brass bowl of rose-scented water there and patting her cheeks and forehead with the pads of her fingers, cooling her face.

"One more and we're out of this mess," she said grimly. She called for her attendant and sent a messenger to bring Cúchulainn to her.

The messenger, cocky and sure of himself with his high standing among the Connachtmen for his recent position in Maeve's household, found Cúchulainn playing *fidchell* with his charioteer, Laeg Mac Ríangabra. Having come so recently to Cruachain from the backcountry, where Maeve had found him on one of her outings, and not knowing the story of Cúchulainn, he strutted into the room without knocking.

"Well, come on, *hero*" he sneered. "My lady wants to speak with you."

"Does she?" Cúchulainn murmured, studying the board. He had nearly trapped Laeg's king in the center of the board.

"Did you hear me, clod?" the messenger said. "I said, *now!*"

Laeg glanced at Cúchulainn, then looked at the messenger. "Best mind your words and ways, toddler, or you may get your down-comance. Don't bandy words with a man unless you can dance to the tune he orders the piper to play."

"And you, freckled-face, mind your lip! I am in the service of Maeve herself!"

"Go away," Cúchulainn said. He nudged a piece onto another square and looked up, grinning at Laeg. "Think I've got you cornered now, old friend."

"Ducks and drakes," Laeg said, frowning at the board. "You've fallen right into my trap." He pushed his king to the side, trapping one of Cúchulainn's pieces.

"Have I?" Cúchulainn reached out to move a piece, but the messenger, incensed at being so casually dismissed, swept the pieces from the board and stormed back to the door, pausing, hands on hips, glowering at Cúchulainn.

"*Now* will you come with me? Or must I send a troop to bring you?"

"Mocking me, eh?" Cúchulainn said. "Take your lies and try

them on a fool somewhere! If she wants to see me, she knows where to find me."

"Idiot! Do you know who you are talking to?" the messenger shouted.

"Yes! A fool!" Cúchulainn said. He seized one of the *fidchell* pieces and threw it across the room at the messenger. It pierced the man's skull and lodged in his brain.

Staggering from his death-wound, the messenger stumbled back to Maeve's rooms and fell across the threshold, mumbling through the small bubbles of foam around his mouth, "By Dagda, the Red One of Perfect Knowledge, but this is a touchy fellow," he gasped and died.

"Rats," Maeve said. She motioned for the others to haul the poor man's body away. "We've brought the wrath of Cúchulainn upon us for sure now, we have. See what work his fit of rage causes us? Poor man. There was hope for him. Ah, well! Foolish men bring about the gods' wrath."

She quickly touched scented oil to her fingertips and ran them down the valley of her breasts. She settled the green *sida* around her and touched kohl to the corners of each eye. Then she walked down the corridor to Cúchulainn's room, where the warrior was again engaged in a game of *fidchell* with his charioteer. Laeg's eyes bulged when he saw her standing in the center of the room, the light behind her shining through the folds of her gown. He cleared his throat twice, and when Cúchulainn looked up, frowning, he waggled his eyebrows comically at her.

"Something is wrong, old friend?" Cúchulainn asked. "You look as if the *Sídhe* had visited upon you, dancing a bewitching step upon your chest while you slept."

"Psst," Laeg said, waggling his eyebrows furiously.

"Hmm?"

"Behind you. Maeve!" he whispered urgently.

Cúchulainn glanced over his shoulder. His eyes drooped with boredom. "Well, you come yourself this time instead of sending a messenger with the tongue of a pig-caller!"

"He won't bother you again," Maeve said. "He's dead."

"A civil tongue would have kept him alive," Cúchulainn said. He shrugged. "But, that's the fate of messengers. Tact is a messenger's armor and when he leaves it behind, he goes naked into battle."

"I know," she said huskily. "But I wanted to talk to you. *Desperately*. So I chose the first one at hand."

"Should I go?" Laeg whispered across the *fidchell* board. Cúchulainn shook his head.

"Well, you're here now," he said brusquely. "So, speak your piece. Have you decided upon another challenge?"

Anger flashed through her at being treated in this manner, but she forced it down and curved her lips in a smile that would cook a salmon with its warmth. She crossed the room and placed her two arms around Cúchulainn's neck, pulling the warrior's head back and under her breasts that lay like two soft melons on his forehead.

"I need you to understand my problem," she said.

"Say what you want, but three's unwelcome company here, and I have no place in these negotiations," Laeg said, grinning. He climbed to his feet.

"Try your lies upon another," Cúchulainn said to Maeve. He looked at Laeg. "Aren't you going to finish the game?"

Laeg rubbed his nose with a callused hand, still grinning. "Naw," he said. "I think I'll drop down to the stables and check Black's harness. I think he needs a new rivet in the lead rein."

"Well," Cúchulainn said. His eyes looked up at Maeve, standing over him, and her legs began to tremble at the lights beginning to dance in his gaze.

Dimly, she heard Laeg close the door behind him as she spoke:

"Glorious son of the Ulstermen
and flame of the heroes of Erin,
We have found to be most deserving
of the Champion's Portion, deserving
of all the rights to its position

and without any other conditions.
So, to you we give this special prize
—oh, but you have most wonderful eyes!—
and beg of you to accept this cup
of chased gold with which to sup
your wine at feast. At the cup's bottom
you will find a gem-carved eagle, a totem
of your worth as champion of Ulster.
Your wife shall also lead all Ulster
women into every feast. This I say:
I wish only you among the three to stay
here in Cruachain with me. Your fame,
bravery, distinction, youth, and glory shame
others who pretend to your superiority.
Beside you, their valor is termerity.
But I have a boon to pick with you.
Please do not abuse my gift and sue
us to recognize you in a feast
and bring out from others the beast
of jealousy. We do not wish to see
our home burnt, our people to be
taken as slaves to your Ulster
because of a warrior's bluster.
I shall send to your king in Macha
a messenger telling that in Connachta
were you chosen as the sole bearer
of Emain's standard, the terror
of her enemies. Now, come with me
and receive your honor. You will see
what you shall gain from Ailill and me
if you agree to this minor ruse
to keep us from suffering abuse."

And Maeve bent to kiss his lips, feeling them tremble at first
like the soft wings of butterflies, then harden into a warrior's kiss.
And her heart melted within her and she felt herself grow weak

from desire, until Cúchulainn laughed and pushed away from her, rising.

"All right," he said. "I'll play your game, for the Champion's Portion means more to others who are dear to me than it means to myself. Honors must be gained on a battlefield and not at a feast with a table fork. Let us go and collect my trophy."

"Yes," Maeve said, trying to catch her breath from the power of Cúchulainn's kiss. "Let's. Now. Er . . . I mean, of course. Follow me."

She led the way out into the cool hallway, feeling the flush on her cheeks, her breasts, begin to ease, but not the pressure of his lips on hers. He followed her into her rooms. She crossed to the sideboard and poured honey-wine into a cup of chased gold with a ruby carved into a raven's likeness at the bottom of the cup. She took a large sip from the cup, then handed it to Cúchulainn.

"Here is your trophy, my Hound," she said. "With it, you may enjoy the feast of a champion, and I hope that for a hundred years more, you may enjoy the same."

"Thank you," he said. He took the cup and drained it in one draught.

Maeve crossed to a chest and opened it, taking out her jewelry box. From inside, she selected a dragonstone as big as his two eyes and handed it to him.

"Take this as well and have it set in a brooch in remembrance of me," she said.

"Ah," Cúchulainn said, shaking his head. "But to do such a thing would mean that I must give you something in return, and I have nothing but my weapons and my armor."

"Oh," Maeve said, the flush rising rapidly again from her breasts into her cheeks. "Perhaps something will come to you. Er . . . I mean, *occur* to you. Yes, occur. But please, do not forget your promise. Do not tell the others what you have received."

"I won't," Cúchulainn said, taking the dragonstone from her. He gave her a large grin. "And I *will* have this set into a brooch, and will wear it to hold my cloak across my chest. But I cannot keep it unless I can return a like favor to you."

"Very well," she said, her voice catching in her throat, the syllables clicking together. "Leave your fires out tonight, keeping the room pitch-dark. I shall come to you then."

"Heat is stronger if fires are properly lit," Cúchulainn said.

"Yes, but, well . . ." She paused, flustered, and he smiled and left, pausing politely at the door to bow his head.

"Oh!" she said, and crossed again to the bronze bowl of scented rosewater. She splashed the water onto her face, feeling the cool water ease the heat pulsing hotly there. Behind her, the door opened. She turned and saw Ailill peeking around the corner.

"Hsst! Is he gone?" he whispered.

"Yes," she said, annoyed. "Why are you creeping around like a mouse? Come on out into the room!"

He opened the door and walked in. "Well?" he demanded. "Any luck?"

"You might say so," she said. "All three of them accepted the conditions by which we named each the champion. Now they can return to Ulster and we can get on with our lives. But I do think you should recall at least one troop of men from the border to place around Cruachain as guards."

"Why?" Ailill asked, alarmed. "Did something go wrong? Tell me! What is it?"

"No, no," she said soothingly. "Nothing went wrong. But if something should happen after they reach Emain Macha and they decide to return here for some reason or another, we should be ready for them. Common sense, now, Ailill. Don't think with your emotions. Use logic."

"Logic. Yes, you're right, of course. Logic. Must use logic," he muttered.

"And," she said casually, "I think a large feast would be in order tonight to wish them farewell on their journey back to Ulster. I will give them the other challenge tonight."

"Huh?" He paused, looking blankly at her. She closed her eyes, counting slowly.

"You know, with Ercol and Garmna? We talked on this."

"I had forgotten," he said. He sighed, rubbing his temples. "The pressure of kingship and all that, you know. By the gods, but I will be glad to be washed of all this!"

"Yes, dear," she said, mollifying him. "Now, run along and make the arrangements. There's much to do."

"Yes, yes. The arrangements. Of course. Five bullocks, I would think."

She nodded and he turned, bustling from the room. A triumphant smile curved deeply into her lips and a strange light of excitement began to burn deeply in the emerald-green depth of her eyes.

As Cúchulainn walked toward the stables to tell Laeg to ready Black and Gray for leaving, he found Loegaire and Conall sprawled under a lime tree, sharing a small cask of beer as they lazed in the shade. The day smelled smoky from the harvest, and Cúchulainn accepted their invitation for a jot.

"I'm think of leaving tomorrow," he sighed as he stretched his legs out beside them. "This has been a tiresome journey, and although Maeve and Ailill have been excellent hosts, I would rather be at home in Ulster."

"I agree," Loegaire said quickly. "It's good to travel, but home is where I've planted my seed."

"My crops, too, have been planted at home," Conall said, agreeing with Loegaire. "I've plowed enough in these foreign fields. Let us go home and put an end to this."

"I'll tell Ailill," Loegaire said, starting to rise. He halted as Cúchulainn held up his hand.

"Excuse me, my friends, if I have presumed too much, but knowing your love for our homeland, I took the liberty of telling Ailill and Maeve that we would be leaving tomorrow. Mind you, I did this only out of love for you. If I have offended you, I apologize."

"No offense," Loegaire said, and was quickly echoed by Conall. "In fact, had I seen them earlier today, I probably would have said the same. The wine is good and so is the beer—"

"The food's good, too," Conall broke in.

"—and the women have a few tricks I haven't seen in Ulster—"

"That's for sure!" Conall said.

"—but a man gets tired of sampling different foods each night. Sometimes he needs familiar fare to relax his digestion."

"Yeah. What you said goes for me, too," Conall said.

Cúchulainn laughed. "Then we agree, cousins, that tomorrow we leave." He rose. "I'll tell Laeg and he'll tell your men. *If* he can find them."

"Oh, he'll find them," Loegaire said carelessly. "They all rut in the same pasture. No secrets among them, you know."

That night, the men from Ulster were entertained by Ailill in a manner in which they had never before been entertained, with three hundred naked women serving them in the mighty feast-hall. Platters heaped with roasted beef and pork were brought in on gilded trays. Rare wines and aged beer flowed copiously, while rich breads baked in raisin sauces and walnut-and-honey mashes. Harpers played soothingly from the corners of the room, while the haunting notes of a flute hovered delicately overhead like birds in flight.

The choice of food was also given to their horses. Conall and Loegaire ordered two-year-old oats to be given to theirs, but Cúchulainn chose barley grains for Black and Gray. Their charioteers slipped away early from the party—first making arrangements with a few of the buxom wenches to meet them in the stables following the feast—to make the chariots ready for morning departure.

After the feast, lots were cast among the women to be divided up among the heroes of Emain Macha. Maeve, however, had taken two of the women—Saeve the Eloquent, one of her daughters with Ailill whose voice in the dark sounded like hers, and Concend, the daughter of Cet Mac Matach, who often amused Maeve's attendants with imitations of her—aside, quietly explaining that tonight they were to pretend to be her after the others had made sure their rooms were dark.

They giggled over the conspiracy and vowed to keep Maeve's secret. Besides, Saeve and Concend had looked with longing upon Loegaire and Conall several times during the time the Ulster warriors had stayed in Cruachain. But Maeve kept her daughter Finnabair ignorant of her plans. When the time came, Finnabair, with fifty damsels in her train, went to Cúchulainn, while Saeve the Eloquent took another fifty with pert breasts to the room of Conall Cernach. Concend led fifty more perfumed and scantily dressed women to the room of Loegaire the Triumphant.

"At last," Ailill said when the rubble of the feast had been cleared away. He sighed. "Now, we can get back to normal. I think."

"It has been a difficult period for you, hasn't it?" Maeve asked solicitously.

"Yes, it has," Ailill said. Bruises seemed to have appeared under his eyes. He yawned. "But I think that tonight I will sleep as I haven't slept in a long time."

"Are you sure?" Maeve asked.

"Oh, yes, my dear. I am sorry, but not tonight. My head is pounding," Ailill said. "Sleep is what I need the most."

"Oh, well," Maeve said. She heaved a deep sigh. "I suppose it wouldn't hurt both of us to get some sleep."

Ailill reached over, patting her hand. "I promise that I will make it up to you tomorrow, my darling. And I think that I might be able to find a little bauble to amuse you as well."

"Good night, Ailill," Maeve said. She rose and bent to kiss him. Then she smiled and walked off to her rooms.

Quickly she bathed and changed into her most becoming gown, a sheer white *sida* without a seam that made her look more naked than dressed. She placed a golden *torc* around her neck and added a slim, gold bracelet to each shapely wrist before padding down quietly to Cúchulainn's room.

She opened the door a crack and saw that the room had been

left in dark as she had ordered. Quietly, she slipped into the chamber, listening to the giggles of the women. She paused, letting the *sida* fall to the floor, then silently she crept among the women, artfully working her way into Cúchulainn's arms.

The next morning, Maeve stood bleary-eyed on the balcony, watching as the three heroes readied their chariots to leave. Ailill stood beside her, fidgeting as they loaded their chariots. At last, he spoke.

"Before you leave, please come bid us farewell in the feasting-hall! We'll have a last cup together!"

Cúchulainn waved as he helped Laeg tie down the straps on their gear, then nodded across at Loegaire and Conall. They shrugged and followed him into the palace and down the long corridor to the feasting-hall.

When they entered, they saw Ailill and Maeve seated at a table, watching young men in warrior-training perform the wheel feat, throwing a heavy, iron-rimmed wheel down the length of the hall.

"Ah!" Ailill cried as he saw the three. "Our guests! We're so sad that you have picked today to leave, but we understand the nudgings of home and hearth. Come! Let us have a final drink to your departure, a cup to wish you the peace of the road!"

"Tuck your elbow under the rim before you throw that thing," Loegaire said to a youth unlimbering his throwing arm. "You'll get a bit more distance that way."

"Oh, you've tried this?" The youth winked at his friends. He offered the wheel to Loegaire, who failed to see the youth's mockery and nodded, taking the wheel from his hands.

"A bit rusty, but I think I've still got the hang of it," he said. He curled his body to the right, then unleashed the wheel. It flew in a wobbly arc until it smashed halfway up the wall at the other end of the room.

"Not bad for your age!" the youths jeered, but Loegaire, in his eagerness to be away, mistook their jeers for applause and smiled, nodding his head in thanks.

"What about you?" the youth said to Conall. Conall glowered at him, but took the wheel and threw it halfway up the ridgepole of the hall. It fell back with a clatter to the slate floor.

"Well-thrown, Graybeard!" they shouted, and Conall permitted himself a smile, thinking that they were awarding him triumphant cheers instead of shouts of scorn.

"I don't suppose you'd care to give it a toss, would you?" the youth said to Cúchulainn. But Cúchulainn saw the mockery behind the guileless mask the youth kept on his face and shook his head.

"Child's games," he said. He walked toward Ailill and Maeve, who had risen upon their entrance.

"Are you as old as that?" the youth taunted, and threw the wheel at Cúchulainn, who whirled, caught the wheel in midair. He crooked his arm and hurled the wheel high into the air. It ricocheted off the top of the ridgepole, caromed across the ceiling, then smashed through the wall and buried itself a man's cubit into the ground outside.

The youths stared round-eyed at Cúchulainn's feat, then broke into cheers. But the cheers were no different from what had been given to the others, and Cúchulainn felt the youths were mocking him. He shook his head.

"That is no test," he said icily to the youths. He walked over to where three of Maeve's attendants stood. He borrowed fifty needles from each, sorted them in his hand, then walked back to the youths.

"If you want a true test, try this," he said. He threw the needles one at a time into the air, his hand moving so rapidly that the youths could not see the fingers on it. Each needle locked itself into the eye of the one thrown before it. Cúchulainn caught the chain when it fell gently toward the ground and dangled it before the youths.

"Now, that isn't so hard," he said casually. "Any fool can do that. But can you remember which needle went to which woman?"

And saying so, he took the chain apart and gave each woman the needles she owned. The youths broke into wild applause.

"Parlor tricks!" Conall sniffed in dismissal. "Something to humor the kids at night!"

Cúchulainn grinned and took the glass that Ailill pressed upon him. He smiled at Maeve and touched the dragonstone brooch holding his cloak to his shoulders. She blushed, and her eyes sparkled from the dark rings around them.

"May your chariot wheels never touch the ground until they touch Ulster's rich earth!" Ailill said loudly.

They drank and placed the glasses upon the table. The men turned to go, but Maeve spoke.

"One moment, please!"

They halted and looked at her speculatively.

"I have one last challenge for each of you," she said.

"Grinders," Conall grumbled. "Just like a woman to wait until the last to change her mind."

"Oh, this is really nothing," Maeve said. "You must stop somewhere on the way to Ulster for I would like you to visit my foster-father, Ercol, and his wife, Garmna. And please do what they bid you. That way, there should be no argument as to who is the rightful champion when you arrive in Emain Macha."

Conall and Loegaire each winked at her words, but Cúchulainn gave her a gentle smile that sent her heart to thumping in her rib cage until she feared it would bang a hole in her chest.

"We will, gladly!" they cried, and turning, left.

"Tell you what, cousins," Loegaire said, climbing into his chariot. He nudged his driver with his elbow, winking. "I'll bet we get to Ercol's house before either of you."

"Them nags of yours is crow-bait for sure, compared to mine," Conall said. He laughed, the sound rolling like thunder off the stone walls of Cruachain's courtyard. "Why, I'll drive rings around you before you get there. Get it? Rings." He guffawed as Id Mac Ríangabra grinned at his brother, Sedlang, who flushed angrily as he twitched the reins of Loegaire's horses between his fingers.

"You all have been sucking on the wine jug too much if you

think that those slew-foots of yours can stay on the road with our Black and Gray," Laeg said, drawing the reins through his callused fingers. "Mind you, we could give you a head start, but it seems to me that you each need a lesson in humility. So," he cocked an eye at Cúchulainn, who grinned and nodded his permission, "without further ado, we accept."

"Then," cried Sedlang, "away with all!" And he slapped the reins smartly across the backs of Loegaire's dappled grays. They leaped forward in their harness and dashed down the highway, followed quickly by Id and Laeg. Within moments, only the dust of the departing chariots hung in the air in the courtyard of Cruachain, the Place of Enchantment.

Chapter 10

THE TEST OF
THE HAG

THE THUNDER OF THE chariot wheels awoke Ercol from
his afternoon nap. He raised a bleary eye, for he had drunk a bit
more beer than he was accustomed to drinking before lying down.
He smacked his lips, wondering at the noise, then felt the bed
shake beneath him. His head felt heavy, and a sharp pain stabbed
him behind his right eye. He winced and pressed the pain away
with his fingers, gently massaging.

The door to his bedroom crashed open, bringing the pain
stabbing back into his head as his wife rushed in, squawking like
a biddy-hen dropping an egg.

"Doom! Doom!" she cried, wringing her hands. She jumped
onto the bed, her weight smashing the air from Ercol's lungs.

"*Oof!*" he gasped. He gagged as sour beer tried to roll back
up from his gullet. "Woman! What is the matter with you?"

"The earth is shaking! Soon it will crack open and we will
fall into the Otherworld, where surely the Donn will punish us!"

"Punish us for *what?*" Ercol asked crankily, pushing her away
from him. She squealed as she landed on the floor. "It's only a
storm approaching."

"Storm, is it?" Gramna said, rising and rubbing her buttocks. "Then why is the sun shining on the fields and the autumn leaves? Tell me *that,* Worldly One."

He rose and pushed the heavy curtains aside from the window of his bedroom and stared out across the plain, blinking in the bright sunlight streaming into the room. In the distance he saw a chariot riding furiously over the plains, its warrior leaping high into the air and balancing on his toes on the chariot-rail. Behind him, two other chariots also raced furiously, their drivers begging the lathered horses for more speed.

"Ah," he said, suddenly refreshed. "It's only the three warriors that our foster-daughter, Maeve of Cruachain, sent word about." He clapped his hands together, rubbing them with relish. He glanced over at the frown on his wife's face. "You remember . . ."

"I remember," she said acidly. "Just like that girl to be taking liberties with our hospitality. Don't recall her sending any coinage along to help with the feasting these boys will need, either!"

"Ah, shut yer gob!" Ercol shouted. "Just tell the cooks to begin preparation. From the looks of them, they'll eat a bullock apiece easily."

"Yes, O Master of the House," she said mockingly, and quickly curtsied. "A simple matter to flap yer lips and snap those orders!" She popped her middle finger against her palm. *Snap!* "But working the cost out of the budget for that girl's whims is enough to drive a person mad. *Madness,* I tell you. Stark madness!"

"Will you get to it, woman?" shouted Ercol. He pulled his stained tunic off and dunked his head in a bucket of water standing on a stall. He blubbered for a minute, then emerged blowing like a whale. He grabbed the tunic and vigorously scrubbed his face. He glanced at his wife, still standing there. "What? You still here? I'll be giving you the back of me hand!"

"And pulling back a stump if you do!" she finished. She turned to the door. "As if you lost your mind of the ways and means of us poor folks!" She mumbled to herself as she lowered her bulk down the stairs. "Feed an army next, we will, he has his way! Don't matter none to him where I get the coinage for it!

Just do it, he says! *Humph!* Rattle his cage, I will, he comes on again with his 'back of me hand!' "

Quickly, Ercol pulled a crimson tunic edged in silver thread from a chest and, struggling, pulled it over his chest and ponderous belly. It fit tightly and he grimaced as he smoothed his damp, gray locks behind his ears. He belched, and cupped his hand and drank thirstily from the bucket, then raced down the stairs to greet the men as they pulled up beside his door.

"Greetings! Greetings!" he cried as Laeg eased Black and Gray to a stop. "The messenger arrived only last night to tell us you were coming. I am Ercol, your host!"

"Cúchulainn," the Hound answered, stepping down lightly from the chariot. He took Ercol's hand politely. "And this is Laeg, my driver."

"Pleased to meet you," Laeg grunted, holding the reins tightly as Black continued to dance, trying to run some more.

"Delighted!" Ercol said, beaming.

Loegaire raced in through the gate and swung to a stop in a cloud of dust beside Cúchulainn's chariot. He stepped down stiffly from his chariot and glared at the younger man.

"You could have pulled in a bit when you crossed that ford back there!" he said. "Near drowned us in water, you did." He seized the bottom of his tunic and wrung it, squeezing a small stream from it.

Cúchulainn laughed. "As I recall," he said, the seven pupils of his eyes dancing, *"you* were the one who egged on the race. Now, Laeg and I were perfectly content to come across the Plain of Spears at a leisurely pace."

Loegaire hawked and spat, then jumped out of the way as Conall Cernach's chariot rumbled heavily through the gate and stopped beside them. His horses hung their heads panting, their sides heaving from the exertion.

"Well!" exclaimed Loegaire. "Here is a latecomer, the sluggard and laggard himself! Tell us, Conall, did you stop for a bite to eat along the way? I cannot understand how otherwise those fine steeds of yours would arrive here so late."

"Keep it up, minion, and I'll squeeze the piss and vinegar from you!" Conall growled threateningly. He shook a huge fist in Loegaire's face. " 'Twas a dirty deed you did back there when you goaded my off-horse at the fork. Took us two miles to bring them both back!"

"Ah, me!" Loegaire said, doubling over with laughter. "I can't help it if you have the poorer brother for a driver."

"I'll stuff me goad in his arse if he keeps up that 'poorer driver' shit!" Conall's charioteer said darkly.

"Stable the horses and rub them down!" Conall ordered. He turned to Ercol. "That is, with your permission?"

"Of course! Of course!" Ercol beamed. "Now, let me see. From Maeve's description, you must be Conall and you Loegaire." He pointed from one to the other. The pair nodded. He laughed. "Yes, yes! I heard about you boys. And you, of course," he added hastily to Cúchulainn. "I take it that your problem hasn't been solved," he added slyly.

"Problem?" Loegaire's brow wrinkled. "What do you know about it?"

"Why, the whole land has heard about Bricriu's tricks upon you and your wives!" Ercol laughed. His belly shook like jelly. "Why, that was one of his worst!" *Hee! Hee!* "I tell you, you should have dropped him into the well and been done with it instead of gallivanting all over the country trying to figure out who's best!"

"No sense poisoning good water," Conall growled, "when we can settle it ourselves."

"Yes, yes, of course," Ercol said. He laughed again. "Come in! Come in! We're preparing a feast in your honor, but I expect that you can use something to cut away the dust, eh?" He laid a thick forefinger aside his bulbous nose and winked. "Thirsty work, coming from Cruachain. Especially at the gallop."

"I could take a taste," Loegaire acknowledged.

"And me," Conall echoed.

"I'll see to my horses first, if you don't mind," Cúchulainn said.

"Oh, your man can do that, surely," Ercol said.

"Perhaps," Cúchulainn said. "But I like to help."

He turned and walked away, heading toward the stables, where Laeg was carefully folding the harness as he unyoked Black and Gray. Ercol frowned as he watched the warrior cross the yard.

"A strange one, he is," he muttered, pulling hard on his thick yellow mustache.

"Stranger the tales about him," Loegaire said. "And I would tell you, but . . . well, me throat is so parched and the sun so hot upon my pate—"

"By all means," Ercol said. He stepped aside and bowed them into his house. He threw a quick glance at Cúchulainn, his lips pursing thoughtfully before he followed.

There's something strange here, there is," Laeg muttered as Cúchulainn came up to help him fold the harness over the chariot-spar.

"Oh? And what's strange here?" Cúchulainn asked.

"Notice that the man has stalls for forty horses, but all he's got in them are two swaybacked nags," Laeg said. "And the shit's been shoveled out and the ground scraped down."

"Strange because the man keeps a neat place?" Cúchulainn asked.

Laeg shook his head. "Naw. Take a look at the hay."

Obediently, Cúchulainn turned his head and looked up into the loft and into the stalls. He shrugged. "So?"

"Green and clean, right?" Cúchulainn nodded. "And *lots* of it, right?" Cúchulainn frowned. He nodded again, slowly this time. "Now, ask yourself this: why so much hay for two nags that couldn't eat a nose bag without falling asleep, and that hay as fresh as if it were cut three days ago?"

"You could be right," Cúchulainn said. He glanced at the other two drivers, Laeg's brothers—Sedlang and Id—as they used old oat sacks to scrub down their masters' horses. He lowered his voice. "But let's keep it to ourselves, you understand?" Laeg's eyes narrowed, and he nodded. "Keep your eyes open, just the same."

"I'll do that. I'll do that," Laeg said. "And you watch yourself up there, young Hound. There's many a slip given when a man puts his lip on the cup."

Cúchulainn laughed and clapped Laeg on his shoulder, staggering the man. "I'll do just that. Water, my friend, only!"

"Well now," Laeg said, sniffing, "I don't know as if you have to go that far!"

Cúchulainn laughed again and strolled from the stable, setting his course across the yard. The smile stayed on his lips, but his thoughts began to hone themselves on the problem Laeg had presented: why would a man need so much fresh hay for two horses like those?

Welcome again!" Ercol cried as Cúchulainn stepped in through the door.

Cúchulainn paused to let his eyes adjust to the gloom. Loegaire and Conall sat sprawled on benches, huge tankards grasped in their fists. Cúchulainn drew a deep breath, smelling heady yeast. Loegaire grinned at him, while Conall lifted his tankard and drank deeply, smacking it back on the bench beside him with a solid *thunk!* His eyes sparkled as he looked at Cúchulainn.

"Well, little warrior! Did you get your ponies tucked in for a spell?" He laughed and jabbed Loegaire with his huge elbow, nearly knocking the slighter man from his perch. Loegaire scowled at him.

"I'll be thanking you to keep your filthy hands to yourself," he said. Conall winked at him.

"Ain't this little cockerel of ours a dandy?" he asked, beaming. He took another drink and wiped his hand across his mouth. "Think of it, Loegaire! Half your age and he's already thinking he's your equal."

"And yours," Loegaire said sulkily. He lifted his tankard, swallowing rapidly, his big Adam's apple bouncing up and down.

"Yes, but yer the one whose pecker's out of joint if he takes yer place at the Red Branch."

"I don't plan on taking anyone's place," Cúchulainn said quietly. "There's room for all of us there."

"Would you be having a jot?" Ercol asked, reaching a matching tankard down from a hook on the beam overhead. It bore a dark red color, nearly black, from having been soaked in ox blood.

"Water," Cúchulainn said.

Ercol's eyebrows lifted. "Water?" Conall sniggered, and even Loegaire managed a smile at Ercol's astonishment.

"But I thought—"

"Water will do just fine," Cúchulainn said, taking the tankard from Ercol's nerveless fingers and crossing to the clay pot beside the doorway. He dipped the tankard into the water, lifted, and drank.

"If that don't put a hum in the hive, I'll not be knowing what will," Ercol said to the others, scratching dirty fingernails deep into his oily hair. They laughed.

"Takes his meals with the Boys' Troop, he does," Conall said, smirking. "Tell me, lad, what by Dagda's balls makes you think to be our equal in this? By all rights, it should be Loegaire and me here tussling about on the sward for that prize."

"I have more trophies than either of you in the Red Branch," Cúchulainn said. "And your horses have yet to come up to Black and Gray's tails in any of the races. Even Conchobor's matched blacks cannot hold hoof to Black and Gray on any turn around Emain Macha."

"Wizardry," Loegaire said, nodding owlishly at Conall. His eyes seemed to be having trouble focusing.

"Yep. Otherworld nonsense," Conall agreed. "Can't do a man's work without ringing in his friends down there."

Cúchulainn's lips drew into a thin line, his nostrils widening. Ercol stepped hastily between them, fluttering his hands like butterflies.

"Now, now! Let's be keeping this friendly here, shall we? Food's what you're needing now. The beer's drained right through your gullet to your head without nothing to be taking the nudge off it. Why, I've got a bullock turning on the spit for each of yuh!"

"A bit of porridge for the young one'd be better for him," Conall said. "Buttermilk!"

"Enough," Cúchulainn said. "You'd do better to keep your wits about you than soaking them in beer! 'Tis a ways to be going before we get back to the Red Branch, and who knows what we'll be having to do before then."

"Well," Ercol said, clearing his throat, "there is a wee thing that is needing your attention, now that your honor speaks of it and all. Not," he added as Cúchulainn stared at him, "that it's something to be doing for the likes of me. Oh, no, not that! Not that! No, it's just a wee happening that our Maeve has asked me to arrange for the three of you."

"A challenge!" cried Loegaire gleefully. He slammed his tankard down on the bench and rose, staggering. "So! You're part of this game as well, eh?"

"Well," Ercol said, "it ain't me what's going on about which part of the meat will be cut upon my plate. Many's the time that I ate less than of the tenderloin and was pleased to be having it, I tell you!" He sniffed. "Been behaving about the country like a bunch of spoiled brats, you have, taking on as to who gets the choice cut from bullock or pork, when there's plenty of either to choose from. But—" he held his hands up and looked away as Conall began spluttering indignantly "—them as are in your business has got the right to do your business the way you want. I'm just a test-maker, that's all. And, if you was wise now, you'd take a bite or two and give your thoughts to what's ahead."

"And what might that be?" Loegaire asked, squinting to keep his host in focus, for seven-year-old beer takes the staying power from many a strong man if properly brewed, and Ercol's had been touched by the Tuatha as it quietly fermented in the springhouse.

Ercol smiled broadly, tapping the side of his nose with a thick, spatulate finger. "Now then, if you be ready for it, then what challenge might it be? Take a bite to eat here, if you will, then go to the House of Samera, which is up and over the hill—just a good stretch of the legs. You'll not be needing your horses," he added. "There's plenty for them to eat here, and after the way you wastrels have been driving them across the plains, they could use a few measures of grain and a healthy nibble or two of grass."

So the three of them went into the feasting-hall to eat, and they gorged themselves fully as Garmna pretended to be upset, but instead, she took secret pleasure at the healthy appetites of the men, who paid good homage to her cooking, cutting large chunks of meat from huge joints laid out before them. Roasted onions lay heaped in a dish along with leeks cooked with nettles, sorrel, and watercress. Wild cherries and elderberries had been piled high in bowls at the hand of each of the champions.

Cúchulainn ate sparingly of the meat and the honeyed loaves of bread from wheat, chasing the bites into his gullet with sips of milk. Loegaire and Conall, though, gorged themselves on meat and bread, chasing each bite with liberal swallows of wheaten beer prepared with honey.

At last they finished and the sun was dipping over the distant Hills of Crom. Garmna handed each a damp towel to cleanse their hands and wipe their faces, then Ercol coughed and stood, folding his hands in great pomp across his ponderous belly.

"Ahem!" He coughed, and cleared his throat. "We have come to the setting of the ways," he intoned solemnly.

"Pompous old quacker!" Garmna sniffed.

"And it is time," he continued, fixing her with a hard look, "for our guests to ready themselves for their trial. Let each warrior take what he feels he might need, for the way is not long, but it could be dangerous. *If* the proprieties are not observed!"

"Well! I wonder what he means by that," Loegaire muttered to Conall.

Conall shrugged. "Who knows? What'll you be taking?"

"The usual, I suppose," Loegaire said doubtfully. "Sword, a couple of javelins. Shield. You taking any brain-balls?"

"That I'm not. They hadn't finished setting before we left. What about you, Cúchulainn?" Conall asked.

The Hound shrugged and shook his head. "I have little use for them," he said carelessly. "Why not use a good stone, if you're so inclined to putting on the use of your sling? Hardier than those lime-dried brains you pluck from the heads of our enemies!"

"He's right," Conall said, looking at Loegaire.

Loegaire rolled his eyes upward, hawked, and spat. "Young ones! Doing away with all tradition, they are! Next thing you know, they'll be giving honeyed stirabout to our slaves." He sighed heavily and shook his head. "It is the times. Be the death of our ways, we don't keep a sharp check on them." Conall ignored him.

"What about your *gae bulga?*" he asked. "Will you be taking that along?"

Cúchulainn shook his head. "No, there should be no need for that here. We're at peace."

"Humph," Conall grunted. " 'Twas me could make that bloody spear work, it'd be singing a pretty song familiarly around."

"What glory in that, then?" Cúchulainn asked. "You know no living thing can avoid its edge when it's thrown."

"When *you* throw it, you mean," Conall said.

"A sword and a javelin or two should be enough," Cúchulainn said firmly.

A soft gloaming was beginning to settle over the land as the three champions emerged from Ercol's house. Swallows darted about overhead, while marsh gas flickered and glowed at the bog at the far end of the home pasture. Somewhere a wolf howled, and Laeg shivered beside Cúchulainn.

"I don't like this. Smacks of the playing of the *Sídhe*, and no good is coming of that, I'm saying. 'Tis a night for curling beside the fire with a buxom wench and letting the wolves howl as they will. *If* they are wolves, I'm thinking," Laeg said.

"Perhaps. But it will do to have another pair of eyes at my back, *I'm* thinking," Cúchulainn said, grinning.

"Now, you wouldn't be doing that to me and forcing me to neglect the little darlings waiting in their stalls for me kindly words, now would you?"

"I would."

Laeg tried again. "Sure, and you wouldn't be forgetting what we found in the stable, would you? It might be well for us if I stayed here and looked after the both of them."

"They'll be all right," Cúchulainn said firmly. He lowered his voice. "And, I don't think the master of the house will be doing himself a favor if he plays boogles with Black and Gray. They'll be fine."

"I'll get me goad," Laeg sighed. " 'Tisn't much, but it will do to fetch a knot on someone's head."

Mumbling, he set off to the barn to take a last look at the mounts before catching up to the three champions.

"Now, you'll be keeping to the right as you curl around the hill," Ercol said warningly. "The bog hasn't dried yet and it wouldn't do to be putting an unwary foot there. But keep to the right as you round the hill and you'll be seeing Samera's lights burning before you down in the vale in front of the wood."

They kept to the path, carefully thumping the ground on either side with the shafts of their javelins as they walked around the hill, forestalling any wandering off into the bog in the dark. Soon they saw lights flickering in front of them and they hurried forward to the house. A haze hung over it like smoke from a garbage dump. Conall raised his javelin and hammered on the oaken door with the butt of the shaft.

"This gives me the creeps," Laeg said, looking around apprehensively.

"What's that?" Conall growled.

"Well, have you noticed that we don't seem to hear the crickets or the folding of the linnets' wings, or even an owl hooting somewhere?" he asked.

"Now that you mention it, no," Cúchulainn answered. "But what difference does it make? Are you thinking the *banhsídhe* might be readying herself for a bit of howling?"

"Now, don't even go to joking on that one!" Loegaire said.

"You may be able to get on and about in the Otherworld, what with your friends and such there, but some of us don't have that influence. We have to take what may come."

"I don't have any influence there," Cúchulainn said testily.

"Right," Conall answered, hammering on the door again until the timbers shivered and threatened to crack. "And taties don't have eyes, neither."

They heard the latch drop on the door and stood silent while the massive oak portal creaked open on its iron hinges. A bent, hooded figure stood silently in the doorway. They couldn't tell if it was man or woman, but eyes burned from the cowled darkness like hot coals.

"Tell your master that Conall, Loegaire, and Cúchulainn of the Red Branch are here!" demanded Conall.

The figure gestured silently to the warriors and stood aside to let them enter. Cautiously they stepped in and waited while the figure placed its shoulder to the door and inched it shut behind them. They found themselves in a huge hall. Battered weapons and shields covered the wall; axes huge enough to have been swung by giants, swords that would strain the sinews of average men, helmets that could have been used for cauldrons, and javelins with shafts the size of hickory trees. At the far end of the hall, a huge fire crackled in a massive stone fireplace the size of a hogshead, sending light to dance among the shadows stretching high into the darkness above them. A table surrounded by four chairs stood in front of the fireplace. A huge jug and four goblets took up the center of the table.

"This is the home of a mighty warrior," Loegaire whispered.

"I don't like this," Laeg complained. "No sir, I don't. Now, if the three of you were thinking men, you'd think it was time for us to get out of here before something happens that we're going to regret. But," he sighed, "since any thinking around here is to be done with sword arms, well, I guess that leaves it to me for the proprieties." He grimaced and turned to the figure waiting.

"Tell me now, my good man, where do you suppose we might be finding your master?"

The figure continued to stare at them.

"Is it something I said, or has the *cailleach beara,* the Hag of Beara, taken your tongue?" Laeg asked, frowning and leaning closer. He suddenly retreated. *"Whew!"*

"What is it?" Loegaire asked anxiously, taking a fresh grip on his javelin.

"Onions," Laeg said in disgust.

"Onions?"

"Aye. And from the smell of them, they've stood around a while in a pot or two longer than what's good for them," Laeg said.

"Nonsense," the figure answered. "They're the best thing for you. Very nourishing and uplifting. Their roundness is a perfect unity that suggests unity to the mind."

"Gods help us, a Druid!" Laeg moaned.

"Maybe," the figure answered. "A philosopher, surely."

"Well, philosophisize us to your master," Conall ordered impatiently. "We don't have all night to be nattering about roots and bulbs!"

"Oh?" A small strip of white flashed from the hood. "What *do* you have time for?"

"Nuts and gracklins!" Conall muttered, wrinkling his heavy forehead. "This one plays in roundabouts as much as Cathbad or Seancha! All we want is your master."

"Then turn around, gentlemen ... *en* ... *en* ..." a voice echoed from behind them.

They obeyed, and at the far end of the hall they saw a stumpy, bowlegged man, swarthy, with a streak of white through his hair, as if someone had smacked him with a whitewash brush. He laughed at their stare.

"Come, gentlemen!" he cried, the sound echoing away from them. *En ... en ...* he laughed again, the sound keening away throughout the cavernous hall. Laeg flinched and stepped forward to stay close beside Cúchulainn's elbow—his *left* elbow, well away from his sword arm.

"Not what you expected, eh? Well, I don't blame you! Sometimes I don't expect myself when I look in the mirror in the mornings." *Ayuck! Ayuck! Ayuck!*

Laeg groaned and whispered, "Just our luck! More metaphysical nonsense. I say we leave him to the spiders and mites in this place and go back to Ercol's house. I still don't trust him with Black and Gray, despite all you say."

"They can take care of themselves," Cúchulainn said. "Let's see what happens here."

"Yes," the man said. "Why not see what happens here, Laeg? You might find it rewarding."

"How did you know my name?" Laeg asked suspiciously.

"Then again, you might not," the man finished. He grinned and rubbed the heel of his hand against his nose. "And, who wouldn't know the prince of charioteers? Your fame has spread as far as your warrior, the Hound of Ulster!"

"A fine, discerning man," Laeg said. He nudged Cúchulainn. "You know, I could have been wrong about him." Cúchulainn grinned.

"Humph!" Conall said. "This patty-caking with words isn't my style."

"No, of course it wouldn't be your style, Conall Cernach the Victorious! I have heard of you, too, and you, Loegaire Búadach the Triumphant!"

"Well," Conall said, sniffing suspiciously. "You have heard about us! All well and good, depending upon what you've heard. But who are you? Hay to one, hay to the other, I always say. Speak!"

The man laughed again and smacked himself on his forehead. He beamed. "Of course! How forgetful of me. Bad manners and all that. I am Samera, your host. And this . . ." He gestured behind them. They turned and looked at a young, slim girl who had magically appeared from the shadows. The Druid was gone. "This is my daughter Búan."

She nodded shyly at each. Then her eyes fastened on Cúchulainn and widened. She took a short, sharp breath. Her eyes softened at the corners, and Laeg sighed deeply.

"Ah, me! Another one falling in heat with my Hound," he said.

"Be quiet, Laeg!" Cúchulainn whispered from the corner of his mouth. "Don't embarrass the young thing."

"I welcome you to my father's house," the young girl said shyly. "Won't you please join him in a glass of wine?"

Ayuck! Ayuck! Ayuck! Samera laughed. He spread his stumpy fingers and grimaced. "'Tis age, nothing more, that makes me forget the Rules of Hospitality! Come, join me for a glass of wine."

He gestured at the chairs and moved around the table to plop into one of them. The others looked at each other for a moment, then Loegaire cleared his throat.

"Er . . . I don't want to seem forward, but there are four of us and only three chairs. An oversight, surely," he said.

Samera looked up from beneath grizzled eyebrows, a smile splitting his full cheeks. "Oversight, you think? No, no oversight!"

"This, uh . . ." Loegaire paused to clear his throat again obviously embarrassed. "You know, this could be seen as . . . well, as an insult. Not," he hastened to add, "that I'm accusing you of anything or not, you understand. It's just that it, well, looks bad. If one of us were to be left standing while the other three sit—of course, Cúchulainn, that would mean your charioteer would stand . . ."

"By Conlaí's Well!" Laeg swore, but stopped short when Cúchulainn dropped his hand on his shoulder.

"Are you casting a slur upon my charioteer?" Cúchulainn asked softly. Lights began to dance and shimmer in each of his seven pupils. "Be aware before you answer, Loegaire, that such an insult casts a slur upon me as well. Sure, a warrior is only as good as his charioteer, who must drive him into battle and place him so he may gain honor with his sword and throwing arm."

"There you go again, Hound! Putting words into my mouth before I've spoken them. Sure, and I meant no shame or slur to your charioteer! It's just that, well, warriors is warriors and charioteers is charioteers. The seats at tables have already been judged by the Brehon." He shrugged. "A herder does not seek to be a

Brehon, a charioteer a warrior."

"I told you!" Laeg said bitterly. He closed his eyes, shaking his head. "Sure, and isn't it this that it has brought us to, this bickering among you for the true champion, when all know that Cúchulainn alone has the right to that name!"

"That has yet to be settled," Loegaire said stoutly.

"Ahem."

They turned to face Samera, who smiled apologetically at them. "It really matters not, there being enough chairs available for all who will be remaining here," he said.

The warriors looked from one to the other, then Loegaire frowned and asked, "Now, what would you be meaning by that?"

"That? Oh." Samera shrugged disarmingly. "Nothing. Except the little thing that Ercol asked me to arrange calls for each one of you to spend a night in the glade where the fairies come and dance at Lughnasa and Samhain."

"And what will happen there?" Loegaire asked.

Samera spread his hands and waggled his thick eyebrows at the hero. "I don't know. But whoever spends the night there successfully will be the greatest of the heroes."

"This is ordained, then?" Conall asked.

"Ordained? Well now, that is something else," Samera said, leaning back and stroking his chin. "When something is ordained, you are playing with cause and effect. It will matter; that much I can safely tell you. But ordained?" He shook his head. "That is something only for Druids and the *Sídhe*. And those who whisper in the mists."

"Then what is the purpose?" Loegaire asked.

"Ah! Purpose! Now that is something else!" Samera cried. "The purpose will be that which you decide it to be."

"Crazier than a loon," Laeg muttered to Cúchulainn. "I'm telling you—"

"Shh," Cúchulainn said, shushing the charioteer. He looked over at Loegaire and Conall. "Will this settle the matter, then? He who first lasts out the night in the glade will be the one for the Champion's Portion?"

"Suits me," Loegaire said. "As good as anything, I suppose."

"I dunno," Conall said, frowning darkly. "What if more than one of us can stay the route? What if all three? Right back where we started from, I say. What then?"

"Oh, I wouldn't worry about that," Samera said. "I mean, well, I really doubt if more than one of you—if *any*—will last the night. *I* wouldn't, that's for sure, and I live here!"

"That bad, hmm?" Loegaire said, his eyes squinting warily, suspiciously, at their host.

"Shall we say that strange doings go on in those woods?" Samera said.

"Then let's each take a night and see who does the greatest challenge against whatever—if anything—happens," Loegaire said.

"You mean that each of you spend a night there alone?" Samera asked.

"Seems only fair and right," Conall said. "After all, just because Loegaire spends the night, it doesn't mean that I couldn't as well. Or our little Hound, for that matter. Still, it is a game to be played."

"Aye, I agree with that," Loegaire said.

"All right with me." Cúchulainn shrugged indifferently. "So, who goes first?"

"Why not Loegaire?" Samera asked. "After all, he is the first to question the number of chairs."

"Are you throwing me own words back at me, now is it?" Loegaire asked.

"No, no," Samera said quickly. "But you are the oldest, are you not? And as the oldest, aren't you entitled to go first?"

"The man speaks reason, he does," Loegaire said quickly. "So, what do I do?"

"Follow my daughter. She will lead you to the glade. But you are *sure* you wish to do this? It isn't for the faint of heart, you know," Samera said.

"Faint of heart, is it?" Loegaire said. He spat on the floor and rubbed it dry with the toe of his sandal. "That, for your faint of heart."

"Then go," Samera said.

Loegaire cinched his sword belt firmly about his waist. "I'll be seeing you old women in the morning," he said and swaggered out behind the silent Búan, who glided across the floor to the door and opened it, disappearing into the night.

"Well then," Samera said, rubbing his hand. "Some wine for us all? And I can have smoked salmon brought if you are feeling peckish."

"Brain-food," Conall said.

"Wouldn't hurt you any," Cúchulainn said.

"Are you calling me—"

"Now, now," Samera said hastily. "Let's have a wee bit of peace in me house. It could be a long night. Or a short one. But wine! That's the ticket!" He poured the goblets to the brim and passed them around. Conall took a small sip and his eyebrows raised instantly. He took a large mouthful, swallowing it in installments.

"Good!" he said. Laeg and Cúchulainn followed suit, nodding their approval.

"From the hives on the bottom of the hill where the clover is the richest," Samera said. "Three years in the making."

"Worth every day," Conall said magnanimously.

"Thank you," Samera said.

The door opened and closed behind them. They craned their necks and watched as Búan glided back across the floor to stand silently beside Cúchulainn. Laeg watched her suspiciously, while Conall gave Cúchulainn a broad wink.

"The warrior is placed, Father," Búan said.

"Good," Samera said with satisfaction. "Now, we wait."

"What is that?" Conall asked curiously, pointing to a corner beside the fireplace where a tall wooden rod stood.

"That? Oh, nothing, nothing," Samera said.

"Something, I think," Conall said. He rose and stepped to the fireplace and picked it up to bring it into the light.

"Careful!" Samera said quickly. "Do not harm it!"

His words came too late as Conall's hands opened, dropping the rod onto the floor. "A *fé!*" he exclaimed, leaping back and away from it. The rod rolled over and nudged Cúchulainn's foot.

"Don't touch it! Bad luck!" Laeg exclaimed.

Cúchulainn ignored him and reached down and picked up the rod. "Aspen," he said. He peered closely at the *Ogham* scratched into it and read the words aloud.

"Beware! I bring sorrow to he
who dares to lift me foolishly.
For I measure the dead today
and the grave where they'll lay.
Warrior! Pass by and leave me."

"Woe! Ah, woe!" cried Laeg, pulling at his hair until it stood at wild angles to his head. "I told you this place had a curse on it!"

"Oh, stop it!" Cúchulainn demanded sharply. He looked at Conall, who had backed away, keeping a wary eye on the staff in Cúchulainn's hand. "It is only a piece of wood with a message written on it."

"A curse," Laeg said.

"There are some who say it is my *geis,*" Samera said resignedly. "Perhaps it is. Perhaps it is."

"Words are words," Cúchulainn said sternly. "It is up to the person to make of them what he will."

"You can make of them what you want," Laeg said stoutly. "I make of them a curse and I'm telling you, I am, that those words are meant to be believed."

"There's something in what he says, Cúchulainn," Conall said warily. "Best be putting it down and away from yourself. 'Tis only a foolish man who plays stick games with the *fé.*"

"You are the grave-digger?" Cúchulainn asked.

Samera sighed and scrubbed his hands across his face. "Aye, that I am. And now you'll be telling me that you'll be going, and thanking me for my hospitality."

Cúchulainn shrugged. He rose and carefully stood the rod back in the corner of the fireplace. Laeg took a step back and away from him. "A man is what he is, nothing more," he said. "He makes himself, and by the way he makes himself, others know him and give him honor or dishonor." He frowned at Laeg and Conall. "It is not for us to be putting the name of Donn upon him."

The door slammed open and shut quickly, the sound reverberating throughout the house. *Boom! . . . om! . . . om!* Startled, Cúchulainn and Conall leaped from their chairs, their swords flashing readily into their hands. Loegaire stood stark-naked in front of them, his back to the door, his eyes as wide as chariot wheels, his legs shaking, his goad quivering from its tangled forest of black hair.

"Loegaire! What happened?" Conall exclaimed.

"Hunh-uh! Hunh-uh!" he answered, his hands flopping weakly at his sides.

"I knew it! I just knew it!" Laeg said dismally.

"Shut up!" Cúchulainn ordered. He rose and walked over to the warrior. He smelled the fear, dank and rancid, as he drew near the man.

"Now, what has happened to you? Get a grip on yourself!" he exclaimed as Loegaire's hands shot out and grabbed his tunic, balling the material into his huge fists.

"Witches!" he blubbered, drool draining from each corner of his mouth. "Horrible! Gad!"

"Crackers, I tell you," Laeg said, tapping his forehead significantly with a blunt forefinger. "Gone crackers. Pity."

Gently, Cúchulainn removed Loegaire's hands and gave him over to Búan for caring. She led him away into the recesses of darkness. The sounds of his blathering echoed back from him as he went down a long hall. *Blann . . . lann . . . lann!*

"Well, that certainly didn't take long," Samera said. He shook his head. "A difficult business, this being a champion and all. Are you sure you two wouldn't just as well share the honor? A tenderloin can be split easily in two and make enough meal for both."

"The Red Branch is one house, not two," Conall said. "One house, one champion, I say."

"Whatever," shrugged Cúchulainn. He picked up his goblet and drained the wine. "Who's next?" he asked Samera.

"No one until tomorrow night," Samera said regretfully. "Maybe by that time, you two will have come to your senses. Meanwhile, I'll show you to your sleeping quarters. Sleep as late as you wish. Tomorrow will be a long night for one of you."

He led them down the long hallway and showed them to the washhouse, where they bathed with soap made from burnt bracken and briars. After they had been refreshed, he led each of them to a narrow room filled with pillows and blankets. Iron hooks had been hammered into the walls to hang their clothes and weapons upon.

Cúchulainn stripped himself naked and hung up his clothes and weapons, then fell onto the soft cushions, stretched and yawned. He was nearly asleep when he heard the door open and feet pad softly across to his bed. His flesh tingled warningly, then he caught the faint rose scent and relaxed, his white teeth flashing in the darkness.

"Most unusual, Búan," he said softly. His eyes caught the gleam of her white body as her gown slipped softly to the floor.

"Do not go into the forest tomorrow night," Búan said quietly. "Mortals cannot stand against what you will find there."

"Maybe," Cúchulainn said. He felt her weight slip onto the cushions, then her warm body curl around his own.

"No mortal can spend the night in the ring when the fairies dance," Búan said. "Especially not when the old woman comes."

"The old woman?" Cúchulainn asked. "Tell me about her."

But the young girl's lips found his and the Hound forgot his question as the night lengthened into morning.

Conall," Samera said. "You will be the next to go into the forest tonight. That is, unless you two have come to some sort of agreement. Hmm?"

"Be good to get this nonsense over," Conall said.

He turned away and began putting a new edge on his javelin and sword with a rock he took from the courtyard. The *scritch . . . scritch . . .* cut into the nerves of all as the day wore to an end and the sun dropped a burning orange ball over the crown of the hill. Again, Samera directed Búan to lead the way to the glade, this time leaving Conall there.

Then Samera sighed and poured goblets of wine for Loegaire and Cúchulainn. Loegaire, dressed in a borrowed robe, took the goblet and drank it down and refilled it himself from the seemingly bottomless pitcher. Laeg muttered to himself and paced back and forth the length of the room, nervously cracking his knuckles, the sound echoing around them: *tlock! . . . ock! . . . ock!*

"I'm afraid for your friends, Cúchulainn," Laeg said. "Loegaire does not seem to be coming out of it, and Conall, well . . ." He shook his head.

"Urk! Witches! Horrible!" Loegaire said. He drained the goblet and reached again for the pitcher.

"Tell me, Loegaire, what did you see? What happened to you?" Cúchulainn asked gently.

"Urk! Witches! Horrible!" He drank another glass of wine. Drool began to roll from the corners of his mouth. His eyeballs rolled wildly in his head.

"Oh, this is a fine one, it is!" moaned Laeg. "That Maeve! Trickery, I tell you! And what are we going to tell the Red Branch when we return? Or if I return with the three of you drooling and pissing? Ach. Conchobor has lost three of his best warriors to what? A fool's game!"

The door opened and closed and Búan reentered the hall. She crossed to stand beside Cúchulainn, her hand dropping lightly upon his shoulder. Her father looked up quizzically, noticing the familiarity. His eyebrows twitched.

"So tell me, Cúchulainn," he said, "how long has it been since you saw your wife, Emer?"

"Why do you ask?" Cúchulainn answered.

Samera sucked his lips in and popped them with a smacking

sound. "Just talk to pass the time. Shouldn't be long now, I would think."

A loud shriek came from the outside, floating hollowly through the hall, making the hairs of all stand up on the back of their necks.

"The *banhsídhe,*" Laeg whispered, the whites of his eyes rolling in his head. "Shit! I knew this would happen. Conall's done for as sure as I'm standing here. That scream's enough to make a eunuch out of any man!"

Hard on his words came the door opening and closing so rapidly that all there would have sworn Conall had materialized through the thick oak had it not been for the noise of its slam echoing through the hall. Like Loegaire, he was stark-naked, the hair on his chest standing straight up, as was the hair on his head. His flesh, pebbled and scratched from thorns, shivered in the room. His goad, as thick as a man's forearm, trembled between his legs, flapping from one thigh to the other.

"Conall!" Cúchulainn said, rising with concern. He pulled his cloak from his shoulders and wrapped it around Conall. "What happened?"

"Oh, the witches got him as sure as I'm—" Laeg said, behind him.

"Be quiet! Well?"

"Be quiet, he says," Laeg muttered, miffed. "Be quiet, and himself so scared his balls click like crickets."

"Hoo! Hoo!" Conall gasped.

"What? What was that?" Cúchulainn asked.

"Hoo! Hoo!" Conall said again. His eyes rolled with madness.

Cúchulainn took a cup from Laeg's fingers and pressed it against Conall's lips. Wine dripped like blood down Conall's chin, soaking into Cúchulainn's cloak.

"Hoo! Hoo!" Conall said again when Cúchulainn took the cup away.

"I'm afraid that's all you're going to get out of him tonight," Samera said regretfully. "Well, I guess that settles it, doesn't it? You're the champion, Cúchulainn. Ain't none of these two gents going to make a challenge upon you now."

"No champion can be named by default," Cúchulainn said. "The name has to be earned. I will go to the forest glade tomorrow night."

"Ah, me," Laeg said, turning aside as Búan came forward and gently took Conall's arm to lead him away. "You got any more wine in that pitcher?" he demanded of Samera as he walked back to the table.

"Sure. And there's more where that came from. A whole tun, if need be," Samera said.

"Ah well, it's a man's work ahead of me tonight," Laeg said without relish. "But, I'll do me best. Still, you might be telling your steward to not nod off with the keys to your cellar in hand in case the tun leaks dry before morning."

"A man after me own heart," Samera said with ardor, gleefully rubbing his hands together. "And, if you're not minding the company, I'll be joining you for a tot or two before the cock crows."

"One man drinking is loneliness; two men drinking is company," Laeg said.

"Keep a clear head for tomorrow," Cúchulainn said. "You will come with me."

"Come with him, he says," Laeg mimicked, shaking his head. He poured a goblet full of the earth's blood, and drained it in one swallow. "Come with him! Sure, and keep a clear head about it while I'm going to my doom? Thank you, no. If I'm to be killed, I'll have a head on me that will make death welcome, that I'm telling you."

Cúchulainn laughed and left the chamber walking quickly down the hall to his room. That night, Búan came again to his bed and when they rested, Cúchulainn's head upon her cone-shaped breasts, the Hound spoke, asking: "Tell me, Búan. What did Loegaire and Conall see that has taken speech away from them?"

"Riders from the *Sídhe,*
and demons from the sea!

Gray-haired witches and hags
leaping over the rocky crags!
Fairy folks dance in a ring
and to mortals they bring
man's worst dream now reality
from Manannán's deep, dark sea
among crashing, foaming waves
that make the bravest man rave.
What do you fear most, my Hound?
For that will be certainly found
when you face the fateful glade
and its terrors with your blade.
But mortal steel cannot work its will
against the specters whose loud cries
freeze blood, burn flesh, and I
can do nothing to help you defeat
the pookahs and hags you will meet.
Witches and warlocks! Beldams and furies!
Harridans and harlots! Witchwives and whoories!
With breasts like empty bladders,
mouths moaning words to scatter
the wits of all men. Only the brave
will remain when they begin to rave!
Barefooted Druids begin to quake
and the ground beneath them shake
when the dreadful sisters speak
and their minions begin to shriek.
Not even Badh, Macha, and Mórrígan
last when the demons have begun!"

"Don't you think you are making just a bit much of this?" Cúchulainn teased. "Why, it sounds as if all the evil in the world was being unleashed upon one person at once."

"No," she said sadly. "Just the evil that lives in one person. His own evil."

"And if no evil lives in a person? What then?" he asked.

"Evil lives in all men where good lives in all men," she answered.

"I don't understand," he said.

"Desire. That is what changes good to evil. What do you desire the most? To be a champion?"

"That is honor," he protested.

"Is it? Or is it the desire to be what man is not meant to be?"

"What is man not meant to be?"

"It differs from man to man. Some must remain men; others are destined to be gods."

"A man chooses, then?"

"A man can always choose. It just depends upon the limitations of his vision."

"And what have I chosen?"

"A short and noble life."

"Can I change?

"No."

"You are sure?"

"Did not Cathbad the Druid tell you this when you first took up arms?"

> "He who is armed upon this day
> will find glory. Though his stay
> upon this earth will be sweet,
> he soon will become raven's meat."

"Are you predicting my death? Have you the sight, then?" Cúchulainn asked.

"Your death will be your own making," she said. "But the time is not far away. That is all I can tell you."

> "Neither time nor place nor way.
> Just that soon will come that day."

"Then, let us take this day while we can," Cúchulainn murmured.

And she sighed and sank down into his arms, but not before a single, solitary tear dropped onto his chest, scalding him with its sadness.

Ah well," Samera said. He coughed and hacked and spat phlegm onto the floor. He scratched his head with a dirty fingernail. His bloodshot eyes looked sadly at Cúchulainn. "You are determined to be doing this?"

"I am," Cúchulainn said. His battle harness gleamed, his sword hanging close at hand, three javelins held loosely between the fingers of his right hand.

"Then there's nothing to it but to let you go," Samera said regretfully. "Take him to the glade, Búan."

"Come, Laeg," Cúchulainn said. He grinned at his charioteer, whose face was drawn and tight, eyes bloodshot, face shadowed with beard stubble.

"Come, he says. As if I'm a dog to be sniffing at the heels of the Hound. I'm coming, though I'm not afraid to be telling you that your wits have flown from you and left you with a stone between your ears," Laeg said.

Búan gave them a sad look, then silently led them out of the house and into the woods. Immediately, the stark limbs reached out for them, clutching and grabbing as they trod a narrow path winding like a serpent's back, deeper and deeper into the woods. Damp and sour smells rose from rotting vegetation, and the sounds of the night seemed ominous: the chirrup of the cricket like the grating of a sword; the hoot of the owl like a hollow war drum; the moan of the wind through the trees, rising to nearly a screech before dropping down to a moan again.

"This is the place where things live that go bump in the night," Laeg moaned. "Oh, my head!"

"I told you not to drink all that wine," Cúchulainn said.

"Aye, but this way, my going will not be so painful as relief," the charioteer said.

Cúchulainn laughed softly. "Watch my back, friend Laeg."

"I'll watch it," Laeg grumbled. "Fat lot of good it will do, though, against air and mist."

"Here we are," Búan said softly, stepping out into a glade silvered by moonlight.

Cúchulainn looked around swiftly, noting the trampled grass, the ashes of a fire in the center of the ring, a rock covered with black stains. He shivered, and the hackles on his neck rose as ancient evil reached out skeleton fingers and caressed his skin.

"I must leave you. They will not come as long as I am here," she said lowly.

"All right. I'll see you in the morning," Cúchulainn said, his eyes shifting around the clearing, probing into the darkness.

She gave him a wan smile and slipped from the clearing, disappearing in an instant. A twig cracked. A stick snapped. Then, for one brief moment, all the air seemed sucked out of the universe, and then a horrible, rancid smell permeated the clearing, and the trees began to shriek.

"I've gotta pee," Laeg muttered.

"Watch, watch," Cúchulainn murmured, his eyes dancing around the clearing.

"I'm watching," Laeg retorted.

The sound of urine splattering against a stone came from behind Cúchulainn. He started to turn, but mist suddenly seemed to roll into the clearing from all sides, a dirty, gray mist, foul like decaying meat, and then wraiths slipped in and out of the curling clouds, and suddenly shrieking faces were in front of him, at his sides, at his . . .

"Watch your back!" Laeg shouted, and cursed.

And Cúchulainn twisted and dodged as bony fingers came out of the mist to snatch at his weapons, his clothes. The javelins were plucked from his hand in an instant, and then cold fingers tore his cloak from him, shredded his tunic. In an instant, he found himself naked, struggling against the cold death-grip of specters that screeched at him, teeth biting at him. He fought back, a mighty fist crashing through a mystical face, sending it reeling into dust. Then, ropes slipped over his shoulders, and in a second, he found himself bound and trussed as neatly as a pig for the spit. And then he saw her, the Hag, slipping through the fingers of mist, shape-shifting, her form first beautiful, with ruby-tipped, cone-shaped breasts, then wrinkled and ugly, with dugs like bladders, brown tips leaking pus.

And then Laeg shouted at him, reminding him of what he was.

"For shame, Cúchulainn, little puppy! Look at you! Helpless weakling! Stripling! Where's your power now? Mewling and pewling, stripped and tied! You call yourself a champion, when mere ghosts can destroy you?"

The Hag spread her legs, squatting above Cúchulainn like the *Síghle na gCíoch.* Her smile gaped wide; a fetid odor crept from her mouth. *Little Hound! Little Hound!* she moaned. And then the *riastradh* came over him. His hair stood on end, each hair tipped with blood. His mouth gaped wide until his liver seemed to flap in his gullet. One eye squeezed shut as tight as a needle, while the other bulged from his head, bloody-veined and horrible. His heart boomed in his chest. Then the hero-halo rose above his head, burning like brimstone. His muscles cracked like a frost-laden tree and the ropes binding him snapped apart. He leaped to his feet, a huge roaring rolling from him, and seized the spirits, tearing them apart until black blood spattered the clearing, the trees, the grass. The Hag shrieked and turned to flee, and Cúchulainn seized a rock and threw it at her, stiking her on the thigh. She gave a great cry of pain and disappeared in a thunderclap, leaving the clearing streaked once again with silver light from the moon.

Laeg advanced cautiously into the clearing, feeling the heat pouring like liquid fire from the naked Cúchulainn. The cloaks of the specters he held in his hand. And then, as quickly as it came over him, the "warp-spasm" disappeared. He took deep, shuddering breaths and stared around the clearing. With disgust, he threw the specters' cloaks from him.

"Well, my friend," he said, "I think it is over."

"Hope so," gulped Laeg.

Cúchulainn glanced down at his naked body and laughed. "I

see now how Loegaire and Conall lost their clothing." He looked ruefully at his clothes, shredded and torn. "Worthless," he said. Then he spied his weapons, and a pile of weapons that he recognized as those belonging to Conall and Loegaire. "Well, at least we'll be able to return their weapons to them. Help me gather them, Laeg."

Together, the pair left the clearing and made their way back along the path to Samera's house. Laeg pushed the door open and they entered, dropping the weapons onto the floor. Laeg pushed the door shut while Cúchulainn strode naked down the hall to the table where Samera sat with the pitcher of wine in front of him. He seized a goblet, draining it.

"You have won," Samera said quietly. "It is my judgment that you will have the Champion's Portion at all feasts from here on. And that your wife shall be the first to enter all rooms of all feasting-halls before all the other women of Ulster. I further decree that your weapons will hang above all others except those of Conchobor and Fergus Mac Róich."

"Cúchulainn?"

They turned to look at Conall. The light of madness slowly left his eyes. He looked puzzled at Cúchulainn, then at Loegaire, who blinked as if suddenly come from the dark into a lighted room.

"Why are you naked?" Conall asked.

Cúchulainn laughed loudly, delighted with the breaking of the spell upon his two friends.

"It's a long story," he said. A rustle came behind him. He turned and looked at Búan. She limped toward him, her lips tightening with each step as her legs slipped through the slit of her *sida*. Through the light of the fireplace, he could see the huge bruise on her left thigh.

The next day, the three heroes returned with Laeg to Ercol's house. Ercol greeted them quietly, reservedly, for he had heard of the results of their fight against the Hag and her specters by mes-

senger before the heroes arrived. Cúchulainn, too, was quiet, reserved, remembering the look of desperation in Búan's face when
he had turned away from her.

"Well," Ercol said, "I'm glad you've managed to return. I've
readied food and drink for you. A messenger has come for you,
Conall."

"What is it, Rathand?" Conall asked as the young lad stepped
from the house.

"I bring greetings to you from Fedelm, your wife," Rathand
said.

"What is it? Is everything all right?" Conall asked.

"Everything is well," the messenger said. "But she wonders
why it is you tarry so long before returning. More than Ailill's
promised three days have passed since the others came back from
Connacht. I have been sent to inquire about your well-being."

"Women!" Loegaire laughed.

"Well, we'll be leaving tomorrow," Cúchulainn said. "Why
don't you wait and go back with us?"

"Glad to have this behind us," Conall grumbled.

"Oh, but one thing remains," Ercol said as the three started
into the house. They stopped and turned as one to stare at him.

"What's that?" Loegaire demanded.

"Well," he sighed. "Tomorrow each of you has one more challenge to face."

"What's that?" Cúchulainn asked.

"Me. And my horse."

"That nag you keep in the stable?" Loegaire broke out in a
peal of relieved laughter. Even Conall laughed, while Cúchulainn
permitted a smile to creep upon his lips.

"Tomorrow at sunrise," Ercol said quietly. "I suggest you eat
and drink your fill, then retire. Now, if you will excuse me, I have
to get ready."

"Take a week's worth of oaths and chanting to get that swaybacked creature ready," Conall said.

Ercol nodded and walked away from them. They watched
him disappear around the corner of the house, then looked at each

other. Slowly, the laughter slipped away from them and they grew thoughtful and pensive.

"What do you think, Cúchulainn?" Conall asked at last.

"I don't know," Cúchulainn said. "But I think we should do as he says: eat and rest."

"I *am* a bit hungry," Loegaire said.

And the three of them entered the house and fed upon the meal laid out on the table for them. No one came to meet them, and at last, the three champions called their charioteers to them and gave orders to prepare one of their horses for the match on the morrow. Then the three champions unrolled pallets they found in a corner and stretched out in front of the fire, their weapons close at hand, and slept.

Sunlight streamed into the room when Laeg shook Conall and Loegaire awake. They glanced at the sleeping Cúchulainn.

"Are you going to awaken him?" Loegaire asked.

"You can, if you want," Laeg said. "Remember what happened the last time someone did that?"

They stepped away carefully from the sleeping Hound, each remembering how Cúchulainn had smashed the head of the servant who had tried to shake him awake. Since that time, he was left to awaken of himself, the *geis* upon him making itself known by the servant's brains left scattered on the wall. Cúchulainn yawned and sat up, rubbing the sleep from his eyes. He spied Laeg and grinned.

"Well, did you ready Gray or Black for today?" he asked.

"Gray," Laeg said. He bit his lip.

"What is it?" Cúchulainn asked.

"A funny thing. Remember all that hay in the barn before we left four days ago?" Cúchulainn nodded. "It's gone."

"What do you mean, it's gone?" Cúchulainn said. He frowned.

"Just what I said. It's gone."

"Our horses couldn't have eaten that much hay in that short a time."

"They didn't eat any of it," Laeg said. Cúchulainn's eyebrows raised. "Sedlang and Id and I found our horses turned out into the pasture. They've been on grass while we've been gone."

"Most peculiar," Cúchulainn said.

"Uh-huh. Watch yourselves," Laeg said.

The other charioteers met them as they stepped out into the bright sunlight. Each had prepared a horse for them.

"Well," Loegaire said, holding onto the bridle of one of his horses. "Where is our brave host today?"

"Oh, I'm here!" called Ercol.

They turned and looked as Ercol rode from around the corner of the stable on his swaybacked gelding. The horse looked with rheumy eyes at them. Its back was so swayed that Ercol's feet nearly touched the ground on each side. Its knobby knees nearly knocked together, and its huge hooves slapped the ground like palms.

"You've got to be joking," Loegaire said. "You really don't think you'll fight either of us with that crow bait?"

"Are you ready? I believe we'll start with you, Loegaire," Ercol said without preamble.

"Mannerless all of a sudden, isn't he? Watch him, Loegaire," Conall muttered.

"This will only take a minute," Loegaire said, vaulting onto the back of his horse. He kicked his heels against the sides of his horse. It reared, pawing the sky, then galloped toward Ercol and his gelding, teeth bared, nostrils flaring blood-red in the morning sun.

Ercol sat quietly upon his gelding. Then the horse began to grow, its back straightening, muscles bulging and leaping beneath sleek skin like taut wires thrumming in the wind. Lips peeled back from yellowed teeth. Its legs grew straight and firm. It screamed a challenge into the air and leaped forward, rearing and pawing at Loegaire's horse. A huge hoof slammed on top of its head, splitting the skull, and Loegaire's horse dropped dead into the dust of the yard.

Loegaire rolled away, leaping to his feet. Ercol drew a sword from the sheath around his waist and rode toward him. Loegaire turned and ran, leaping over the corral, the stream meandering around the hill, and darted off into the trees behind the house, his charioteer hammering hard upon his heels.

Ercol reined his horse around, his grin splitting his face from ear to ear. "Crow-bait, huh? You're next, Conall!"

The warrior vaulted onto his horse's back and galloped toward Ercol. He pulled back on the reins, lifting his black into a rearing dance toward Ercol, hooves pawing the air. Ercol's horse turned and lashed out with both hooves, smashing the ribs of Conall's horse, and it dropped dead in its tracks.

Ercol leaned down, slashing with his sword at Conall, who dodged and suddenly sprinted down the road toward Emain Macha. Rathand, the messenger sent from Emain Macha by his wife, raced after him, with Id hard beside him. The three crossed Snám Rathaind, and there Rathand drowned in the river, and that is why that place is called Snám Rathaind to this day.

Meanwhile, Ercol looked back at Cúchulainn. He shook his head. "That forest took more from them than I thought. Looks like it's just me and you now, Hound."

"A horse of the *Sídhe?*" Cúchulainn asked, slowly mounting Gray. Laeg silently handed him the reins and his sword.

"Actually, a gift from Manannán Mac Lir, the Sea God, to my mother," Ercol said.

"I see," Cúchulainn said. He lifted the reins, and Gray began to dance daintily, head up, lips beginning to curl back from bold, white teeth. "Are you sure you want to do this? You are betraying the Rules of Hospitality, you know."

"Bothersome drivel!" Ercol said.

"The Brehon is quite explicit upon this," Cúchulainn said.

"Oh, let's just get on with it, shall we?" Ercol said.

His heels drummed the sides of the gelding and the mount leaped forward. Gray ducked under its charge and seized the nape of the gelding's neck in his teeth, biting hard, shaking his head. The neck bone snapped and the gelding fell lifeless into the dust. Cúchulainn leaped from the back of Gray, his fist striking Ercol under the ear, knocking him senseless.

Laeg sprang forward with leather strips in his hand. Together, he and Cúchulainn bound Ercol tightly, while Gray wandered off to nuzzle a tuft of grass.

"Well," Laeg said, raising his eyebrows. "Now what?"

"We go home," Cúchulainn said. He rose and squinted off into the distance. "Perhaps we can catch Loegaire and Conall and your brothers before they get to Emain Macha."

"I'll harness up," Laeg said, turning toward the barn.

"Tie Ercol in Loegaire's chariot. You drive Conall's and I'll bring Black and Gray. I'll lead Loegaire's chariot," Cúchulainn ordered. "I'll pack up inside." Laeg waved and disappeared into the stable.

Within the hour, the two were on the road toward Emain Macha. Unbeknown to them, they were followed by Búan, who knew the track of the chariot of Cúchulainn, for it left no narrow trail but heaped the soft earth up on either side and extended itself to leap over chasms where bridges had fallen and fords had become too deep with rushing water to be eased across.

She nearly caught up with the chariots when Cúchulainn stopped for Conall and traded chariots with him, with Laeg taking Loegaire's chariot to drive. She made a leap after Cúchulainn's chariot, but missed and struck her head against a rock. She died there, and to this day, the place is called Úaig Búana, "Búan's Grave."

The two heroes rode into Emain Macha and found the Red Branch in mourning, for Loegaire, ashamed of what he had done, had reported the two warriors killed by Ercol. When Cúchulainn and Conall gave their reports to Conchobor, the king reproached Loegaire sternly for his lies, scolding him for his falsehoods. Cúchulainn, however, returned Loegaire's weapons and chariot and horse to him, raising himself in the esteem of all, and the feast of mourning was quickly turned that night into a feast of welcome.

Chapter 11

THE
BEHEADING
GAME

TALK CEASED AS CÚCHULAINN stepped from the twilight into the dark feasting-hall and made his way down the center aisle to Conchobor's throne. He took his place and glanced over at Conall and Loegaire, slumped on their sides, each with a tankard clutched in one meaty fist. Loegaire stared into his tankard, one eye blacker than the other, sulking, while Conall grinned at Cúchulainn and waggled his eyebrows at Loegaire. Cúchulainn hid his smile behind his fist, pretending to cough. He quickly looked over at Seancha, at his scraggly, red-yellow beard and sharp Adam's apple, his gaze staring myopically at the well-rounded hip of a buxom serving wench.

"Seancha, my friend," Cúchulainn said, "what are you thinking?"

"Many things," Seancha answered dreamily.

"Oh?" Cúchulainn accepted a tankard of ale from one wench who took special pains in bending over farther than necessary to give him a look down the valley between two hillocks that rivaled the Paps of Anu. "Such as?"

"Power. Passion. Position. Puissance. Pelf. Property. Politics.

Puberty. Pudency. Pussy. They all are related, but pussy, ah. That has substance. All the rest are blatant illusion, drunken ideologies." He sighed sadly. "Alas, too old, too old. Now I think of puns instead of puds, and my pod is used for puddling instead of pricking. But, I do have thoughts—ah, fine thoughts, and sometimes— rarely, but that only makes it more exquisite—usually at the rising of the moon—I feel my youth again, ponderous and potent, and then I find myself believing in no gods, satisfying myself with substance."

"Or maybe it is a gift of the gods?" Cúchulainn said, smiling into his tankard.

"No! No! The gods give you hope, then—*crack!*—they step on your neck or make you impotent, tantalize you with lascivious thoughts, but alas, performance becomes nothing. Youth and old men have no use for the gods. The youth because of his arrogance, the old man because he recognizes that for all his hooting and pompous praying, and sacrifices, the gods will answer only when they feel like it." He leaned closer, breathing onion fumes at Cúchulainn. "Don't tell Cathbad or any of the other Druids, but I'm beginning to think that their religion is only a system of mechanical hoots and howls and posturing in the pale moonlight. One can get the same answers from stones or manure piles. Or garbage." He belched softly, his eyes turning inward. "Of course, it is caution to play with cant and causes—one cannot be too careful, you know—but one must remember that the *idea* of something is not worth two hoots with the *substance* of something. Gods are ideas; pussy is substance. Now, you take Bricriu, for example. For all his pompous panderings, playing, preening, and politics, we know him to be only a pleonast, a court jester parading his cockade before his king. It is, however, his idea of *himself* that makes him dangerous. You understand?"

"Vaguely," Cúchulainn said. "You keep on thinking, though, Seancha. That's what you're good at."

Seancha's eyes slicked down to where Loegaire sat in disgrace. He winked slyly at Cúchulainn. "You know how Loegaire got that black eye?" Cúchulainn shook his head. "He brought back a few tricks from Connacht that he learned from Maeve's busty wenches and made the mistake of telling Fedelm. Oh, she isn't called the Fresh Heart for nothing! The tongue of a fishwife, she has! Threw a temper tantrum that had the horses moving restlessly in the stables.

" 'Should I have told Ailill no when he offered the Rules of Hospitality? Should I have insulted my host?' Loegaire demanded of her. Bad mistake, that. *Bonk!* She brained him with a bronze pan! You could hear the sound all over Emain Macha. Now, you see, it wasn't that Loegaire slept with those women that mattered so much to Fedelm, but the idea that he thought so little of her as to bring back the, ah, little tricks. Dumb. Dumb."

Conchobor struck his silver wand against the bronze plate beside him, and the talk ceased. Sualdam Mac Roig, Cúchulainn's father, brought the food to Conchobor, setting aside the Champion's Portion on a separate platter.

"Chestnuts and apples!" Dubthach Chafertongue said. "Who is to get the Champion's Portion tonight? I tell you what: give it to one of the other heroes."

"And why should another receive it?" Seancha demanded. "I heard no other making a claim on it at Bricriu's feast, when it was left ready for any who dared to contest it. And none did, save for Loegaire Búadach, Conall Cernach, and Cúchulainn, the Hound of Culann."

"But," Dubthach sniffed, "I do not see any proof that they received judgment from either Ailill or Maeve. After all, isn't that why they were sent there? Surely, one of them would not have returned from Crúachain without some token, *something,* to show that the Champion's Portion should be awarded to him. You ask me, we should put it on a platter and share it around. Or, give it to someone else."

Loegaire slammed his tankard down on the bench beside him and rose, and brandished a bronze cup, tilting it so the silver bird in the bottom shone in the light from the feasting-hall fires. His lips curled as he glared in triumph around the room, saying, "So, it's a token you want, is it? Well, here it is! This was placed into my hands by Maeve herself!" His eyes flickered automatically to where his wife sat, glowering at him. "This is the token of my triumph as champion over all, and as such, I claim the Champion's Portion and the right of my wife to walk first into all gatherings!" He glanced again at Fedelm, who lifted her chin and stared around her with great satisfaction.

"Never would have thought that Maeve would've picked him," Seancha muttered. "Like picking a colt to race a stallion."

Conall Cernach rose, glanced disdainfully at Loegaire, then held his cup high above the shorter man. "Sit down, wee one! The Champion's Portion is no more yours than a babe still sucking on his nurse's teat! Maeve was playing foxes and geese with you! Here is the trophy befitting a champion! Your token is only bronze, while mine is white gold. Who ever heard of placing bronze over that, now? Eh?"

Loegaire glowered at Conall and started to speak angrily, but Cúchulainn rose and held his cup high in the air. Even in the dimness of light, all could see that his cup was far superior to the other two. He smiled down at the two from his place beside Conchobor and said:

> "Pretty trinkets, that I see,
> but little to this given to me.
> Bronze and white gold, I confess,
> are nice, but given in duress,
> for Maeve and Ailill did no one
> a favor. The deed they have done
> was to avoid possible hostility
> between the three of us. You and me
> have been duped by, her clever ways.
> Yet it is clear that for all days,
> the Champion's Portion should be
> mine, for all here can surely see
> that my cup of red gold with a bird
> of precious stone is better by a third
> than either of yours. And this stone

of two dragon eyes, given by Maeve,
is more worthy than any cup she gave
to either of you. Therefore, I say
the portion is surely mine today."

The feasting-hall exploded into hot debate as the cups were measured one against the other, and although many friends of both Loegaire and Conall were there to support their champions, all could see that Cúchulainn's trophies were far superior to those brandished by the other two.

At last Conchobor rose and struck his wand against the post, calling for order in the hall. All fell silent and turned expectantly to him as he gathered the folds of his cloak over one arm and said:

"Let justice be done, I say!
It is evident that this day
has been more than fairly won
by our Hound, whose deeds have won
him the Champion's Portion. So I
award you the portion until you die,
at which time it shall go to he
who shall avenge your death
in open battle, not with stealth,
as a true champion. This token
is yours! So have I spoken!"

Fergus pushed his bulk erect and stood beside Conchobor, glowering at the room. His shaggy eyebrows came together in a thick line across his forehead as he growled:

"Listen, you puppies! I say
that Cúchulainn has won the day
from all in this feasting-hall.
This is over! Do not try to stall
giving him what is his due. He's won

the right to the portion. It's done!
And his wife may now walk into
this hall first without any to-do
about her godly right to precede
them, thanks to her husband's deed."

And Seancha rose to stand on the other side of Conchobor, saying:

"Well spoken, my oafish friend!
I had no idea your tongue could bend
its way around words! I, too, say
that the Hound has earned this day
the right to the champion's meat
to be delivered to his seat
during all our feasts and days
in accordance to the Brehon's ways!
No one shall have due course to say
that he, instead, should in any way
have precedence to our Cúchulainn.
I am satisfied: the deed is done."

"Bullshit!" Loegaire spat. He threw his cup down. It bounced and rolled to come to a stop at the feet of the three. Conchobor's eyes narrowed dangerously, but Loegaire ignored him. He stared angrily at Cúchulainn.

"I swear by all that people swear that you bought that cup from Maeve with jewels and treasures and one night that you spent in her arms so that she could brag she slept with the Hound of Ulster! Oh, yes," he continued as the hall began to buzz angrily from his words. "Yes! You bought that cup from Ailill and Maeve so that you wouldn't be disgraced when I showed my cup! I don't know how you found out about my promise to Maeve not to say anything until we arrived back home here in Emain Macha—unless that viperish bitch played tongue games with me—but I say that you did this so the Champion's Portion would not be rightfully mine!"

"Liar!" someone called from the far end of the room.

"Who said that?" Loegaire demanded, stepping into the walkway, fists clenched threateningly by his side. "Who dares to call me a liar?"

"I do!"

"And I!"

Several stood up in support of Cúchulainn, but Conchobor quickly struck the side of his throne with his wand, calling for order in the hall. The shouts dribbled down to angry murmurs. Then, Conall rose.

"I, too, swear that the Champion's Portion should be mine and not our little Hound's. The judgment you have brought back from Connacht is not a judgment, but obviously a clever way of turning the tables back upon our king to make his own decision and not foist it off on someone else. Besides," he added, contemptuously tossing his cup after Loegaire's, "I claim the portion to be mine. Both of you are liars, as far as I'm concerned."

Cúchulainn's face reddened and he leaped to his feet, his sword flashing out in his hand as the other two drew their swords and stepped into the middle of the room. He started to leap forward, but Conchobor and Fergus moved quickly between the three of them, their kingly presence demanding an end to all argument. The three immediately sheathed their swords and sat down.

"Very well," Seancha sighed. He pinched the bridge of his nose, rubbing gently. "Let my will decide this, if I may." The three exchanged grins and slowly nodded.

"We agree," Conall said. "Speak!"

"Listen carefully now, for I don't want a repeat of this unsightly demonstration in the hall. All three of you could be censured for what you have done, and I say that if Bricriu was here, he should be boiled in his own bile for bringing this upon the head of the Red Branch! This bickering is not only becoming very dangerous, but tiresome! The bitter words of a rancored man who stews all day in high dudgeon, seeking ways of tying a red rag to a bull's butt, should not be tolerated! But he has succeeded in turning this house against itself. I hope the teeth fall out of his cankerous mouth!" He drew a deep breath. "Therefore I say that each of you go to the ford of Budi Mac M-Bain and ask Budi for judgment. Until you return, the Champion's Portion shall be served to all! Though a poor piece it will be in the mouth of he who has not earned it," he added.

Loegaire and Conall exchanged looks with Cúchulainn, and together, the three rose and silently left the hall. Fergus drew a deep breath and let it out with a hard *whoosh!*

"By the beard of Maeve! That was a fine thought you had, Seancha!" He clapped the poet hard upon his shoulder, staggering him. "I'd never have thought of ol' Budi!"

"Not surprising! Thought is a strange animal to you," Seancha snarled, wincing and rubbing his shoulder. "You can't work your way through the world with your sword and that club between your legs."

"Well now," Fergus said comfortably, scratching the mentioned member through his tunic. "The world doesn't spin on thought, only action."

Seancha's eyebrows shot up as Fergus lumbered back to his couch. "Sometimes even babes have insight of vision," he said.

Lugh's chariot had passed the meridian height, and long shadows cast themselves upon the ground outside the old house of split oak. The champions' horses stood, heads drooping sleepily, in the dappled shade of aspens. Inside the house, empty tankards sat on tables by the three warriors, who stared expectantly across the small room to where their host Budi sat still, legs crossed, staring at them with the unblinking gaze of a lizard. His face was lined and as gray as ashes beneath his scraggly beard with ringworm holes cut into it. At last he sighed, scratched his belly beneath his dirty tunic and unlocked his legs, joints popping like bent branches. He stuck a foot out with thick yellow calluses on the bottom and wiggled his toes.

"Well, isn't this an interesting state of affairs? Well." He sucked in the ends of his mustaches and blew them out again.

"Will you help us or not?" Loegaire asked crossly.

"Didn't you go to Ailill for judgment?" Budi asked.

"Yes, but—" Loegaire started impatiently.

"But what?" Budi interrupted. "Didn't you get judgment? Did you not get the bronze cup, and you, Conall, the white-gold cup, while Cúchulainn received the red-gold cup? And is not white gold more expensive than brass, and red gold more expensive than the other two? It would seem to me that judgment has been given. Your problem is that you don't like the judgment, even after you agreed to it. Didn't get what you expected. So you went home like a mewling babe puking in his mother's arms and sulked when the Champion's Portion didn't come your way."

"I did not sulk!" Loegaire protested.

"Oh? Then why are you here?" Budi shrugged. "What are your plans? To flit around Eire like a whippoorwill, stopping here and there on a whim until you find someone who will say yes, Loegaire, you are the champion?"

"Yes. No. I mean, no. Er . . ." Loegaire wrinkled his forehead. "What was the question again?"

Budi sighed. "And you, Conall. First you say you want judgment, then you don't. Tell me, what is it that you want?"

"I don't understand you. What do you think I'm here for? Of course I want judgment!" Conall snarled.

"But did you not get it in Connacht?"

"Politics! That's what we got. And games of chance. Nothing to test a man's bravery, his worthiness! Blade against blade, I say. That's the true test of a champion!"

"Right. There was no judgment," Loegaire chimed in. "Only ducks and drakes."

"So a champion isn't supposed to be intelligent?" Budi asked mildly. He pulled a louse from his hair and cracked its shell with a thumbnail like yellowed horn. "He's just a brute to go swinging and hacking his way through the universe without direction?"

"No. But I leave that to the Druids and poets and such," Conall said.

"Dumb as an ox," muttered Loegaire in disgust. "Look here, will you give us judgment or not?"

"I don't know," Budi said. His gaze shifted over to Cúchulainn, who sat quietly, slightly away from the other two. "We haven't heard from our young Hound here. What do you think, Cúchulainn?"

"I think this nonsense has gone on long enough," Cúchulainn said.

Budi grinned, his teeth snaggled yellow stumps in his mouth. "Then, what do you propose we do?"

"I have no objection to another test, I suppose," Cúchulainn said. "I have won all those we have taken—"

"Magical intervention!" Loegaire said quickly. "Not fair!"

"Yes, magic," Conall said, then pursed his lips, thinking, as if he didn't quite believe what he had said.

"But the entire cosmos is founded on magic," Budi objected. "Surely you don't deny that?"

"All I want is an equal shot," Conall said.

"Me too," Loegaire chimed in quickly.

"Free will? The exercise of. You will accept this as binding?" Budi asked.

"If you mean that we all have a choice or not, yes," Loegaire answered, casting a hard sidelong look at Cúchulainn. "As long as there's not magical election involved. We each get a turn and that's it."

Conall and Cúchulainn nodded their acceptance. Budi's eyebrows waggled like fat caterpillars. "It isn't easy to judge those who will not accept the judgment of Ailill and Maeve, for I think they hit on a very clever tactic. An impossible situation, you see, is a bit more touchy than simply setting a log in front of each of you and naming the one who hacks through first the winner. Why, one of you would complain that his wood had more knots in it and therefore it wasn't a fair challenge. I'd let each of you guzzle a tankard of beer, but one of you who lost would say it wasn't fair because your tankard had more beer than foam, thereby placing you at a disadvantage. Very clever, this play with cups.

"But," he sighed, "you apparently weren't intelligent enough to see that you were being given a chance to decide for yourselves who was the worthiest. Even stopping by Maeve's foster-father's house was a test designed to let you see your faults and fallacies. But that didn't work because two of you are too proud to see what the other can do! Pride! It'll be the downfall of us all, you'll see. Excuses, excuses! In the old days, an excuse wasn't given. A person played with the tools the gods gave him instead of pissing and moaning about fairness and all. But you want judgment. I don't think you'd accept anything that I came up with, given that you've refused the judgment of Ailill and Maeve, and even of your own king, among others."

"So, go see Uath Mac Imomain, who lives down by the lake. He'll make a decision for you. But be aware," he said, holding up an admonishing forefinger. "You'd better accept his decision! He's not as understanding or as philosophical as I am. And don't bother coming back here whining about unfair challenges. I have other things to do than to arbitrate silly games such as this. You will all accept Uath's decision, or you will not. And if you do not, why then, I don't want to hear any more of your sniveling and whining like snot-nosed brats! The champion will be decided. See that you are wise enough to accept Uath's decision!"

He rose, joints popping, waved the three away and stumped out of the room, back into the depths of his house. Loegaire and Conall exchanged looks.

"Grumpy old fart, isn't he?" Loegaire asked. Conall shrugged and glanced over at Cúchulainn.

"You know there isn't anything personal about all this," he said apologetically. "It's just something that has to be settled, that's all."

"Not personal," Cúchulainn said dryly. "Uh-huh. Well, I'm glad you didn't make it personal. I'd hate to have to beat a friend."

"So am I," Conall said. Then his face darkened. "Don't you worry about that!"

"Are we going to sit around arguing, or are we going down to the lake and see this Uath fellow and let him make his choice?" Loegaire asked. "Time's wasting!"

They rose and went out of Budi's house. Their charioteers looked up hopefully, then sighed and hunkered down on their haunches when each shook his head.

"Becoming a joke, this is," Id said, yawning.

"That it is," Laeg answered. "That it is."

The three warriors found a path along the shore and set out to follow it, twisting and turning through stands of aspen and birch and willow. Slowly the trees thinned out, then suddenly stopped, leaving a bare stretch of ground before a stand of hazel and oak. In the middle they could see a huge, rambling hall that seemed to wink and waver in the bright sunlight. They stood indecisive for a long moment. At last Conall broke the silence.

"I don't like this," he said. "Something seems fishy here."

"You're standing beside the water," Loegaire said.

"That ain't what I meant," Conall said. "I smell something rotten and it ain't fish."

"Maybe you should wash your feet," Cúchulainn suggested, moving toward the house.

"Har-de-har-har," Conall said sarcastically.

"He does have a point," Loegaire said pointedly. "You could stand a bath."

"I'll—"

"Be quiet," Cúchulainn said. "You sound like a couple of washerwomen arguing about the rinse, not like Red Branch warriors."

They fell silent, giving each other threatening looks as they came up in front of the house. From somewhere they heard the sweet tune of a fife, the notes seeming to hang in the air like brilliant fall leaves, russets, browns, and golds. A huge knocker hung on the door, carved in the shape of a harp. What the three of them did not know was that Uath was more than a simple arbitrator, one who could come up with interesting challenges to test the mettle of men, but a seer of great and protean powers.

He was a bit of a shape-shifter, too, and—although he kept this fairly hidden from Loegaire and Conall—a bit of a wizard. He was the specter after which Bélac Muni in tSiriti was named.

Cúchulainn reached out, lifted the knocker and let it fall. *Boom!* And distant thunder rolled back softly from across the lake. *Bo-o-o-m-om!* The music stopped. A loon called anxiously from the lake, and somewhere deep in the forest behind the house, a squirrel chattered angrily at being awakened from its nap. Slowly, the ponderous door opened and a tall, stoop-shouldered man looked out, a fife tucked under one arm. He smiled at them.

"Yes? May I help you?" he asked. His voice was low and soft, buttery.

"Budi told us you would pass judgment on us," Conall said abruptly.

The man blinked. "Ah, yes. I see. Well, won't you come in and have a glass of wine? I have some fresh-pressed rose hips."

"Beer's more a man's drink," Loegaire grumbled aside to Cúchulainn. "Took me near a week to get that sweet Cruachain crap out of my gullet. *Phaugh!* Give me something with body to it, not pap juice!"

Cúchulainn ignored him and stepped across the threshold, thanking the man for his thoughtfulness. Instantly, a coldness brushed over him, making his flesh pebble. A musty but pleasant odor of sloe berries tickled his nose, making him sneeze.

"Bad sign, that," Loegaire said. He shivered. "Why is it so cold?"

"Won't you have a seat?" the man said, motioning down a dim corridor. They could see light flickering at the far end. "I'll only be a minute with your refreshment."

The three warriors walked warily down the hall and emerged into a large, well-kept room. The floor had been freshly swept and a fire burned brightly in the stone fireplace at the end of the room. Thick chairs, each carved from a single oak tree, stood in a semicircle in front of the fire.

"Do you notice anything strange?" Cúchulainn murmured when the three of them stood in front of the fire, holding their hands out to its warmth.

"It's cold," Conall said. "Other than that, what?"

"Four chairs," Cúchulainn said.

"So?" Loegaire said, glancing apprehensively over his shoulder. "There're four chairs. There're four of us. What's so unusual about that?"

"How did he know there were three of us coming?" Cúchulainn asked. "And why isn't this fire burning through the log?"

They all looked down at the fire burning from the log, yet the surface remained unscorched.

"Oh, no," groaned Loegaire, pressing his palms against his temples. "Another fucking magician!"

"Not exactly," the man said, coming up to them, balancing a tray on one huge hand. "But I do have a few tricks I can do to entertain you, if you wish."

"Such as the fire?" Conall asked.

"Oh, that," he said modestly. "No, that isn't me. It's the wood."

"Special wood, huh?" Loegaire asked hopefully. The man handed him a mug.

"I believe you said you would prefer beer," he said, "I took the liberty."

"Thank you," Loegaire said and sipped suspiciously, his eyes brightening as the golden beverage slipped smoothly down his gullet.

"Bees," the man said in answer to the unspoken question in Loegaire's eyes. "From an island in the lake. I believe that you would prefer a mug, too?" he asked Conall. "You didn't say, but you look like one who would prefer that. If not—"

"Beer's fine," Conall said. His huge hand took the tankard and he drank deeply, but when he took the tankard away from his lips, the level of the beer was the same as before. He frowned and cautiously ran his tongue around the inside of his mouth, tasting, wondering if he'd dreamed the swallowing or had indeed swallowed.

"And I thought you might like to try my rose-hip wine," the

man said, handing a glass to Cúchulainn.

"Thank you. I would," Cúchulainn said graciously. He sipped and nodded appreciatively. The man beamed.

"Good. Sit. Sit." He motioned to the chairs and took the one at the end so he could look at all at once. "Now then, you were saying something about 'judgment,' I believe?"

"Excuse me," Loegaire said, "but I don't think you've told us your name."

"Oh, I'm sorry," the man said. "Since you are here, I was certain you had been told. I am Uath. And I have certainly heard about you, Loegaire Búadach. Who hasn't heard stories about your deeds?" Loegaire puffed his cheeks out, immensely pleased and trying to hide it. "And you," Uath continued, shifting his look to Conall Cernach. "I have heard of you as well, mighty warrior who keeps every night with a Connachtman's head hanging from his belt!"

"A wise man," Conall said and took another deep drink of the beer, looking mystified when the level again remained the same. "Good beer," he added lamely.

"But even now, legends are being built around Cúchulainn, the Hound of Ulster," Uath said, beaming at the youngest warrior. "My, my! What stories!"

Cúchulainn smiled, his cheeks growing warm as he tried not to show his pleasure at the man's enthusiasm. "Then you know why we are here?" he asked. Uath smiled and shook his head.

"I have an idea," he answered. "But it is you who must make the request."

"Well, what do you want us to say?" Loegaire asked brusquely.

"Whatever it is you wish," Uath answered.

"Stuff and nonsense!" Conall growled, taking another large draught from his tankard, determined to lower the level beneath the brim. "We want you to decide which of us is worthy of the Champion's Portion." He glanced at the tankard and saw no change in the level. He sighed happily; this could be the gift of the gods to the one they had chosen as the champion. He glanced furtively at Cúchulainn and Loegaire; they had not noticed the level in his tankard. Loegaire kept glancing down at his tankard and frowning, while Cúchulainn sipped the wine, glanced at the goblet, then quietly placed it aside.

"Do you not care for my wine?" Uath asked politely, his brow furrowing in concern.

"It is very good," Cúchulainn said. "But a man could become a slave to it if he is not careful. I have been refreshed. That is enough."

Uath nodded, a faint smile touching his lips. He looked over at Loegaire and Conall. "And have you found the beer to your liking?"

"Very fine," Conall and Loegaire said in unison. They glanced at each other and covertly moved their tankards so the other could not see.

"Very well," Uath said. He fell silent for a moment, then coughed, clearing his throat, and said: "So, I suppose that without further ado, we should get down to the purpose of your coming. Now, you all wish me to make the decision?" They nodded. "Even though this decision has been made more than once before?"

"Tricks," Conall said.

"Magic," Loegaire concurred.

"Not a true test of a man," Conall said. "A champion should be one tested against men."

"Ah, then you do agree that a test is needed to determine the champion?" Uath asked.

"Of course," Loegaire answered.

"And one that an ordinary man would not be able to perform?"

"Ordinary men can't be champions," Conall answered.

"But," Uath said, looking at Cúchulainn, "we haven't heard from our Hound. What do you think should decide the champion?"

"People," Cúchulainn answered promptly. "The people should decide. But," he shrugged, "since they cannot come to an agreement, then an arbitrator must decide."

"Haven't you tried this before?" Uath asked.

"Yes."

"I see. So it must be a test, therefore, that the other two will agree only a certain individual could perform," Uath mused, looking up at the ceiling and stroking his chin. "That should be a simple thing to arrange."

"Good," Loegaire said. He looked blearily at Uath, the beer having proved extremely heady. "Everyone wants to make everything so complicated. The simpler, the better, I say."

"Right!" Uath cried, clapping his hands together. He rose, went to the fire and took down a mighty ax from black hooks above the mantel piece. Its head was twice the span of an ordinary man's arm from top to bottom, and its edge gleamed with sharpness. "I have just the thing!"

"Here now!" Conall said. "What are you aiming to do with that ax?"

"Why," Uath cried merrily, "it is simple. You cut off my head today and give me a whack at yours on the morrow. What could be simpler than that?"

"Nuts! Why, what sort of test is that?" Loegaire demanded. "Whoever loses his head today will not find it by the morrow, you can bet on that! 'Sides," he added, squinting suspiciously, "this smacks of more wizardry. I thought we were done with that!"

"Oh, life itself is full of magic, don't you think?" Uath said, laughing. "Why, just think how magical it is that you are here today instead of lounging beside a fire at Emain Macha, telling lies about how brave you are."

"Lies? Lies?" Conall said, growing angry.

"No offense. But just think about how magical life is," Uath continued blithely. "It takes a certain mare and a certain stallion to produce a certain colt. No other combination could produce the same colt. Or take a look at the blades your smithy hammers out for you. No two are alike any more than any two butterflies are alike, or any two fishes or deer or boars or—"

"Metaphysics," Loegaire moaned. "We're at loggerheads again. Enough! We get the picture."

"Sorry," Uath said, lowering his head sheepishly. "I get carried away a bit at times. A fault of mine."

"But only a fool would agree to your conditions, metaphysics or not," Conall said. "I've cut enough heads from shoulders to know that they don't grow back again. Once off, they're off. That's all there's to it!"

"Then, what do you have to lose?" Uath asked, his eyes opening wide.

"All right," Loegaire sighed, setting aside his tankard. He rose, wobbled on his legs for a second, then steadied himself and held out his hand. "Gimme that thing and bend over this table here. I'll give you the first blow."

"And I may give you one in return on the morrow?" Uath asked.

"Oh, sure," Loegaire said, winking at Conall.

"Then," Uath laughed, "take your swing, my friend!"

He bent forward at the waist, grabbing each side of the thick black oak table with his hands and stretching his head out as far as he could to give Loegaire a clean swipe with the ax. Loegaire measured carefully, then swung the ax back and around, slicing through the man's neck. The axhead buried itself in the table, the force of the blow causing it to ring like a bell. Uath's head flew from his shoulders, bouncing into a corner of the room. Blood fountained high in a steaming arc.

"Ho! Well struck!"

Loegaire glanced around, searching for the source of the voice, then stepped back, his eyebrows waggling in surprise at his hairline as Uath straightened from the table and calmly walked over to pick up his head, tucking it under his arm. Loegaire looked in amazement as the lips grinned and parted to speak.

"We'll meet here tomorrow morning to settle this once and for all," Uath said. "Now, I beg of you to take a room at the other end of the hall and my servant will bring you food and drink."

He blinked happily at each of them, then turned and walked from the hall, singing:

"And so we divide the ladies fair
Among those who waited there;
The slender and dimpled and round
Pleasured every man they found..."

His voice trailed off as he disappeared down the hall. Loegaire looked from the ax in his hand to the other two. He shook his head and left the ax in the table, reaching for his tankard.

"More damned witchcraft! Now we'll have to find someone else to make the decision. Enough to bring the thirst out upon any man!" he said mournfully. He raised his tankard and drank.

The next morning, however, when the three champions appeared in the Great Hall, they found a cheerful Uath waiting beside the table, whistling a merry tune. They glanced at the ax; its head had been cleaned of blood, the table and hall scrubbed and smelling fresh.

"Close your mouth, my good man!" Uath laughed as Loegaire stared openmouthed at him. "You'll catch all the flies in Ireland!"

"How...how..." Loegaire stammered.

"Witchcraft," Conall finished in satisfaction. "Told you no good would come of this!"

"Well now, I don't know about that," Uath said. "We have the makings of a good contest going right now!" He looked at Loegaire and smiled. "Don't see any reason to postpone it. Stretch out, my good man, and I'll take my swing. Then we can all have breakfast!"

"In a pig's ass!" Loegaire exclaimed. He turned and ran from the house. He ran into the forest and burrowed deep into a pile of moldy oak leaves, hiding.

"Hmm. I must say that I thought he'd make a better show than that," Uath said sadly, shaking his head. "But—" he brightened, "—we can still have a time. Come now! Who's next?"

"Enough of this nonsense!" Conall exclaimed. He spat into his palms and seized the ax. "Stretch out, *vathi!* We'll see if you come back after this one!"

Uath raised his eyebrows and glanced at Cúchulainn. "Sorry," he grinned, "but you'll have to wait your turn."

"Ain't gonna be no more turns after this," Conall grunted, raising the ax. Uath smiled and stretched out on the table. Conall brought the ax down with such force that Uath's head caromed off two walls before bouncing like a wicker ball under the table.

"That should settle this, once and for all!" Conall sniffed disdainfully. With contempt, he tossed the ax onto the table and clapped his hands together, dusting them off.

Uath rose and fumbled under the table for his head, and again tucked it under his arm. "Well then! I shall see you in the morning for my stroke, friend Conall," he cried, and stumped off down the hall.

"I'll . . . I'll . . ." Conall strangled, his face red with apoplexy. Cúchulainn thumped him heartily upon the back. "Loegaire was right, this is no test. Witchery!" Conall squawked.

"You made the deal," Cúchulainn said admonishingly. "By the honor of the Red Branch, you must uphold your words, your brag!"

"Against a man, yes!" Conall spat. "But against a . . . a . . . *bonánach?* My mother raised no foolish children!" He ran from the hall and dashed down to the lake and dove into it, swimming deep into the rushes to hide.

Cúchulainn sighed. "Honor," he said softly. "Fleeting as a hare!" And he turned and went sadly back to his room, waiting for the morning.

The next morning, Cúchulainn walked into the hall and found, as he expected, Uath waiting cheerfully for him.

"I take it, then, that Conall has had second thoughts? Well, no matter. It is up to you now, my Hound! Will you have a try with my ax?" Uath asked.

"I will," Cúchulainn said softly. "Though I know you to be

one of the *Sídhe* and so this is truly no test of mortal men, I will play with you."

"That's the spirit!" Uath said, handing him the ax. He stretched out upon the table and firmly gripped the sides of the table.

Cúchulainn swung the ax with all his strength, severing Uath's head, smashing through the table and burying the ax head deep into the stone of the floor. Uath's head flew up, banging against the wall across the room, then ricocheted back off the other wall, then bounced twice before coming to rest in the fire.

"Ow! Ow! Help! Help!" it cried as Uath's body fumbled, trying to separate itself from the wreckage of the table. Cúchulainn took a quick step to the fireplace and thrust his hand into the flames. He seized Uath's head by the hair and pulled it free, smothering the smoldering hair with his other hand.

"Thank you," Uath breathed. "That is one thing that I hadn't counted on. Quite a blow! Quite a blow! Well, I'll be seeing you on the morrow. And, thanks!" he called as his body reclaimed his head and lumbered down the hall away from Cúchulainn.

"I'll be here," Cúchulainn called softly.

But instead of going to his room, he went down to the lake and walked along the shore, spending the day watching the ducks and geese land on the calm water. He breathed deeply, smelling the smoke of the fall day, the crisp of the coming evening.

"Psst!"

He looked around and found Conall parting the rushes, looking at him.

"You took your try?" Cúchulainn nodded. "Aye, then there's nothing to keep us here! Where's Loegaire?"

"Here!" came a soft call from the woods. They watched as he pulled himself from the pile of rotting leaves. "This has been a wasted journey. Let's away!"

But Cúchulainn shook his head.

"What's the matter?" Conall demanded, pulling himself from the rushes. He sat down and squeezed the water from his clothes.

"I must wait for the morning so Uath may have his try,"

Cúchulainn said softly.

"What!" Loegaire exclaimed. "Surely you are making a jest!"

"You know that you ain't like him," Conall said. "You can't make your head attach itself back to your shoulders. At least," he added, "I don't think you can." His eyes narrowed suspiciously.

"I can't," Cúchulainn said sadly.

"Then waiting is foolishness!" Loegaire said abruptly.

"Perhaps. But I gave my word," Cúchulainn explained.

"It ain't like you promised a *bó airech*—one of the nobility—that you would," Conall said. "There ain't no honor in trying to outwit the magic ones. Just plain foolishness."

"You tried," Cúchulainn said pointedly.

"So that you could see the foolishness of doing it yourself," blustered Loegaire. The others looked at him. "Well, I did! I can't help it if you two don't take my actions to heart. I do my best."

"Uh-huh," Conall said acidly. "And that's why you hid under the leaves?"

Loegaire's face burned burnished bronze. His eyes narrowed into slits. "You calling me a liar?" he demanded.

"Uh-huh," Conall said. "You hid the same as I."

"You both can go if you wish," Cúchulainn said quickly to avert a battle between the two. "I must wait until tomorrow."

"Damn your hardheadedness!" Loegaire said. Conall sneezed, his eyes watering. "We'll wait until your body is separated from your common sense. Then we'll take what's left back to Emer and let her keen over the idiot she once knew."

"You're all heart," Cúchulainn said. He turned and walked back into Uath's house.

"Come on, oh, ox!" Loegaire said roughly to Conall. "I heard some bees buzzing while I was, ah, being discreet. I think we can find something to eat over there." He pointed off to the west, to the woods. Together, the two walked deeper into the forest.

Ah!" Uath exclaimed happily as Cúchulainn presented himself in the hall the next morning. "You are ready?"

"I am," Cúchulainn said. He took a deep breath and glanced toward the window. Conall and Loegaire peeked in over the sill. He gave them a faint smile and stretched out upon the patched table, took another deep breath and said: "Take your swing!"

Three times Uath lifted the ax, dropping it swiftly upon Cúchulainn's bare neck. Each time, the ax bounced back as if striking an iron anvil, the sound ringing louder with each stroke.

"Arise, Cúchulainn!" Uath exclaimed. He turned and hung the ax back on the iron hooks over the fireplace. "Come in, Conall and Loegaire, and meet your champion! I pronounce Cúchulainn the champion of Ulster and give to him all the rights of the champion. Now, there's an end to it all! Each has seen what the other would do, and only one among the three of you stood the test. And a fair test it was, for only a man without fear is worthy of bearing the honor of the Red Branch upon his shoulders! Each of you has been the witness for the other. Take word of what has happened here back to Conchobor! It is over."

But when the three returned to the Red Branch, Loegaire and Conall stoutly denied Cúchulainn's story, claiming that they had been napping when Cúchulainn had been tested by Uath, and laughing when Cúchulainn claimed they had run from their obligation.

"Now," Loegaire said scornfully as Cúchulainn looked on in disgust, "Would any of you think that a man would be picking up his noggin and putting it back on his head? All of you have cut enough heads from shoulders to know that it is pure foolishness to think that someone would be around to test me after I lopped his head from himself. Go to the trophy house and look at the heads with my mark on them among the rafters!"

"And mine," Conall said, glancing at Cúchulainn but refusing to meet his eye. "I still claim the Champion's Portion!"

Conchobor sighed and gently rubbed his temples with the pads of his fingers. He glanced over at Seancha. "Well?" he demanded. "Any other ideas?"

"You'll have to go to the house of Cúroi," Seancha said wearily. "I can think of nothing else."

And so the three warriors drove their chariots to the house of Cúroi and were met by Cúroi's wife Bláthnait, the daughter of Mend. Loegaire looked with admiration as the tall, heavy-breasted Bláthnait threw open the door for them.

"Welcome!" she cried. Her breasts bounced violently beneath her thin shift, the nipples showing large and dark like plump whortleberries. The light behind her showed her shapely limbs. Loegaire groaned softly at the heavy, dark shadow between her legs.

"I regret that my husband is not here to welcome you, but he left word for me to give each of you directions," she said, a smile curving her full lips deeply into dimples.

"He knew we were coming?" Conall asked with misgiving.

"Oh, yes," she said. "He was called away to Scythia—for you know that he cannot redden his sword in Erin blood and that no food from Erin has passed his lips since he was seven—such is his strength and valor, pride and courage, and...where was I? Oh, yes...he left instructions for your testing. Do not act so surprised, Conall. All of Erin knows of the contest between you and Loegaire and Cúchulainn. Frankly, I think you are making too much of a piece of meat, but I'm only a woman, not a man."

"Yes," Loegaire said, clearing his throat. "I can see that."

"Aren't you the naughty one?" she laughed. She put her hands on her hips and swayed saucily. "Unyoke your horses and put them in the stables. Feed and grain them. Then make your way to the bathhouse." She nodded to her right. "I'll have food and drink waiting for you afterward." She beamed and winked, then turned and flounced back into the house.

"Well, my friends, shall we?" Cúchulainn asked. He leaned over, spoke into Black's ear, then stepped back while Black tossed his head and trotted with Gray to the stables.

"I don't think," Loegaire said regretfully, "that I have ever seen a pair of bountiful bubbies to match those! Not even Mugain's, which all of Emain Macha saw, thanks to you, Cúchulainn, when you came back on your first day under arms. Remember?"

"Bubbies?" Cúchulainn frowned. Then his face cleared. "Oh,

yes. Sorry. I was distracted."

"With your horses," Conall sighed. "Really, little Hound! Don't you ever think of the priorities of life?"

He and Loegaire shook their heads and led their horses to the stables. Cúchulainn laughed and followed.

When the warriors entered the feasting-hall of Cúroi's house, they paused and breathed thankfully of the smell of roasting meat and baked bread. Bláthnait beamed and bounced forward on the balls of her dainty feet, her breasts bowling like melons beneath her shift, her hips heaving like a heavy sea.

"Come! Come!" she said. "Everything is ready. Eat! Beds have been made ready for you. I think it may rain tonight, so I have ordered extra furs for you."

"I really should check on Black and Gray first," Cúchulainn said apologetically.

"Impossible!" she said. "It will interfere with the testing, which begins right after dinner. But I assure you that your horses have been well cared for. I promise." She placed her hand beneath one breast, lifting it gently. Loegaire made a strangled noise deep in his throat.

"What might that be?" Conall asked. She cocked her head quizzically at him. "The test?" he added.

"Oh, that!" she laughed. "Why, nothing. An insignificant little thing! Simply keep watch over my husband's fortress, one of you each night! Guard it well until his return, at which time he will make his decision upon which of you shall be named the champion."

"That's all?" Cúchulainn asked. "Guard the fortress?"

"Yes. Well, you never know what may happen," she said. She winked at him. He smiled slightly, patiently. She raised an eyebrow, then looked at Loegaire. "And you, you lucky man, get to be first!"

"Why me?" Loegaire asked, suddenly suspicious.

"You are the oldest!" Bláthnait said. "Now, eat hearty and get some sleep, for when night comes, you will have to go outside and you won't be able to come in again until morning. You see," she continued at the puzzled look in their eyes, "my husband sings a spell over the fortress to keep it—and me—" she added modestly "—safe from harm whenever he's away. The spell makes it spin as rapidly as a mill wheel grinding flour, so that its entrance can never be found until Lugh's rays touch it from the east."

"That's it?" Conall asked. "No witchcraft? Other, I mean, than the spell upon the fort?"

"I don't know," she said, shrugging her shoulders. Loegaire looked away, drawing a deep breath. "I've never been outside the walls after dark. Oh, the courtyard is safe enough, but . . . who knows?" she finished brightly.

"Let's eat, then," Conall said. His stomach rumbled. "I could eat a whole bullock by myself and drink a tun to wash it down."

"Water, please," Cúchulainn said.

"Humph!" Conall and Loegaire muttered as they moved toward the table.

Bláthnait grinned and handed a goblet to Cúchulainn. Their fingers touched, hers cool, yet warm, and Cúchulainn felt his flesh gooseflesh.

Loegaire Búadach stomped his feet and blew on his fingers to keep them warm as he stood guard outside the fortress walls. As the night wore on, he fought to keep his eyes open, silently cursing his luck as he thought of Bláthnait lying naked in a pile of furs in front of a roaring fire. He sighed and watched the east, willing the sun to rise.

He heard a noise behind him and turned to the west and saw an angry giant striding from the waves of the sea, his head nearly touching the clouds, his hands filled with javelins as thick as oak trees, sharpened and the points fire-hardened.

"Urk!" Loegaire squawked. "What do you want?"

The giant's face wrinkled into a furious mask. He threw the javelins at Loegaire, who dodged and ducked. In desperation, Loegaire threw his own javelin, but missed. The giant's face broke into a scornful smile and he reached out a huge hand, so large that it spanned three ridges, and seized Loegaire.

"Hey! Ark!" Loegaire struggled, finding his strength no more than a babe's in the giant's hand as the giant curled his fingers around him like a *fidchell* piece between millstones.

Loegaire struggled as the giant slowly squeezed. Bright lights bounced in his head. He gasped. Then the giant reached and dropped him over the wall into the courtyard of the fortress, where he lay gasping, smelling the bitter soil where a manure pile had been cleaned away. The walls began to slow their spinning. He drew a deep breath and rose shakily to his feet as the door opened and Conall and Cúchulainn stepped out. They looked in surprise at him, then at the wall.

"Everything all right?" Cúchulainn asked.

"Of course," Loegaire said. He took a deep breath, trying to ignore the pain in his ribs.

"How did you get in? The gate is still barred," Conall asked.

"Oh, I jumped over the wall," Loegaire said. "See if you can do the same."

He walked past them and went into the house. Conall shook his head.

"That Loegaire," he said. He hawked and spat and measured the height of the wall with a practiced eye. "That's quite a jump."

"You can try it in the morning," Cúchulainn grinned.

"Maybe I will," Conall answered. "If Loegaire can do it, so can I."

That night, Conall stumped around the walls of the fortress, pausing every other turn to eye the wall, squinting against the top of it in the darkness. He shook his head. How Loegaire had cleared that height, he hadn't the foggiest idea. *He must've had help,* Conall thought at last. *Ain't no how he could jump over that!*

A slight splashing noise came to him and he whirled, his eyes bugging out at the sight of the giant wading swiftly ashore from the sea, his hand clutching a bunch of javelins the size of oak trees as if they were matchsticks. The giant threw his javelins at Conall, who dodged and threw his own javelin back as hard as he could. The giant swatted it aside and grabbed Conall, squeezing hard.

Conall cried out in pain and tried to push the giant's fingers open, but though his shoulders cracked with the strain, he could not budge the giant's grip. Black spots swam in front of his eyes as he labored for air. Then the giant reached over the parapet and contemptuously dropped Conall in front of the doorway.

The warrior lay gasping on the ground as gray light showed in the east and the walls slowed their spinning. Painfully, he hauled himself erect and brushed the dirt from him. The door opened and Loegaire and Cúchulainn stepped out. Cúchulainn looked from him to the top of the wall and raised an eyebrow.

"Told you if he could do it, so could I," Conall mumbled and straightened his shoulders and marched into the hall.

Cúchulainn looked at Loegaire, who shrugged and said, "Well, lad, it looks like it's up to you!"

That evening, Bláthnait caught Cúchulainn before he left the fortress. She leaned her heavy breasts against his arm, saying, "Now, my Hound, watch carefully, for this is the night of the full moon!" She licked his ear.

"And?" Cúchulainn asked, gently pulling his arm free.

"Every night of the full moon, the Three Grays of Sescend Úairbéoil, the Three Cowherders of Brega, and the Three Sons of Dornmár Céoil gather to try and destroy my husband's stronghold!" she said. "Hmm. Aren't you the strong one, though?" She licked her lips and tried to kiss him, but Cúchulainn drew back. She pouted.

"I'll keep close watch," he promised.

"It is also the first moon after Samhain," she said. "And an ancient prophecy brings a monster from the lake that will devour everything in the fortress, man and beast, unless a brave man can drive it away. My husband has always managed that, but," she hesitated, then suddenly kissed him full on the lips, "he's gone."

"I'll remember that," Cúchulainn said, and hastily left before she could throw her white arms around his neck. He stood alone in the dark, taking comfort in the stillness between the sounds of linnets and crickets and the hunting calls of the nighthawks and shrikes and the long *whoooos* from the owls circling on silent wings. "Nuttier than a three-balled ox," he muttered to himself, then stiffened as the soft pad of a footstep came to him. His hair tingled as he dropped to one knee, peering through the dark, searching for the stepper.

"Shit!" came a soft curse out of the darkness, followed by a cautious, "Shhhh! You know there're guards about!"

"Stubbed me toe! Damn!"

"Quiet!"

Cúchulainn smiled in the darkness and quietly drew *Cruaidin Cailidcheann* from its sheath. A soft, bluish glow came from its burnished blade and it began to vibrate in his hand. His senses suddenly sharpened, the seven pupils in his eyes enlarging, drinking in the light from the stars until an unearthly aura came from the objects. He looked to the south and saw men creeping quietly on the balls of their feet toward the fortress. A happy smile curved his lips. He took a firm grip on his *dubán,* drew a deep breath, let it out slowly, then cried:

"Who's there? Speak! Or I attack!"

"Discovery!" a loud voice bellowed.

"Attack and be damned!" another cried.

And Cúchulainn sprang at them, dancing on the balls of his feet, leaping like a salmon over their spears and javelins. He danced on the rims of their shields to strike down upon them, *Cruaidin Cailidcheann* singing happily as it crashed hard against shields, splitting bosses, cutting heads two at a time until, at last, all remained lifeless around him.

He drew a deep breath, feeling joy rush through his veins. Then he took their heads and placed them on his watch seat so that they formed a small pyramid of nine. He had barely returned to his watch when another nine leaped out of the darkness at him, and he cleaved their heads from their shoulders with ease and piled their heads against the others. Then yet another nine and a fourth nine came at him.

At last he stood alone in the darkness, blood steaming from the ground in a fog that rose to his knees. He felt sticky and smelled the brass of blood and fear in the darkness and nodded with tired satisfaction over what had happened in the night.

The hours drew on until false dawn appeared in the sky. Then Cúchulainn heard the lapping and surging of water in the lake behind the fortress, rising up as if it were a heavy sea. At first he thought not to look, then curiosity overcame him and he walked wide around the corner of the spinning fortress and came upon a dragon rising from the waves, its ugly yellow eyes glowing in the darkness, scales large and mossy green. A stench of rotting meat came toward him as it rose thirty cubits high over the lake, dreadful and decadent, depraved and damned.

"Stay!" Cúchulainn shouted sternly. "Back into your foul mere! Return to the blackness from whence you came!"

"My, my!" said the dragon, chuckling. *Hum! Hum!* "What have we here? A tadpole? And a toothpick?"

"I am Cúchulainn," the Hound said. "Surely you have heard about me."

"No. No. Can't say that I have. Is there some mystical implication for the giving of your name? Some power for calling on the secrets of the magic *Ogham?*"

"There are no secrets to the *Ogham,*" Cúchulainn said, stepping sideways to keep the dragon from edging to his right. "I can read them as well as you."

"Oh, educated! Well, what a delightful change of events, to meet an educated man instead of the buffoons usually left to guard this place. Tell me, did they name me for you?" the dragon asked.

"No. But why should they? Worms are worms, big or small!"

"Careful!" the dragon warned, its eyes closing to a glint. "You are close to insulting me. You don't want to do that, wee one! You look like," a chuckle rumbled again from its throat, "... like a . . . —*gasp*—puppy!" It chortled. *Haw! Haw! Haw!*

"Are you going to talk this to death, or are you going to do something?" Cúchulainn asked, yawning.

"Insolence!" the dragon shouted. It roared and leaped at the fortress, its mouth gaped so wide that one of the royal houses could have fit easily into its gullet, bright tongue flickering like darting dragonflies.

Cúchulainn suddenly remembered his coursing feat and, leaping high into the air, he circled the beast as fast as a winnowing sieve. Then he seized the dragon's neck with one hand and thrust the other down the dragon's gullet, seizing the beating heart. He ripped it from the dragon's breast and cast it on the ground. A great gout of blood burst from the dragon's mouth.

"I am killed!" it croaked, and toppled sideways to the ground, its claws digging ditches deep into the dank ground. Cúchulainn drew *Cruaidin Cailidcheann* again and diced the dragon into tiny pieces, then took the dragon's head and placed it with the rest of the night's trophies.

At last dawn broke over the horizon, and Cúchulainn, weary from his efforts, turned to look at the sea and his heart fell, wretched and broken, as he watched the giant step from the sea. The giant paused, shaking water drops from him like a flood. He glanced at the pile of heads and laughed harshly. *Har! Har! Har!*

"This has been a bad night for you, wee one!" he boomed.

"And for you, *bachlach!*" Cúchulainn snarled.

The giant glowered and heaved a javelin at him, but Cúchulainn danced on its point, avoiding it. The giant's thick eyebrows leaped up; then he shouted and threw three and four more javelins at Cúchulainn, but the Hound easily avoided them. The giant roared with anger and reached out his huge hand to seize Cúchulainn as he had Loegaire and Conall, but Cúchulainn performed his salmon leap and his coursing feat at the same time, drawing *Cruaidin Cailidcheann* as he hovered in the air, spinning like a mill wheel, above the giant's head.

"A boon!" the giant said quickly. "My life for yours?"

"A deal?" Cúchulainn asked. "Only if you grant my requests!"

"Name them!" the giant shouted. His eyes crossed as he tried to keep Cúchulainn in focus. He grew dizzy. "They're yours!"

"Grant me supremacy over Erin's warriors and the Champion's Portion without contest. And the right of my wife to enter the hall before all others in Ulster!"

"Granted!" cried the giant. "You have my word!"

"Others may contest it!"

"Then their challenge shall be mine!"

"Very well," Cúchulainn said, and he sheathed his sword, dropping lightly to the ground. As soon as his toes touched the sod, the giant vanished.

"Curiouser and curiouser," Cúchulainn said, scratching his head. His fingers touched the dried blood on his head and he grimaced, remembering the bath waiting for him inside the fortress. He looked at the fortress wall and thought about the leap that Loegaire and Conall had made over it. He fetched a tremendous leap and slammed against the side of the wall.

"Higher than I thought," he muttered, picking himself up off the ground. He tasted blood on his lips and wiped it free. Twice more he tried to leap the wall, and twice more he failed.

"What's this?" he scolded himself. "You have won the Champion's Portion and you can't even leap a piddling wall that your partners easily scaled? For shame!"

He sprang back from the wall the length of a spearcast and, dancing lightly forward to where he had been standing until his forehead touched the wall, he leaped straight up until he could see over the wall. Everyone was still asleep. His toes scrambled wildly for the edge of the wall, but he missed and fell back down into the thick grass at the foot of the wall, sinking into the ground up to his knees. So smooth was his fall, though, that not a single bead of dew was shaken from the grass.

A fury came over him and suddenly the "warp-spasm," the *riastradh*, came over him, and a tiny drop of blood appeared on each strand of hair, standing straight up from his crown. One eye squeezed shut and the other fell out along his cheek. His lips peeled back until his liver flapped in his gullet, and the warrior's shriek that came from his throat froze a deer solid in fear seven miles away. He leaped the wall, and so high was his jump that the sun rose before his toes touched the ground inside the fortress.

He drew a deep breath, calming the singing of his blood with an effort, then entered the royal house and heaved a great sigh that caused Bláthnait to exclaim, "Ah! Our warrior has had a great victory and triumph!"

And the others looked at her in amazement, for they did not know that the daughter of Inis Fer Falga knew the trials that Cúchulainn had endured during the night.

Soon, Cúchulainn had bathed and was resting in the warmth of the outside with his fellow warriors. He leaned against the fortress wall, blinking sleepily as he watched Cúroi ride toward them with the war gear of the nines killed by Cúchulainn. After taking the heads and placing them in the center of the house, he glanced at the three and said, "Well now! As my wife has told you, I know why you're here, and so I'll be telling you my decision."

"What's this?" Loegaire demanded. "No more mystical nonsense?"

Cúroi laughed, the sound rumbling like thunder in his deep chest. "No, no. No magic. The lad who collected these heads in one night is the one who is fit to guard a king's house. The Champion's Portion truly belongs to Cúchulainn, for I see that none of your sword marks," he added to Conall and Loegaire, "are on any of them. I grant Cúchulainn, the Hound of Ulster, the right to the Champion's Portion from now until eternity, for not one of you, nor any of the others in Erin, can meet him fairly in combat. I have spoken. This is my wish," he said sternly as Loegaire opened his mouth to object.

"Well, that's settled at last," Cúchulainn muttered. "Thank you."

"My pleasure," Cúroi said. And he gave Cúchulainn seven *cumals* of gold and silver as a mark of his good word for the deeds the Hound had done in the dark of the night where Loegaire and Conall had failed.

But when the three heroes returned to Emain Macha, Dubthach the Chafer tongued teased Loegaire and Conall, saying, "Well now! We will not be dividing the Champion's Portion tonight, I'm thinking, for you have all received judgment, I see, from the magic of Cúroi."

"Magic? Magic? Yes, yes! That's what it was! Magic!" Loegaire said loudly. He hawked and spat. "Who could claim anything because of that?"

He glowered at Cúchulainn, and the Hound threw his hands up in disgust and anger.

"That's it! Take the portion and award it to everyone here!" he said.

"No," Loegaire said. "I claim the—"

"Do not play word games with me, Loegaire," Cúchulainn said. A strange light passed over him in the flicker of an eyelash, but all there in the Red Branch saw it and a chill wind seemed to blow over them, freezing their hearts in their chests.

Cúchulainn stormed from the feasting-hall and climbed into his chariot. Laeg lifted the reins, and Black and Gray leaped forward, galloping wildly from Emain Macha.

"Now where," Conall asked, "do you suppose he's going?"

"To ride the border and cleanse himself with honest deeds, for a change," Seancha said, disgusted.

"And the Champion's Portion? What about that?" Conall asked.

"We shall wait on it," Conchobor said, glancing at Seancha, who nodded his agreement. "I have a strange feeling that this hasn't been settled yet. Not by a long sling's throw. And until it is," he added firmly, "each of you will patrol a section of our borders. Perhaps that way, we shall have some peace around here instead of being forced to listen to each of you yammer about how you are worthy of the Champion's Portion. Wasn't for tradition and the ways, why, I'd have it diced up and given to all. Conall, you take the south; Loegaire, you the north."

"The north!" Loegaire exclaimed. "Ain't nothing up there but cold winds blowing off the sea. A man can freeze his balls up there!"

"Enough!" Conchobor roared. The hall lapsed into an uneasy silence, remembering well when Conchobor fell into a rage once before and ten men had died. "I have spoken!"

Wisely, Loegaire held his tongue, grabbing a flagon of wine and draining it as he sat in disgust at the end of the feasting-hall. Conall shook his head and rolled his eyes to the heavens, then took a long drink of his tankard.

So the warriors of the Red Branch sat down to an uneasy meal, remembering the feast at Bricriu's house, and the sly words that had brought dissension to the peace and harmony that had been the Red Branch.

Chapter 12

THE *BACHLACH'S* DECISION

WHILE CÚCHULAINN, CONALL, and Loegaire were patrolling the borders, the Ulster warriors spent their idle time on the sporting field playing hurling, while Conchobor and Fergus Mac Roích played *fidchell* while lolling under a linden tree at the far end of the playing field.

One hot day, Conchobor and Fergus Mac Roích, with Ulster's nobles as well, left the sporting field and entered the Red Branch Quarters for a cooling drink before supper. As eventide came and they seated themselves for the drawing of the close, a huge, rude-looking man, as ugly as sin, approached them. He seemed twice their height and wore an old cowhide with a dark dun mantle wrapped around him. Over his shoulder he carried a great club, the head the size of a winter shed that could house thirty bulls. Mad yellow eyes protruded from his head, each eye the size of an ox-cart wheel, and each of his fingers was easily the size of another's wrist. In his left hand he carried a stock that would be a burden for twenty yoke of oxen, while in his right hand he bore an ax with the head weighing enough to form one hundred fifty glowing masses of metal with which to forge single ax heads, and the edge sharp enough to shave hairs if the wind blew them against it. A yoke of six hitched to a plow would be needed to move the ax handle.

Without speaking, he came into the room and moved to the fork-beam beside the fire to warm himself, blocking the heat with his bulk. At first no one spoke; then Dubthach the Sharp-Tongued recovered his boldness and said:

"Isn't there enough room in the hall for you? Or do you stand beside the fork-beam because you wish to be our servant? I expect a blaze will come to the house more upon its own legs than will you bring brightness to the household with your mug and manners."

The stranger waited for the nervous giggles to subside before speaking. His voice rumbled out like thunder rolling over the hills.

"Well now! Aren't you the brave one to be flapping your lips like the flatulating cheeks of your ass! What property I have is my own—no man calls me servant. Hear that, dunderhead? Soon you will all agree that despite my size, the household will indeed be enlightened by my presence and—" he paused to shrug, his yellow eyes roaming about the room, considering "—the hall unburnt."

Dubthach tried to answer, but the stranger made an abrupt motion with his hand, continuing:

"Be quiet, little puppy! I have other plans in mind, a challenge to put before you. But before I give it to you, know this well: in no place, not in Erin, Alba, Europe, Africa, Asia—including Greece, but you know how those Greeks are: all hemming and hawing here and there about the place, contemplating the meanings of atoms in the universe, senseless fools!—Scythia, the Isles of Gades, the Pillars of Hercules, or Bregon's Tower—that which we now call Brigantium, a high-sounding name for a jumble of rocks, I say—have I found one to stand fairly with me. Now, I have heard," and his lips curled in a sneer, "of how you Ulster warriors are supposed to be stronger, more powerful, and braver than any others, and of how your values of truth, generosity, and worth far exceed all others, for your dignity and honor will not let you be lesser than another. So I have come to you with my challenge. Select one among you to play a little game with me that I have devised to pass the time." He twirled the ax in his fingers like straw.

Fergus Mac Roích heard these words and threw his head back to gaze in scorn at the intruder, saying:

"This challenge you speak of, long-winded stranger, is not one that just affects the honor of one man if he should fail to answer you, but affects as well the honor of all Emain Macha. And should he not uphold the honor to which he is sworn, why then, death will be no stranger to him. I don't shun death, mind you, but I would have your challenge known. If I deem the challenge to be fair play, why, I am your man!" He lifted a huge haunch and trumpeted a fart loudly to show his disdain.

"I, too, am your man if you but promise fair play," said Ailill's son Seancha quickly so that he would not seem to be less a warrior than Fergus. "No Red Branch warrior would give his word, then break the covenant with an unknown person. Even with a churl like you. Any here will answer your challenge if you make it known!"

"Brave words, little puppy!" He laughed, the sound booming in the hall. "Well, let's see now." He glowered around the room. "I exclude Conchobor from this," the man said arrogantly. "His sovereign reign excuses him, and likewise Fergus Mac Roích—for he, too, has worn the crown in the past—although I wouldn't mind testing the mettle of someone who claims seven women a night with a winkle for a goad. But for the rest of you, all of you who dare to take part in this venture, come forward and let me cut off your head. Tomorrow night, you may give me a like stroke in return. Come now! Where's the vaunted daring of the Red Branch darlings?"

"What nonsense!" said Dubthach with scorn. "Do you take us for fools? There is no warrior here to challenge that except these two, who are protected by their throne."

"By Gods' balls! Here's one," said Munremur, the Fat-Neck, son of Short-Head. He leaped angrily out into the center of the hall to face the stranger. Munremur had the strength of a hundred warriors, and each arm held the strength of a hundred centaurs. He stretched his arms and curled his hands into threatening fists. The *bachlach* watched him, a faint smile upon his lips.

"Kneel, clodhopper," Munremur said insultingly. "I'll cut off your head tonight, and tomorrow you may give me a like stroke in return."

"I can get that arrangement anywhere," the man said. He laughed derisively. "I came here expecting the Red Branch knights to be different from the others," he taunted. "Come now! You should accept my challenge as I put it to you: let me cut off your head tonight and you to return the stroke in kind tomorrow night."

"What sort of challenge is this to make?" scoffed Dubthach of the Sharp Tongue. "You accuse us of trying to avoid death like beardless youths, but apparently you have no desire for the idea yourself. You have the brains of a rock if you think that the man killed tonight will return to kill you in turn tomorrow night. If you have such power to be killed every night and avenge it the next day, why then, prove it! Give one of us the first stroke."

"So this is to be the way of it, is it?" the other said. He laughed loud and long in the Great Hall. "Then," he said merrily, "let us proceed, if say all of you. That is, if your bowels haven't turned to jelly."

He then made the others promise that if he allowed them to sever his head tonight, they would allow him to return on the morrow and deliver a return stroke to them. All agreed to these conditions, and Munremur took the ax from the *bachlach*'s hand. Its two edges were a clean seven feet apart. The *bachlach* laughed again and put his head across a block brought forth for that purpose. Munremur spat into his hands and raised the huge ax, delivering a blow across the man's neck, severing his head, the ax head ringing as it stuck in the block beneath. The man's head bounced like a hurley-ball until it lay next to the fork-beam base, while blood fountained from the neck stump, washing the Great Hall with its crimson flood.

The *bachlach* rose, picked up his head, gathered his ax, and left the Great Hall, blood coursing down behind him, filling the Red Branch on every side. The knights lifted their feet against the wash of his blood and watched his departure with loathing, wondering at the trickery that had just been witnessed by all.

"By the gods," said Dubthach of the Sharp Tongue. "If that man returns tomorrow following such a stroke, there will be none left alive in Ulster after playing his game. There's something fishy here. And I'm not smelling smoked salmon, either!"

The *bachlach* returned the next night, however, and claimed the right of his return blow to Munremur, but the warrior blanched at the prospect of honoring the covenant that he had made with the man, knowing that he had no magic to help him regain his head once it was severed from his body. He hid in the washhouse behind a tub, waiting for the churl to leave.

"What honor is there in this?" the *bachlach* scoffed. "This man owes me a return stroke and refuses to let me deliver it. Well then, so let it be. I have heard a lot about three of the Red Branch who claim the Champion's Portion from Conchobor's meat. Bring them on! Let one of them—or all three, for that matter—stand in this coward's place and fulfill the covenant that all made in this very room last night. Where is Loegaire the Triumphant?"

"I am here," said Loegaire, he and Conall having returned the day before from patrolling the border. Loegaire was stung that he would be singled out from all the other warriors present. He swaggered forward, held his nose delicately between thumb and forefinger and blew snot onto the ground. He snarkled and hawked and spat a gob near the *bachlach*'s shoe. "And I will have a chance with you."

"Feeling your oats, are you? Very well. Have at it! Need any help in lifting the ax?" he asked, laughing at the flush of red in Loegaire's face. Again, the *bachlach* bared his neck, and again his head was struck from his shoulders, but when he returned the next night, Loegaire, too, refused to honor the covenant made, disguising himself in women's clothes and swathing his face to the eyebrows in veils.

This time, when the *bachlach* sneered and ridiculed them, Conall Cernach growled, "All right, pig-face! You want to play blades, why, I'll cross with you."

"Ah, but will you keep your word better than that wee one who came before you? The one with the blow of a gnat in his fist?"

Conall seized the ax from the *bachlach*—nearly staggering when the weight of it struck his arms—and said, "Stretch out that neck and let's see if you can pick up that ugly mug after I've bounced it from the walls a time or two!"

The *bachlach* stretched out his neck upon the block and laughed as Conall raised the ax high and brought it down. The *bachlach*'s head bounced from his shoulders and Conall swung again, driving it into the walls, *wham!* Then again, *wham!*

"That'll give us some peace around here, I'm thinking," Conall growled. His face and clothes were matted from the *bachlach*'s blood, and steam rose from the floor where the blood had flooded it to a hand's depth.

He watched in amazement as the *bachlach* stood and fumbled around until he found his head and tucked it under his arm. One eye closed in an obscene wink and the mouth opened, saying, "Tomorrow, brave one, I'll return for my turn with the ax. If, that is, you're still humping around the hall, pretending to be brave."

"I'll be here," Conall shouted. "Come when you wish. I'll be here."

The next evening, the lookout shouted that the *bachlach* was nearing Emain Macha's gate, and suddenly Conall's courage leaked out the soles of his sandals and he ran and hid in the dung-pile behind the stables waiting until the *bachlach* left.

The *bachlach* strode into the hall, demanding Conall to come forth, but no one gave the lie to him as to where Conall had gone. The *bachlach* grinned at Conchobor and said, "Brave warriors you have here! I should wonder that you can find enough to patrol your borders, what with their knitting and needling."

"Shit," Fergus spat. He stepped from his couch, hitching up

his belt over his bulk. "Gimme that blade and let's cut the foxes and hounds! I'm for you!"

But the *bachlach* shook his head. "No, you are exempted from the game as due your right, for no one can put the coward's mark on you. Or on you, Conchobor. But I would think you would do better to have some men here instead of surrounding yourselves with weak-hearted curs. Ah, well. Not one ounce of courage among you, eh? Very well. I'll give you a chance to find some courage. Maybe with some of that honeyed wine you brag about, Conchobor! Enough false courage may give a bit of false backbone to one of your warriors!"

He laughed and swaggered from the hall, whistling a merry tune as he strode through the gates, twirling the ax in one hand. He came again on the fourth night to deliver his challenge to the Red Branch, his voice furious and loud and taunting with its challenge.

The next day, Cúchulainn returned and heard the story about the *bachlach* and of how Loegaire and Conall had started the game but gave up the pips and hid when it came time to pay the penalty. He shook his head as he moved toward the washhouse to clean himself from patrolling along Ulster's western border.

"Now, you're not going to be foolish enough to play at that game, are you?" Laeg demanded.

"I haven't been asked to," Cúchulainn said quietly.

"You will be, I'm thinking," Laeg said sourly. "Seems to me that this is one of them tricks of that bitch Maeve. Biggest mistake Conchobor did was listening to that damned Druid and take all this squabble and lay it in the lap of Ailill and his whore. Damned inconsiderate, you ask me."

"Nobody asked you," Cúchulainn said.

"That's true," Laeg admitted, but came back with, "and rightfully so. They might be hearing a bit of the truth and all had they. Why, you have twice the heads of Conall, three times the heads of Loegaire, hanging in the hall. That alone should count for something."

"Should," Cúchulainn said.

"Ah," Laeg spat in disgust. "You'd talk the leg off a bard. I need a drink!"

That night, all the women came to watch and giggled among themselves as the stranger toyed with the stalwart Red Branch knights, whose loud boasts had rung from the rafters in the past. Cúchulainn sat and listened quietly to the *bachlach* as he denounced the body present.

"What sort of men are you?" he demanded, swaggering among them. None dared to meet his stare. "There is no valor or honor here. The mighty Red Branch!" He spat in disgust. "Your powers are gone. All of you greatly covet the Champion's Portion, yet none dare to contest it. Where is this poor mad wight you call Cúchulainn, whose fame is spread across the land? I wonder if his word is better than any of yours."

"I have no wish to play this game with you," Cúchulainn said quietly. The *bachlach* whirled to face him. "There is no sense to it. You are likely to flee if I give you the stroke you wish, for if I deliver the stroke, you will die."

His words had the ring of truth to them, and those in the hall held their breath as the *bachlach* stared at Cúchulainn for a long moment. Fergus finally broke the silence, saying, "Be careful of that one, churl! There's a bit of the magic about him, as anyone knows who has seen him work his way among the armies of our enemies. No minion, there!"

The man silently held out the ax to him. Cúchulainn leaped lightly to the center of the floor and took the ax from the man's fingers and dealt him a blow, hurling his head to the top rafter of the feasting-hall of the Red Branch. Such was Cúchulainn's strength that when the head struck the rafter, the entire hall shuddered from the power of the blow, and the head fell to the floor, bounced once, then rested at Cúchulainn's feet. The young warrior delivered another blow to it, smashing it. Then the *bachlach* rose, gathered his head and ax, and quietly departed.

The next night, all the Ulster warriors gathered early to see if Cúchulainn would deny the *bachlach* as the others had before him. Cúchulainn waited silently in his place beside the knee of

Conchobor, his face a stern mask. A great blackness descended upon him. The others whispered among themselves, debating whether to sing his death-song, for they could see from the black cloud settling over Cúchulainn's brow that he intended to give the stranger the right of a return blow as he had promised. At last Cúchulainn sighed and said to Conchobor:

"None of you will leave until after the stroke I owe is delivered. I do not fear death, only death with dishonor."

They watched as twilight filled the feasting-hall. Suddenly the doorway darkened and the stranger approached.

"Well? Where is Cúchulainn, the Boy-Warrior?" he growled, his yellow eyes raking the knights, who looked away from his glare.

"I am here," Cúchulainn said coolly, stepping forward to face the *bachlach*.

The man laughed and twirled the mighty ax in his fingers until it whirred and sang.

"You appear to be a bit slow with your words tonight," he sneered. "What's the matter? Milk in your spine, now? It is obvious that you are afraid to die. Yet—" he said slowly, his eye holding the level stare from Cúchulainn's eyes "—no, I could be wrong. You seem quite ready to honor your pledge to me as well."

Cúchulainn remained silent and stretched out his neck upon the block. So huge was the block that his neck but reached halfway across. The stranger laughed and sneered at the warrior.

"Come now, wretch!" said the stranger. "Stretch your neck out full."

"Do not torment me with your sneers!" Cúchulainn said angrily. "Shut your gob and take your stroke quickly, as I gave you yours last night. I didn't play gadabout with you, did I? I didn't torment you with worthless words."

"I cannot slay you," said the stranger, "as the block is much larger than your neck. There is not enough room for the ax to fall."

With that, Cúchulainn strained and stretched out his neck until a warrior's full-grown foot would have fit easily between two of his ribs. His neck finally reached the other side of the block, and the *bachlach* raised his ax until the head touched the roof-tree of the hall above him. With all his might, he brought down the ax with a crash as loud as a wood tempest-tossed in a night of violent fury. Down fell the ax head onto Cúchulainn's neck, its blunt side below, while all the nobles of Ulster watched amazed as the blade bounced back up from the muscles in Cúchulainn's neck.

"Rise, Cúchulainn, brave warrior!" said the stranger. "Of all the warriors in Ulster and Erin, no one can be found to compare with you in valor, bravery, and honor. From this hour forward, the Champion's Portion will not be denied you by any, and your woman will always be the leader of the Ulster ladies into the feasting-hall. And whoever will challenge your right from this moment on will forfeit his life. This I swear upon my ancestors' bones." He glared around the hall. "And," he added, "since all here have seen the truth of the comings and goings the past few days, why, no one can give you the lie as to what happened. I do not see them, but Conall and Loegaire, take heed! None of your word trickery can take away this man's right this time! Leave your false words to the linnets and crickets!"

Then he told of the deceitfulness of Conall and Loegaire, who had agreed that Cúchulainn was not to receive the Champion's Portion, even after Cúchulainn had fairly won it during a similar wager with Terror, the son of Great Fear, who had challenged the three to the beheading game a month past. And when Conall and Loegaire had denied Cúchulainn's victory in that game, the judgment had passed to him to settle it. Conall and Loegaire, who had by this time returned to the feasting-hall, were shamed by this revelation of their connivance and were sent to sit at the end of the table, where the youngest knights, who had to be tried, waited for their moment in glory.

The *bachlach* vanished suddenly from the hall, leaving a slight wisp of fog behind. Later, it was learned that he was none other than Cúroi Mac Dairi, who had come in disguise to fulfill the promise he had early given to Cúchulainn that he would be the bravest of men and all would know him for that bravery.

And so the end finally came to Bricriu's feast.

Glossary of Terms

Ailill: king of Connacht whose wealth was enormous. His wife, Maeve, refused to believe that a man had more wealth than she, and because of the differences in their wealth, the famous war for the Brown Bull of Cooley occurred.

An tsleg boi ac Lugh: Lugh's spear of light.

Anu: identified also as Danu. Two mountaintops near Killarney in Co. Kerry are called *Dá Chich nAnann,* literally "the Two Paps of Anu." She is seen as the Mother Goddess.

Aodh: Goddess of Fire.

Aove (also Aodh in some texts): a poet who has an affair with Mugain, wife of Conchobor. Angered at this, Conchobor decrees his death and Aove asks that he be drowned. Conchobor agrees, but every lake that the poet is taken to, he manages to cast a spell over, which causes it to dry up. At last he is taken to Lake Loí, which is owned by Loegaire Búadbach and cannot be affected by the poet's song. But he is saved when Loegaire, mortally wounded when he bangs his head against a lintel and knocks his brains out, manages to slay Aove's thirty guards before he dies and the poet goes free.

Badb: identified as the most terrible of the battle goddesses; a part of the Mórrígná, a triple goddess of whom the other two are Macha and Mórrígan. She is also known as Badb Catha, or "battle raven," and although both sinister and sexual, she is usually identified with prophecies concerning the end of the world and chaos.

Badb Catha: See above.

banhsídhe (*banshee, bannshee,* or *bean sídhe*): female spirits who cry when death is imminent.

bards: from *aes dána*, or "Men of Art."

ben urnadna: a contracted wife whose tenure is short, usually for one year.

Black of Saingliu: one of Cúchulainn's horses, born, according to some legends, at the same time as he. Along with the Gray of Macha, the Black came out of a lake to test Cúchulainn's worthiness. Cúchulainn rode the mount all over Ireland in one day as it tried to dislodge him. After failing, it accepted him as its master. Together with the Gray, the Black became yet another weapon for Cúchulainn. Their birth and appearance from the lake suggest magic and are part of the mysticism of the epic.

Bláthnait: daughter of Mend, the wife of Cúroí.

bodhrán: a leather drum beaten by the hand that gives forth a booming sound almost like thunder.

bonánach: goblins; demons of the air.

Breas: God of Agriculture.

Brehon: a judge among the Druids; one who interprets the law.

Bricriu: called "the Bitter-Tongue," or "the Poison-Tongued One." He is one of the Ulster Exiles and has a castigating manner of speech. Filled with bitterness toward the world, he throws a magnificent feast *(Fled Bricrend)* in a story before the *Táin*, found in *Lebor na hUidre (Book of the Dun Cow)*, in which he challenges three warriors—Loegaire Búadach, Conall Cernach, and Cúchulainn—to prove their right to the Champion's Portion of the feast. He is compared to the Greek satirist Thersites, and Lókí, the mischief-maker in the *Eddas*. He is associated with Lough Brickland, Co. Down, near which was his palace of Dún Rudraige.

buanbach: a game like draughts or checkers.

Budi Mac m-Bain: the Yellow son of Fair. He is a traditional settler of quarrels, although his judgment is sometimes fatal. *Bain*: dig out; extract; reap. This suggests that he is the one to discover the truth.

caílleach: an old hag, but also a shape-shifter to a young woman.

The place of the old hag in Irish literature is usually connected to magic.

caiseal: a stone wall around a fort.

Carbad Seardha: Cúchulainn's scythed chariot, bristling with knives attached to the wheels, which become weapons themselves when Cúchulainn charges through the Connacht men, scything them down like wheat.

cathair: a group of buildings surrounded by a high stone wall.

Cathbad the Druid: a Druid at the court of Conchobor Mac Nessa and, according to some accounts, the father of Conchobor. He was the most powerful of Druids.

Coirpre: several individuals, among whom is the father of Eric, Conchobor's grandson through his daughter Fedelm. Conchobor and Coirpre are sworn enemies. Cúchulainn kills Coirpre in *Cath Ruis na Ríg*, or "The Battle of Ros na Ríg," which is the story of Ulster's war after the raid for the Brown Bull.

Conall Cernach: one of the major heroes of the Red Branch. His name "Conall" derives from *cuno-valos*, which roughly translates to "strong like a wolf." Although he appears among Maeve's soldiers in *Táin Bó Cuailnge* in the early part of the epic, this appears to be an error, as he is a stalwart fighter for Conchobor in the latter part. Some critics have suggested that he was part of the Exiles, only to renounce them after Maeve broke her word and the pact involving the Connachtmen and single combat with Cúchulainn and returned to the Red Branch. His name is associated with many legends, including one in which he joined the Roman army and was present at Christ's crucifixion. He revenges Cúchulainn's death, caused by trickery, by trailing the murderers and disposing them one by one, until finally he meets Lugaid Mac Con Roi in a classic combat by a ford.

Conchobor Mac Nessa: king of Ulster in the first century B.C. His palace at Emain Macha is now known as Navan Fort, located west of the city of Armagh. He became king after his mother Ness agreed to live with Fergus Mac Róich, then king of

Emain Macha, for a year on condition that Conchobor be allowed to rule during that time. She deceived Fergus, however, by giving away riches to the knights of the Red Branch so that when it became time for Conchobor to return the throne to Fergus, the knights voted to keep him as king. His father is alleged to have been Cathbad, and although he is generally seen as a wise king, it is his vanity that ultimately brings about the "pangs of the Ulstermen" and leaves them helpless when the Connacht army invades their borders. This came about when he refused to be swayed by Macha's plea that she not be forced to race his horses since she was pregnant. Although she defeated Conchobor's team in a footrace, the exertion brought about the birth of twins, and her death after she cursed the Red Branch. During times of severe crisis, the Ulstermen and all of their generations would suffer her identical pains for five days and four nights.

Conlaí's Well: where the Nuts of Knowledge grow. They are described as a rich crimson in color and appear to be hazelnuts, since the hazel wand is associated with knowledge and magic. Nine hazel trees of wisdom grew over the well and the nuts dropped into the water, causing bubbles to appear. A person with the "sight" could look into the bubbles and successfully predict the future. The location of the well is sometimes given as the source of the Boyne or Shannon rivers. One of the more famous stories connected with the well concerns the Well of Segais, which chased the goddess Boann to form the river named after her. She took the salmon Fintan with her. The salmon had eaten of the Nuts of Knowledge so that when the Druid Finegas caught it and gave it to Finn Mac Cumhail to cook, the salmon's fin stabbed Finn in the thumb. When Finn sucked at the spot, he gained knowledge. Although this story appears in the Fenian Cycle, several stories of the Nuts of Knowledge undoubtedly appeared during the Ulster Cycle.

Connacht: one of the four historic provinces of Ireland in the Ulster Cycle, it still exists to this day. The other three provinces were Leinster, Munster, and Ulster. But the word for a province had become *cóiceda*, or "a fifth," and a fifth province was soon established during the reign of the High-King Tuathal Teachtmhair (the Acceptable) in A.D. 130–160 and called "Meath." This became a province that was solely the territory of the ancient high-kings, and so the political center of Ireland. According to the *Book of Invasions*, the Fir Bolg, the first invaders to establish social and political order in the land, also established five provinces, Munster actually being two provinces under the same name. The idea of a powerful Connacht invading helpless Ulster became a symbol during Ireland's fight for independence from England.

Crom Deroil: Maeve's Druid.

Cruachain: the "Place of Enchantment," where Maeve and Ailill had their home. Maeve, one of the most sensuous and sexual figures in literature—called "Maeve of the Thirty Men" in some stories for her nymphomaniacal need of thirty men a night to sate her sexual urgencies—took great pains to make her palace here an enchanted place where songs could be sung, stories told, the arts pursued. It was a soothing place where the pleasures of the flesh and spirit took precedence over war. It is situated over an area of about ten square miles near Tulsk, Co. Roscommon. Interestingly, it is here that the legendary cave to the Otherworld is found. In Christian lore, this place is known as the Hell's Gate of Ireland.

Cruachan Aí: See CRUACHAIN above.

Cruaidin Cailidcheann: Cúchulainn's sword.

cruitire: a harpist.

Crunniuc Mac Agnomain: the lonely farmer visited by the lovely Macha. He made her pregnant, then bragged that she was swifter of foot than Conchobor's horses, thus bringing about the Curse of Ulster.

Cúroi: king of Munster whose fortress is associated with Caher Conree, Co. Kerry. He appears as a *bachlach* (churl) in *Fled Bricrend*. Apparently he is a magical figure, a shape-shifter, often called upon to arbitrate arguments. He is a reluctant participant in the *Táin* (the Cattle-raid of Cooley) for the Connacht forces, which leads some to suggest that he is taking part in the raid only through a truce or treaty with Connacht.

Cúchulainn: the Boy-Warrior whose parentage is shrouded in mystery, thus giving him powers far beyond those of ordinary mortal men or heroes. His lone stand and guerrilla warfare against the invading Connacht forces became symbols for Irishmen fighting for Ireland's independence from England.

Cuillius: Ailill's charioteer, who steals Fergus's sword while the latter is making love to Maeve. Later, he is killed by Cúchulainn. His reappearance in the final battle can be seen as an example of the mysticism of the epic. Some, however, suggest that it is his son who appears in the final battle and not Cuillius.

Culann: the blacksmith, or wheelwright, whose hound is killed by Cúchulainn. Cúchulainn, then the boy Sétanta, volunteers to serve as Culann's hound until he can train another to take the hound's place. Culann had bitterly lamented the loss of his hound, which had served as a guard to his property. Culann is the smith who forged Conchobor's weapons; consequently, it was extremely important that Conchobor attend a feast that Culann held for him. On an impulse, Conchobor invited the boy Sétanta to come with him, but the boy wished to finish his game of hurling before he left. He promised to follow Conchobor as soon as he finished. When Conchobor arrived at the house of Culann, he had forgotten about the boy. Culann unleashed his mighty hound outside the gates to his house to guard them while his guests feasted. When the hound attacked Sétanta, the youth killed it by driving his hurling ball down the animal's throat and out its anus, then grabbing the dog and smashing it against the pillar of the house. Cathbad gave Sétanta the name of "Cúchulainn" after that, the Hound of Culann, the Hound of Ulster. Culann is also thought to be Manannán Mac Lir, the God of the Sea, in human form, and is referred to as an Otherworld smith dwelling in the *Sídhe* of Slievegallion.

cumal: a woman slave.

curaid: a group of faithful followers, similar to the "comitatus" of *Beowulf.*

Cúscraid Menn Macha: the One Who Stammers, a son of Conchobor and pupil of Conall Cernach. He possesses a magnificent spear, with ferrules of silver that of their own accord whirl around bands of gold on the spear to warn of coming conflict.

Dagda: the chief of the Gaelic pantheon of gods, the equivalent of Zeus, Jupiter, and Odin. He is considered to be the "Father of All" and the "Father of Perfect Knowledge." He led the *Tuatha Dé Danann* into Ireland against the Fir Bolg. He is considered to be the "good god," but not so much in the sense of virtue as that he is good in all things.

Dáire Mac Fiachna: the owner of the cow that gives birth to the Brown Bull.

Dallán Forgaill: "blind man of eloquence," a sobriquet reminiscent of Homer. He was a sixth-century poet who, on his death bed, pronounced Seanchán, the man who rediscovered the *Táin,* as chief poet of Ireland.

Deichtine: Conchobor's sister and mother of Cúchulainn. Supposedly, she was abducted by, or went with, the Sun God, Lugh, who became Cúchulainn's father. Other accounts give Cúchulainn's father as Sualdam, and yet others as Conchobor. In the latter instance, however, that would have been a *geis,* a ban, of the worst sort, so little value is given to Conchobor as being the father of his own nephew.

del chliss: literally "the dart of feats," a javelin of extraordinary powers but not quite as powerful as the *gae bulga.*

Donn: the Black God of Death.

Druids: an ancient caste whose origins and functions are debatable but generally assumed to be of the learned caste, or priestly profession, in Irish culture. The proper name "Druid" is probably derived from "druid," which means "very knowledgeable." References are found in the writings of Julius Caesar. They are said to have traced their origin to Japhet, son of Noah, and took their philosophy from Pythagoras. They were at the center of society and made decisions on matters of tradition, custom, and law, in addition to interpreting the portents that came by day, week, month, and year. According to classical writers, they also taught the doctrine of the transmigration of the soul.

dubán: Cúchulainn's shield, which is described as being crimson-red with knobs and bands of silver, but turning black when in battle, thus to terrify the enemy. This example of "shield-changing" is very similar to Achilles' shield in the *Iliad*.

Dubthach: the Chafer of Ulster, the Beetle of Ulster, the Black-Tongued, all epic similes that describe Dubthach Daol Uladh, a member of the Ulster Exiles. He joined Fergus in sacking the Red Branch, but he was particularly ruthless in that he killed several women in the foray. In retaliation, all of his family were put to death and he became forever a sworn enemy against Ulster. He is portrayed as having rough, jet-black hair, a bloody eye, and the head of a ravenous wolf on each shoulder of his armor. He possessed the great spear *Cealtchair*, which he bathed in a vat of dark blood. His name and appearance sparked horror in Ulstermen. According to legend, his speech was so bitter that his tongue grew black in his head.

Emain Macha: the seat of the Red Branch; Ulster. The name meant the "twins of Macha." (See CONCHOBOR.)

Fann: sometimes "Fand," an Otherworld lady with whom Cúchulainn falls in love; the wife of Manannán, the Sea God. Fann appears to Cúchulainn because she has fallen in love with him, and she weaves a magical spell around him. He lives with her for a month before Manannán breaks up the relationship by appearing to her in a "magic mist." When she saw him, she said:

"When Manannán the Great married me,
A worthy wife for the God of the Sea,

He gave me a wristlet of doubly pressed gold
For my blushes to him that I sold."

When Manannán took her away, he shook his cloak between
her and Cúchulainn so that they would not fall in love again.

fé: aspen rod used for measuring corpses and graves. *Ogham* in-
scriptions were inscribed upon it to protect the man doing
the measuring. It was regarded with horror and no one
would touch it except the one who was to measure the corpse
and the grave.

Fedelm Noichride: a daughter of Conchobor. In *Fled Bricrend*, she
is the wife of Loegaire.

Fergus Mac Róich: a mythical king and *seneschal*. Fearghus (viril-
ity) and Ró-ech (great stallion) give him his name, for he was
known to have genitals five times the size of ordinary men.
According to legend, seven women were needed each night
to satisfy him until he met Nessa, Conchobor's mother, who
was so experienced in love that she alone could sate his lust.
But her price for sharing his bed was for him to appoint her
son Conchobor king for a year so that he would have royalty
behind his name. Fergus, weary of the demands of kingship
and curious about Nessa's bed prowess, agreed, but at the
end of a year, Conchobor had proven to be such a good king
that Fergus was unable to return to the throne. He then
became *seneschal*. Later, after Conchobor breaks his promise
to Deirdre and Niasi, Fergus leads part of the Red Branch
away from Ulster to Connacht and the court of Ailill, where
Maeve, whose lust needed thirty men a night to satisfy, found
a willing stallion in Fergus, who became the head of the
army on the *Taín*. He is seen not only as a mighty warrior,
but as an object of humor as well after his sword is stolen
while he is dallying with Maeve. (See CONCHOBOR.)

Finnabair: literally "fair eyebrows," the daughter of Ailill and
Maeve; she is like her mother in all things sensual. A figure
of great beauty, she is used as the reward for anyone who
can kill Cúchulainn.

Fir Bolg: sometimes Firbolg. (See CONNACHT.)

Fomorians: lords of darkness and death.

gae bulga: Cuchulainn's spear, which supposedly derives its name from Ailill Érann, also called Bolga. It appears to be a weapon not unlike a harpoon but with magical qualities in that once thrown, it will unerringly find its mark no matter how its victim tries to dodge and turn. It has been translated as a "forked spear" and a "two-fold spear" and "the spear of the goddess Bolg," meaning associated somehow with the Fir Bolg.

geis: a Druidic curse capable of forcing someone to either perform or stop performing an act for the rest of his or her life. The two most famous *geisa* were those that forbade Cúchulainn to eat dog meat, and the *geis* that forbade Fergus Mac Róich to refuse a feast or a drink. It is Fergus's *geis* that brings about the disaster on Deirdre and the sons of Uisliu.

Gray of Macha: one of Cúchulainn's magical horses. (See BLACK OF SAINGLIU.)

head-hunting (*ceanntóir*): The Celts believed that the heads they collected from their enemies were more than simply war trophies; they believed that the head was the dwelling place of the soul and the very center of a person's being. It symbolized divinity itself. By displaying and worshiping the heads of their enemies, they believed that they were gaining protection from the magical powers that could be released once the person was dead. Heads were thought to keep evil at bay and to talk, sing, or prophesy. In later years, the turnip lantern of Halloween (See SAMHAIN) became a substitute for a head. In the United States, pumpkins took the place of turnips. An example of a head prophesying is seen in the *Táin* when Sualdam tries to rally the Red Branch knights to come to the aid of Cúchulainn. The knights, however, are too weak with their "pangs" to respond. Sualdam turns away in anger and tries to spur his horse back to help Cúchulainn. Startled, the horse rears and knocks Sualdam's shield against his neck. The sharp edge of the shield severs his head and it falls upon his shield, which is carried into the Red Branch, where it speaks, saying: "Beware, men of Emain Macha! Beware Ailill and the Connacht army!" The curse is broken and the Ulstermen remember themselves as they were— mighty warriors—and speed to the aid of Cúchulainn.

Ibar: Conchobor's charioteer, who drives Cúchulainn on his first series of adventures as a young boy.

imbas forasnai: the gift of prophesy.

In Caladbolg: Fergus's sword, whose stroke is "like lightning and as mighty as a rainbow."

Laeg Ríangabra: Cúchulainn's charioteer, the only one outside of Cúchulainn who can handle his horses.

Lia Faíl: stone with magic properties. Brought to Ireland from Greece by the Thatha.

Loegaire Búadbach: a warrior in the Ulster Cycle who challenges Cúchulainn for the Champion's Portion in *Fled Bricrend*. His father is identified as Connave Buídhe. He is usually seen as a brave enough warrior if a bit pompous, with a high opinion of himself. He fails in all the tests put to him in *Fled Bricrend* and insists that all except the last of the tests were unfair. He appears also in an eleventh-century text wherein he owns the only lake (*Loch Laí*) in which the poet, Aove, can be drowned in accordance with Conchobor's decree after Aove was caught making love with Mugain, Conchobor's wife. Angry that his lake is to be defiled by the drowning of a poet, Loegaire rushes from the house with sword in hand. But he strikes his head against the lintel and his brains are spattered all over his clothes and cloak. Mortally wounded, he still manages to kill the thirty men who have brought the poet to be drowned and the poet goes free.

Lugh: the Sun God, the Otherworldly father of Cúchulainn.

Macha: one of the three warrior goddesses, along with Badb and Mórrígan, but more closely associated with fertility than the other two. It is she who pronounces the Ulster Curse. (See CONCHOBOR.)

Maeve: the wife of Ailill, often called "Queen of Connacht," al-

though the Celtic tribes during this time did not recognize
queens. She is associated with promiscuity and sexuality,
along with abstinance and cruelty. Many epic similes are attached to her name, such as "White Shoulders," "Gentle
Thighs," "Generous Thighs," "of the Thirty Men," generally
all epithets having to do with sex. She uses sex and whatever
else she can to get her way. She is allied in an ambiguous
sense to both Light and Dark in a sort of euphemerized
divinity. Maeve killed her sister Clothru, who was pregnant
with Conchobor's son, and the child was removed Caesarian-
fashion with swords. Maeve then assumed sovereignty from
Clothru with her husband Ailill. She is a leading character
not only in *Táin Bó Cuailnge*, but in *Scél Mucce Meic Da Thó*
and *Fled Bricrend*. The most earthy of Irish pagan "queens,"
she is interpreted as a goddess of war and fertility. She is
eventually killed by Furbaide, son of Clothru, who avenged
his mother's death by putting a piece of cheese in his sling
and hurling it at Maeve while she is bathing in the River
Shannon.

Manannán Mac Lir: the Irish Sea God.

Mórrígan: one of the battle goddesses, usually seen as a raven. She
is often referred to as "the great queen" and is identified
with Anu, the mother of the Irish gods. She met Dagda, the
God King, while she was washing herself at the River Unius
during the great pagan feast of Samhain. She had one foot
on the south bank and the other on the north bank and in
this position, she made love to Dagda, mating over water,
this being part of the ancient fertility ritual. She is the most
sensual of the Mórrigu, the triple war goddesses, of whom
the others are Macha and Badb.

Mugain: the wife of Conchobor. She is usually seen as a symbol
of voluptuousness. Although she is married to Conchobor,
she is highly attracted to others, especially to Cúchulainn.

Muirtheimhna: a province separate from Ulster, although owing
allegiance to it. Cúchulainn is from here, and this, plus his

youthfulness, keeps him from becoming a victim of the "pangs."

Nessa: the mother of Conchobor. (See CONCHOBOR and FERGUS.)

Ogham: a form of writing in which the letters are represented by combinations of parallel strokes in number from one to five and set in varied positions along a central line.

Paps of Anu (Paps of Danu): two mountains in Co. Kerry that look like the breasts of the great goddess, Anu (Danu). The suggestion is that the land is the recumbent goddess, fertile and loving.

rath: an earthen bank surrounding a fort.

Red Branch knights: the *Craeb Ruad* of Emain Macha. Conchobor's warriors who were the defenders of Ulster. The *Craeb Ruad* was only one of the three houses of Emain Macha, which included the Hostel of Kings at present-day Navan Fort, Co. Armagh, and *Craeb Derg*, where the skulls of enemies slain and other war trophies were stored.

riastradh: the "warp-spasm" of Cúchulainn that sets him apart from other men.

Samhain: a celebration at the same time as today's Halloween. It was held to celebrate the end of a harvest. Since harvest time was an end to the growing cycle, it quickly became known as a time when the dead came out to dance with the fairies. In ancient times, fires were extinguished and rebuilt from fire kindled upon the Hill of Tlachtga as a thanksgiving to the sun at the end of the harvest. The Gaelic term for spirits of the dead is *sluagh sith*, or "peaceful host," for this is how the spirits are seen, not in a destructive mode as has become fashionable. Samhain marks the Celtic New Year and the beginning of the agricultural year. Samhain was also seen as the guardian of the dead. (See HEAD-HUNTING.)

samildánach: a Master of All Arts.

Seancha (Sencha): Conchobor's chief poet, whose name suggests "man of lore."

seanchaí (seanechie, seanachie): a storyteller.

Sétanta: the boyhood name of Cúchulainn before he was given his "man name."

sida: a thin, silk gown; gossamer.

Sídhe: the fairy people; mound; hill. When the *Tuatha Dé Danann* were defeated by the Milesians, they entered the underground beneath the hills, each taking possession of his or her own area.

souterains: underground passages connecting buildings in forts. Probably used as hiding places in time of danger.

Sualdam Mac Roig: the mortal father of Cúchulainn. (See HEAD-HUNTING.)

torc: a circlet worn around the throat, marking the head of a family or a member of his immediate family. The manner in which it was made was indicative of one's station. Kings and their wives had *torcs* of gold.

Tuatha Dé Danann: the "Children of Danu," the gods of Ireland, the old gods whose stories reflect the beliefs not only of the ancient Irish, but of a large part of prehistoric Europe as well. They are the direct descendants of Nemed through his grandson, who had left Ireland and settled in northern Greece. When they returned to Ireland, they brought with them four sacred objects: the *Lia Fail,* a stone that shrieks at the inauguration of the rightful king; the spear of Lugh; the deadly sword of Nuada; and the ever-plentiful cauldron of the Dagda, the Father God of Ireland. It is they who defeat the Fir Bolg.

Uath Mac Imomain: horror son of Great Fair. He gives judgment to those seeking settlement. He is able to transform himself into any shape that he wishes. As a *sirite*, he has tremendous power. He is the first to play the head-game with the three heroes Loegaire, Conall, and Cúchulainn in *Fled Bricrend*. This foreshadows the appearance of the *bachlach* at Emain Macha in the final section of *Fled Bricrend*.

Ulster: See RED BRANCH KNIGHTS.

Ulster Curse: See CONCHOBOR, FERGUS, and MACHA.

vathi: seers; the heads of enemies slain in battle were often thought to provide dreams and visions if mounted in the victor's home.